advance praise for *Like Lig*

"*It's only going to get worse,* one of Lee Thomas's characters tells another, in his bold new collection *Like Light For Flies*...and believe you me, it does. Yet Thomas writes so beautifully and immediately that he can make the most atrocious images seem not only familiar, but somehow welcoming. His is a world of dreadful pleasures and awful delights, wreathed in meat and muck, driven by odd desires. The characters in these tales are universally broken people, flawed in ways every reader will understand if not entirely sympathize with, and the fates they meet are often exactly as cruel as they are just. And again: *nothing forgotten and nothing forgiven,* reads the (slightly paraphrased) last line of one story, a quote that could well be Thomas's motto, the overarching philosophical thread behind his work—since most readers will, indeed, find it hard to do either."

—GEMMA FILES, author of the Hexslinger Series

"Lee Thomas' expertly crafted *Like Light for Flies* is horror literature at its best: intense, gripping, and weirdly beautiful. These visceral and violent nightmares haunt and disturb, lingering long after the initial reading."

—JEFF MANN, author of *Desire and Devour*

"Lee Thomas writes with an artist's skill and a revolutionary's heart. His prose entertains, cuts, inspires, and terrorizes. With *Like Light for Flies*, Thomas continues to prove himself as a master of his craft, planting a flag at the top of the horror genre and daring pretenders to climb to such heights."

—NATE SOUTHARD, author of *Down* and *Red Sky*

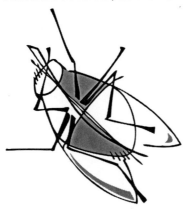

Like
Light
for
Flies

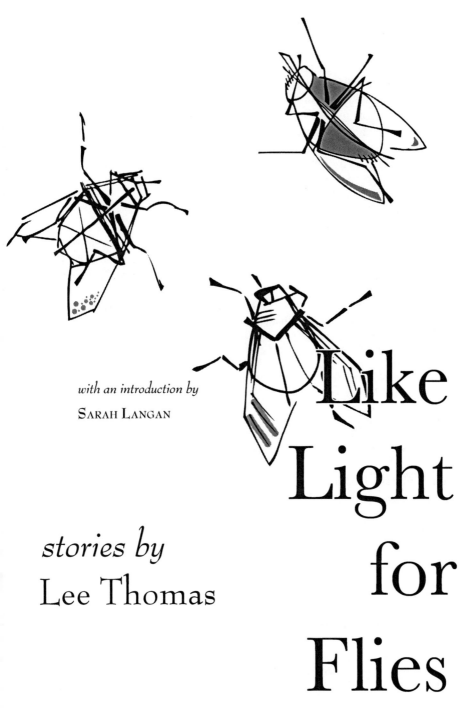

with an introduction by
SARAH LANGAN

Like
Light
for
Flies

stories by
Lee Thomas

LETHE PRESS
MAPLE SHADE, NEW JERSEY

Published in 2013 by Lethe Press, Inc.
118 Heritage Avenue • Maple Shade, NJ 08052-3018
www.lethepressbooks.com • lethepress@aol.com
ISBN: 978-1-59021-026-0 / 1-59021-026-3
e-ISBN: 978-1-59021-167-0 / 1-59021-167-7

These stories are works of fiction. Names, characters, places, and incidents are products of the author's imagination or are used fictitiously.

"Comfortable in Her Skin" © 2011, first appeared in *Supernatural Noir* / "The Butcher's Block" is original to this volume / "Testify" © 2010, first appeared in *Blood Splattered and Politically Incorrect* / "The Dodd Contrivance" © 2011, first appeared in *Swallowed by the Cracks* / "Flicker" © 2010, first appeared in *The Horror Library, Vol. 4* / "Inside Where It's Warm" © 2010, first appeared in *Dead Set* / "Nothing Forgiven" © 2011, first appeared in *Darkness on the Edge* / "Fine in the Fire" is original to this volume / "The House by the Park" © 2011, first appeared in *Tales from the Den* / "Turtle" © 2008, first appeared in the January 2008 issue of *Doorways Magazine* / "Landfall '35: A Prequel to Parish Damned" is original to this volume / "Tuesday" © 2008, first appeared in *Bits of the Dead*

Set in Garvis, Baskerville, & Bernhard Modern.
Interior design: Alex Jeffers.
Interior illustrations: tanja_ru, iStockphoto.
Cover design and image: Joe Carson Smith, royallionphotography.com.

LIBRARY OF CONGRESS
CATALOGING-IN-PUBLICATION DATA

Thomas, Lee, 1965-
[Short stories. Selections]
Like light for flies : stories / by Lee Thomas ; with an introduction by Sarah Langan.
pages ; cm.
ISBN 978-1-59021-026-0 (pbk. : alk. paper) -- ISBN 978-1-59021-167-0 (ebook)
I. Thomas, Lee, 1965- Comfortable in her skin. II. Title.
PS3620.H6317L55 2013
813'.6--dc23
2013005807

Contents

Introduction *by Sarah Langan*   ix
Comfortable in Her Skin   1
The Butcher's Block   25
Testify   45
The Dodd Contrivance   61
Flicker   87
Inside Where It's Warm   109
Nothing Forgiven   125
Fine in the Fire   139
The House by the Park   161
Turtle   191
Landfall '35: *A Prequel to Parish Damned*   203
Tuesday   247

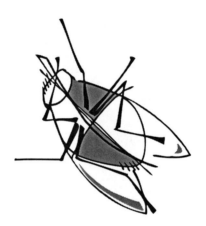

Introduction

I've known Lee Thomas for more than a decade. He's got this big brother vibe—at least toward me. I'd just started dating the man I would eventually marry during the World Horror Convention, 2005, in New York. Thomas was the first person to meet him, and immediately gave him a once-over, followed by an approving handshake. There's a good reason everybody loves Thomas and I'm honored to be writing this introduction.

Thomas and I were in a critique group together back in 2004. The first time I read his stuff, I wondered if it was porn. Then I went home, and thought about it. Then I woke up thinking about it. It stuck in my head—this story. The people in it weren't nice to each other. Married couples weren't in love. Dads resented their children. Everybody screwed around. They were also kind of...screwy. Then, and some of you are familiar with this story—there was the nectar. The jerking off. The bees. Oh, boy.

By the time the critique group met up again, I'd read the story five times. I was dumbfounded. What should I say? My reaction was horror. Distress. *How could he do this?* How could he write such weird, terrible things? But by then I also understood the contrary: *how could he not?*

We are horror writers. Like ancient mariners, we go to dark places, and come back, compelled to tell our tales. It just so happens that Thomas has visited some really hellish worlds. Lucky for us.

I've long felt that Thomas' work ought to be more widely read. It's good enough in prose and originality that it deserves the reviews and awards—not just from the genre community, but from the wider literary community. The man's a natural story-teller in the most classic sense: he understands plot, and how to draw a reader's attention. He also knows how to end things with a bang. If he chose to write thrillers with alpha dog man characters, he'd be a best seller.

My guess is that it's the subject matter that has kept him out of the mainstream. He doesn't just write horror; about a third of his characters are gay. It's a double whammy. Reading this, you might think I'm out of touch—that publishers don't care. Trust me, they do. Even now, in 2013, mainstream houses don't want gay main characters. Jesus, UPS won't even donate to the boy scouts now that gays are allowed. There's a lotta douches out there.

What further complicates it—Thomas's characters aren't refreshingly happy gay men. They don't share fancy condos and egg/sperm donors. We're not invited to witness their normalcy, and the kids are definitely not all right. No, these guys are veterans of a hate war. They're haunted; afflicted by their place in society, as represented by monstrous machines and devils next door. What's worse, in Thomas' world, we're all fucked up. The heteros, the kids, the little old ladies, and even the family pets. We're flawed creatures, molded from a flawed God.

I suspect that the social barriers that make fiction like Thomas' taboo will soon fall. There is room and demand for the stories he so lovingly fashions, even if the three big houses haven't yet caught on. As readers we want the best of our fiction to pull us into new worlds. We want to sympathize with strangers. Here, Thomas succeeds every time.

In these twelve stunning stories from *Like Light for Flies*, you'll see a wide range. From masochist-turned post-modern actress, to Lovecraftian send-up, to vampire origin tale, to hardboiled horror-crime a la Barker, it's a genre soup full of memorable characters and wildly original plots. But the true thread that runs through them is that particular charm residing in Thomas himself.

Despite the darkness, there's something about Thomas's writing that is generous, smart, and above all, *concerned*. That's where the big brother thing comes in. When I read about the monstrous couple who get their come-uppance for not helping a girl in distress, I can almost see Thomas frowning at the end, saying: *I know. It's horrible. I'm so sorry I had to tell you. But you did go looking, my dear.*

Even if there's no such thing as a happily ever after, and it turns out that the world beneath this one is darker than any of us had imagined, there's a bright side, too. Thomas holds our hands through the awful truth, and imparts what wisdom he can. He's not going to lie to us, but he is going to make sure we make it out okay, even if our friends on the page do not.

It's this concern that lifts Thomas's fiction above whatever label gets branded to it. It might even be the impetus for the stories. He tells them because they are his version of truth, and because his morality insists on it. Like the ancient mariner, he must. And how can we read something as brilliant as "Nothing Forgiven" and not be changed? How can we not look askance at the world after that?

There's something disturbingly magical about Thomas' duality—he wants to corrupt us, but he also wants us to become richer people for it. He's a soul preacher. I have no idea where he gets these fascinating ideas. But I believe them.

In these pages, you'll find some of the most original work of this decade. "Landfall '35," the excellent prequel to *Parish Damned*, concerns disposable veterans on the eve of a terrible storm. We've got a sweet couple falling in love in "The House by the Park," but like all couples, they've got baggage. "The Dodd Contrivance" opens doors to new worlds, and we wonder whether the present world or the monster-filled one is worse. All are subtle, and smart, and eschew the obvious. The subject of "Testify" is a Christian leader forced from the closet. It's easy to lampoon the side you're not on, but harder to show all sides with compassion. That's what Thomas does, because he can't help it. Because it's the truth of the story that matters to him, no matter where it takes us, or him.

I hope you enjoy these pages as much as I did. Until we meet again, Mr. Thomas.

—SARAH LANGAN, JANUARY, 2013

Acknowledgements

First and foremost, I'd like to acknowledge the hard work and vision of Lethe Press, a publishing house that has sown its own field and made it bountiful—a rare and wonderful thing. My thanks to Steve, Toby, Kip, and Alex. Special thanks to Daulton for pulling this manuscript from the slush pile and greenlighting its publication.

Much love to Sarah Langan for taking the time to read this work and provide an ideal Foreword for the volume.

Thanks to Abby Frucht, Richard McCann, and Nate Southard, who endured early versions of a few of these stories.

Special thanks to Ellen Datlow, Vince Liaguno, Norman Prentiss, John Everson, Bill Breedlove, RJ Cavendar, Boyd Harris, Harrison Howe, and R. Jackson: editors who were kind enough to buy some of these stories the first time around.

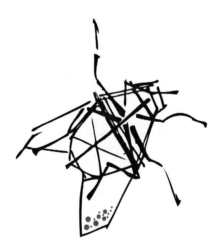

For Steve Berman,

Unspeakable, unpredictable, and unequaled.

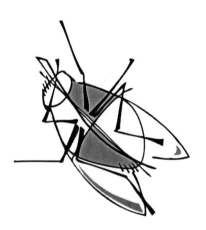

Comfortable
in Her Skin

Sylvia Newman strolls along the boulevard. She is already
late for her rendezvous with Louis Towne, but the delay
is calculated. The nights she makes Louis wait are always
the most exciting, so she takes her time, stopping at brightly lit
shop windows along the street to peer in at the teasing displays.
At *Genevieve's* a glittering stream of diamonds pulls her to the
glass like a magnet. The necklace is draped over a black velvet
bust, and the clear gems twinkle like tiny stars. At their center is
a perfect ruby the size of a postage stamp. Sylvia has never seen
anything so beautiful in her life, and though Louis is rich, She
knows he will never be diamonds-and-rubies generous with her.
Besides, the shop owners in this part of town know Louis well.
They also know his wife.

Leaving behind the beautiful gems, she continues to the corner. Sylvia spots Louis standing by his car under a street lamp
across the intersection. His angry expression is emphasized by
the shadows, and the sight of his frown sends a thrill through her.

He will complain about being made to wait in a neighborhood where he is so well known. He'll sulk over dinner and threaten to dump Sylvia on her ass for being such a pain in his, and when he fucks her, it will be brutal without a hint of tenderness, and Louis will think he's punishing her. Sylvia is more than happy to allow him the illusion.

Louis stands up straight and throws his shoulders back when he sees her across the street. He is an odd looking man with chipmunk cheeks and a perpetual coffee-ground stubble covering them. His ears are abnormally small and stick away from his head. He is not repellent to look at but nearly so. For Sylvia, the attributes that make him attractive—his power and his money—sufficiently offset his passing resemblance to a rodent. Besides, he is a natty dresser always wearing crisp Italian suits, perfectly tailored to his stout form, so he looks sharp if not handsome.

When she reaches the corner, Sylvia lifts her hand to wave. Louis shoves his hands in the pocket of his slacks in a gesture meant to show his irritation.

Behind Louis, a tall, burly man, wearing a black woolen overcoat and a wide brimmed hat pulled low to hide his face, appears on the sidewalk. His stride is purposeful. With his left hand he draws a handgun from the pocket of his coat and swings it up in a smooth arc. Sylvia's heart and lungs turn to ice water, and she opens her mouth to call a warning.

The muzzle of the gun flares. Then in unison with the *crack* of the pistol's report, a hole appears in Louis's face, producing a spray of brain and blood and teeth to shower the sidewalk before he collapses. The giant of a man leans down and puts another bullet in the head of Sylvia Newman's lover.

Sylvia pivots on her toes and hurries back the way she came.

Sylvia did not attend Louis Towne's funeral, but I did. Being Towne's lawyer, I felt a professional obligation to say farewell to my client; the decision certainly had nothing to do with respect or affection for the man.

The service was held at St. Michael's Cathedral, an institution to which Towne had donated considerably over the years. A Bishop presided over the ceremony, standing behind the altar and speaking exalted words above a polished mahogany coffin that contained the earthly remains of a base and violent man—a man I had come to see as evil in every possible way. The irony that the church should so laud such a monster seemed lost on the other mourners. Members of the congregation wept and held each other for comfort. Hard faces, streaked with tears, looked heavenward for answers. "Why?" a woman sobbed in the pew ahead of mine.

I too asked why. Why had it taken so long for god to rid the world of this filth? At least they'd kept the coffin closed for the mass so I didn't have to lay on eyes on him again.

Louis Towne had come to me fifteen years ago to hire my services. Despite ample clues—unheeded because of my naiveté and a certain level of professional denial—it took me a year to discover the nature of my client's business, and I'd almost dropped him on the spot once I did. But the truth was Towne paid well. He paid on time. And Towne scared me. Part of the fear was rational; he was a gun-toting thug, whose curriculum vitae included maiming and murder and a hundred lesser crimes. In this he was not unique. More than likely, dozens of men who had acquired the same level of brutal experience occupied the cathedral's pews, but his intimidation did not end with the obvious. There was another level to his threat, one which I could only call mystical. Even before he entered a room I would feel the air thicken, growing dense with his detestable presence. Sometimes in the middle of a conversation, Towne's eyes would harden and he'd begin speaking phrases in Latin. Occasionally a familiar word would emerge from the babble, and though I could never put together exactly what he was saying, hearing him quote this dead language soon had the power to shrivel my skin into gooseflesh.

Ahead of me and to the left, a man with broad shoulders bowed his head, revealing a scarred nape. I wondered if he had carried his gun into the cathedral, and then I wondered how many murderers shared the room with me, and the mockery of god and his house settled in my gut like writhing worms.

I didn't buy into the macho glamour of the mobs. I saw nothing honorable in the rackets, and the lifestyle they promoted—easy wealth carried over the bodies of the ignorant and unfortunate. They talked about respect and brotherhood and family, but it was all grease for the cogs, making sure the greed machine didn't break down. Friends were as expendable as rivals if it cleared the path to a buck.

At the altar, the Bishop began a prayer in Latin. I shuddered.

Sylvia carries a photograph of her father in her purse. He is tall and wiry and his flat nose and lipless mouth call to mind the face of a python.

Sylvia is nine-years old. She is on the floor watching television when she hears her father shouting. Her body tenses and a web of ice-cold filaments locks to the back of her skull. Matt, her older brother, shouts and a great crash follows. Her father bellows, his voice shaking the thin walls of the house like an approaching train.

This scene is familiar to Sylvia. Her father is at turns sweet and doting and cruel and violent. Alcohol flicks the switch. At least once a week her father beats her siblings, laying them flat like a scythe moving through wheat. He has never raised his hand to Sylvia but that fact does nothing to alleviate her fear. Even so young she understands the indiscretion of blind rage.

Matt comes charging into the living room and barrels into the kitchen. He throws open the back door and vanishes into the night.

Sylvia's father stumbles into the room, growling deep in his throat like an angry dog. He swings his head from side to side and then his eyes lock on Sylvia, causing the icy web at her skull to spread over her entire body. She crawls away from the man and climbs to her feet as her father stomps forward. Confused and frightened, she follows Matt's path, but she stops in the kitchen.

She doesn't want to run from her father, shouldn't *have* to run from him.

"You brats ruined my life," he says. Spit foams at the corner of his mouth. His eyes are hard as glass and burn hate as if lit from within. "I could have gone places."

Backed to the stove, Sylvia pulls a saucepan of boiling water off the burner. She ignores the too-hot handle, and splashes her father's crotch with the contents, and when he bends over, howling in pain, she cracks the saucepan across his skull. He drops to his knees, and she hits him again.

Sylvia checks her hair in the reflection of the glass door before pulling it open. She enters Club Barlow like a movie star walking the red carpet—wearing the awkward smile of grief she has spent hours practicing in front of a mirror. Makes a show of waving at familiar faces, some of whom aren't even looking her way. She walks through the room, her steps landing in perfect time to the bossa nova track pouring from the club's speakers. She takes a small booth on the far side of the dance floor with a gilt mirror at her back, and when the waitress comes for her order, she says, "Martini. Dry."

The dance floor is empty. Nobody dances anymore. Sylvia thinks that's a shame.

As she sips her drink a series of men come to her table. They do not sit beside her. Instead, they lean in close and tell Sylvia they are sorry for her loss, and if she ever needs anything—anything at all—she should call them. She promises to do so, though she never will. Their definition of "needing anything" goes no further than her crotch. Louis's murder has left her a pretty shell, vacant on the sand, and every fucking hermit crab on the beach would be trying to wriggle its way in. Sylvia expects this. In fact, she knows it will work to her advantage, but not with these men. None of them has what Sylvia needs. They run their numbers and sell their smack and boost electronics from the backs of trucks.

Graceless. Useless. Before her first drink is gone, she has already tucked five business cards into her handbag.

Across the room she sees Mickey Rossini, the man she was hoping to find. He is a large man with thick salt and pepper hair brushed back from his brow in a lush wave. His suit is ash gray and cheap. With his arm around a bleach-job half his age, he looks as happy as a bear with a mouth full of honey. His overly broad grin and hooded eyes show he's devoted much of his night to drinking. He has a reputation among the ladies—gentle, sweet, affectionate. Sylvia thinks that's a shame, though she can live with it until she gets what she needs. She stands from the booth and smoothes the sides of her dress before lifting her handbag and crossing to Rossini's table.

The blonde is the first to notice Sylvia. She looks up with a bright, wide-eyed smile, which quickly vanishes. The girl recognizes the threat and immediately scowls, knowing she will have to defend her territory from another predator. Sylvia is unfazed.

When Rossini's eyes fall on Sylvia a noticeable amount of the intoxication clears from them. He's wanted Sylvia for years, but she'd shot him down at every turn. Rossini was a thief; he jacked locks and cracked safes for Louis, making a fraction of a fraction of the money the things he stole were worth. She'd never needed him before.

"Hello, Mickey," she says.

Rossini straightens himself in the booth, removing his palm from the bottle-job's thigh.

He leans back in the booth and says, "Sylvia, it's good to see you."

"Is this your wife?" the blonde asks. She is sulking because Rossini's expression tells her that she has already been subtracted from this equation.

"No," he says.

"Then who the fuck is she?" the blonde wants to know.

"She's a friend. Don't worry about it."

"I didn't mean to interrupt," Sylvia says, playing demure. She locks eyes with Rossini and dips her chin bashfully, knowing the effect it will have on the man. "I'll let you back to your evening."

"Wait. Wait." He nudges the blonde and says, "Why don't you go powder your nose. I need to have a word with Sylvia here."

"Mickey," the girl whines.

"It's business," he tells her. "Be a sweetheart and give us a couple of minutes, okay?"

He gives her a sloppy peck on the lips and produces a fifty-dollar bill and hands it to the young woman, who quickly drops the note into her purse. She scoots her butt across the booth, and as she stands, she fixes a glare on Sylvia, who pretends to ignore the girl's attitude, but decides in that second to put a serious *fuck you* in the little cunt's night.

These amateur bitches, Sylvia thinks. They didn't understand the game, and that's why it ate them alive, leaving them shaking their tits in low rent knocker shops by the docks to feed the bastard brats of sailors and warehousemen, waiting for some disease to slowly snuff their candles. Over the years, Sylvia had seen a hundred similar pieces of trash blown into the gutter, and she didn't pity a single one of them.

"I really didn't mean to interrupt," Sylvia says, sliding into the booth next to Rossini. "It's just that since...well, you know...I've been a little lost."

"I know," Rossini says, placing his hand on Sylvia's knee in a salacious move he masks as mere comfort. "It's gotta be tough. How are you holding up?"

"Fine," she says. Already she has managed to work tears into her eyes. She sniffs lightly and retrieves a napkin from the table to dab her cheeks.

"Oh now, Sylvia," says Rossini scooting closer to her. He puts his arm around her shoulders and slides his hand higher on her thigh, recreating the pose he'd assumed with the bottle-job before Sylvia's arrival. In a handful of moments, Sylvia has replaced the blonde in the booth, in Rossini's thoughts, and in the thief's plans for the night.

Rossini is typical, a man led by his ego and his cock, who believes himself the cure-all for a woman's pain. His need to rescue her is an evolutionary blindfold, and though she finds his predictability unsatisfying, it serves her purpose.

Sylvia is twenty years old. For two years she has enjoyed an affair with Joe Tocci, a handsome and sophisticated man who would soon be named boss of his own crew. He is her lover and her employer, sending her on trips across the city, muling drugs and cash. Sylvia takes pride in her work, feeling she is paying her dues and earning respect within the rackets, unlike the other women who satisfy themselves in the roles of whore, wife, or victim.

One night she returns to the apartment Tocci has rented for her to find Joe and six of his friends three sheets to the completely fucked up, and before she can set down her handbag, a scrawny prick with buck teeth and the bumpy skin of a gourd by the name of Toady turns to Joe and says, "Mind if I take a ride?"

To her amusement, Joe replies, "I'd kind'a like to see that."

Sylvia believes her lover is joking, except that he isn't.

Before she knows what is happening, the men approach her. They grab her arms painfully and hoist her from the floor. Then she is pinned to the dining room table, men holding her arms and her legs while Toady rips away her clothes. Sylvia screams and Joe Tocci slaps her and tells her to keep her, "whore mouth shut." Toady climbs on her first and as he begins the rape, Sylvia spits in his face. Toady balls up his fist and punches her in the mouth. The violence so thrills him he hits her again and again. Dazed by concussion, Sylvia squeezes her eyes closed. She imagines herself in an ocean, except it is a sea of stones. She is batted this way and that by granite waves that stink of men. Opening her eyes Sylvia sees a series of faces hovering above her, blurred and monstrous in their lust. One man kneels on the dining room table and lifts her head by a fistful of hair before forcing his cock in her mouth, and the scents of urine and sweat fill her nose and she thinks she might drown in them. Hot spray lands on her face and thighs and belly, and they turn her over so that her burning cheek is momentarily soothed by the coolness of the polished wood, and then she is afloat again, tossed about like flotsam on fever-hot swells of stone. And later, so much later, as a dozen muffled aches throb across her body she hears Tocci laughing. He says, "I guess I better get a new one. This one's broken."

Sylvia rarely thinks of this night. She tells herself the memories were scraped away with the brat one of those cocksuckers had put inside of her.

Morning light streams through thin curtains, bathing Sylvia's face. She wipes her eyes and hears footsteps. Rossini enters the bedroom holding two mugs of coffee. He is naked and though bulky, his added pounds are solid and intimidating, and she likes the way his body looks.

He hands her one of the mugs and sits on the edge of the bed beside her.

"So tell me what you're doing here," he says, taking her off guard.

She holds the mug in both hands, like a little girl sipping cocoa and offers Rossini an innocent gaze, which makes him laugh like a mule. His reaction annoys her but she refuses to let the lie fall.

"Look Syl," Rossini says once his amusement is under control, "You think I'm a dumb Wop fucker, but I'm not *that* dumb. I saw the way you twisted Louis around your finger. You drove him out of his fucking mind. I never saw anything like it. So while I can play along with some horseshit to get a roll, and maybe even believe you were lonely and needed a bit of hard to make it through the night, the fact you're still here tells me you want more than my cock."

"Maybe I like you," Sylvia says over the lip of her coffee mug.

"And maybe I'll sprout tits and be the happiest girl in the whole USA," he says, still exhibiting great amusement at the game. "What do you think? You think I'm going to sprout tits?"

"Fine," she says. She places her mug on the nightstand and leans back on the headboard. "I want you to help me with a job."

"That's more like it," Rossini says. He drinks from his mug and looks out the window.

"Are you angry?"

"Relieved," he says. "I like to know where I stand. What's the job?"

She hesitates because Louis and Mickey had been close. She doesn't know if the thief retains loyalty to his dead boss, but she cannot drop the subject now. If Rossini declines, she will find a way to convince him as she has convinced other men in the past.

"I want to hit Louis's house," she says.

The night after the funeral Mary Towne, Louis's widow, called me to say she was in Miami with her two sons. I was sitting on the sofa with my arm around my wife, and we were watching an animated film about dogs, and when the phone rang I thought it might have been our daughter who called frequently from her college dorm. To hear Mary Towne's shrill voice—instead of my daughter's—irritated the hell out of me.

"It's those papers you gave me," Mary said.

"About the estate?" I asked.

"Well, what other papers did you give me to sign?" Her voice was like a scalpel scraping bone.

Mary had insisted on reading Louis's will the day after his murder. The fat widow had spent two hours in my office going over the details of Towne's financial holdings, picking and pecking at the numbers like a starving bird, instead of staying home to comfort her children. At the funeral she'd put on a fine show of grief. Empty. Meaningless. I'd been appalled and wondered how a human being's moral compass could waver so far from true north.

Not that Towne was a man who deserved authentic mourning from his wife. I'd told him a hundred times I had no interest in his sexual conquests, but Towne was a braggart and insisted I

endure his tales of whoring and perversion. I'd always felt sorry
for his cheated wife. And then I met her.

"What about the papers, Mary?"

"I signed them the way you said, but we were running late for
our flight."

"So you didn't have them messengered to my office?"

"I *told* you, we were late for our fight. I didn't have time. Just go
by the house in the morning and pick them up."

"Mary, that's highly irregular."

"Well, you'd better do something. I don't want those papers
sitting around for two weeks holding everything up. There's a
key in the planter on the back porch and the security code is
Louis's birthday—day and month. You can bill me for your precious time."

Then she hung up, cutting off the protests climbing up my
tongue.

Sylvia sits in the passenger seat of a stolen sedan. Rossini finishes a cigarette and grinds it out in the ashtray and turns in
the seat to face her.

"He's got no real security," the thief says. "Obviously he's not
going to have cameras recording who comes and goes. He's got a
simple contact system that will take all of a minute to kill."

"He wasn't very cautious," Sylvia says.

"He was scary enough that he didn't have to be. No one was going to fuck Louis over—no one that wanted to stay alive anyway.
The guy was more than connected."

"What does that mean?"

"You telling me you don't know about Louis's hobby?

"You mean his oogedy boogedy mumbo jumbo?"

"It was a hell of a lot more than that," Rossini says. "He put
the fear of god, or the devil, or whatever he worshiped into the
whole crew. Guys that crossed Louis ended up dog food. You
heard about Joe Tocci, right? Last year he disrespected Louis at a
meeting and his men found Tocci shredded like barbecue pork in

the john of his apartment. They said he wasn't in there for more than a few minutes, and there was no other way into that crapper but the one door. Louis got to him anyway."

"Tocci got what he deserved," Sylvia mutters.

"We all get what we deserve," Rossini says. "But the thing is, Louis Towne was not a made man. He was never going to be a made man because he didn't have the blood, but Tocci was a made man. You hit a made man and you're landfill, but no one retaliated on Tocci's behalf. No one. Not his crew. Not the organization. They knew Louis did it, but they knew what Louis was capable of so they let him alone."

"Until someone put two in his head."

"Over a year later," Rossini says. "I'm just saying he didn't have security because he knew he was scarier than anything that could get in his house."

Sylvia follows the thief into the dining room and through an opulent living room. She feels anger, seeing the statuary and the silk-upholstered sofa, and the crystal vases on marble tables. This should have been hers. She should have been sitting on that sofa with a glass of champagne, not prowling the house looking for scraps. She follows Rossini up the stairs and runs a hand along the ornately carved mahogany banister.

"His safe is in his study," Rossini says.

After his words fade, Sylvia feels uneasy. The air grows thick and envelops her, and she believes she can feel it jostled, hitting her like ripples on the surface of a lake. Even the subtle movements of Rossini on the stairs ahead play over her skin, but there is another body at work, displacing the air. She remembers a similar sensation she had felt whenever Louis entered a room, a heaviness as if his presence curdled the atmosphere.

Uncertain, with her skin alit by anxiety, Sylvia follows the thief to the landing and down a black hallway. The sharp ray of a flashlight momentarily blinds her. Rossini offers a rapid apology and puts the cylinder in his mouth. At the center of the beam, is a deadbolt lock. Rossini attacks it with his picks and in a few moments he has the bolt retracted. Then he sets to work on the cheaper, less-complicated lock recessed in the knob.

After opening the door, Rossini leaves Sylvia on the threshold and starts across the room, his silhouette playing against the bobbing disc of light from his lantern. She watches him open a closet door and is surprised to see a shining metal panel beyond, a panel with a combination dial and a three-pronged handle. Louis's safe takes up an entire closet. Sylvia's trepidation turns to excitement as she anticipates the sheer volume of wealth such a vault could hold.

"This is going to take some time," he tells her. "I helped him pick this model, so I know what I'm up against. You might want to keep an eye on the window."

Sylvia does. She pulls back the drapes and leans against the wall. The landscape beyond the window is carved of shadows. The only light comes from the far end of the drive, beyond the gate, where an arc lamp hangs over the street. Everything between this illumination and Sylvia is gloom. She looks into it and finds nothing. She looks back at Rossini and considers her choice of accomplice.

She decides he can't be trusted. The thief is too eager. He hadn't needed a bit of convincing to agree to this job, and as with all things that came too easy, Sylvia looks for an angle.

She slides her hand down the side of her jacket and is reassured when her fingers trace over the outline of the handgun in the pocket.

The shrill cry of Rossini's drill startles her. Sylvia steps away from the window and crosses the den. Nervous, she lights a cigarette and stands by the door. She leans into the hall and is grateful to see the darkened corridor is empty.

Still she cannot shake the feeling that she and the thief are not alone in the house. The air continues to move like an invisible beast, sidling past her. Drawing deeply on the cigarette, she holds the smoke in her lungs and then blows a cloud into the hall. Amid the whorls of smoke, she pictures Louis's face and whispers, "Fuck you," to the dissipating haze. He had lavished a fortune on his wife, had given her every damn thing she had ever whined about, including this house, and what had Sylvia seen for her time and effort?

Finishing the cigarette, she drops it on the carpet. She grinds the ember into the carved Berber and hopes an ember will smolder deep in the pile, causing a fire that levels the Towne mansion about five minutes after she and the thief have driven away with the contents of Louis's safe.

She leaves the doorway and walks to where Mickey is kneeling. He wears goggles as he guides the barrel of a complicated drill rig. Sparks fly from the safe's door, showering the carpet. The air around her shifts again and Sylvia spins on her heels to check the room. Nothing. She hugs herself nervously and returns to the window.

Staring over the dark landscape, she rubs the back of her neck, trying to dislodge the feeling that something rests against it. She tries to convince herself that she's being paranoid. If anyone else were in the house they'd have shown themselves by now, or the drive would be thick with police cars, but logic does nothing to alleviate her fear. By the time the drill's shriek dies, Sylvia is near panic with the certainty someone prowls the house.

"That's it," Mickey says, throwing open the safe. He sets his drill rig on Louis's desk and returns to the open closet door.

Sylvia races across the room to see the extent of the fortune Louis has locked away from the world and to begin its collection. She presses up against Rossini's back and peers around him only to find herself confused by the vault's contents. She had expected to find stacks of hundred dollar bills, stock certificates, a jewelry store's inventory of gems, and though there is some cash—three small stacks on the third shelf of the safe—the bulk of the space is empty. The money sits on one shelf and another is devoted to a bizarre assortment of baubles.

The collection is comprised of six metallic statues. Each is no larger than Sylvia's pinkie finger, and they are ugly like randomly shaped wads of iron with points and blobs.

"I don't understand," Sylvia whispers.

"Amazing," Rossini replies.

"What is this shit?" Sylvia asks. She reaches around Rossini to retrieve one of the unattractive statues.

His hand shoots out and grabs her wrist painfully. "Don't touch those," he says. "You get the cash and the jewelry. That was the deal."

"The cash? There's only about ten grand there and there isn't any jewelry."

Rossini squeezes her wrist until she feels the bones grinding. "That was the deal," he repeats. "The icons are mine."

A hot mask of rage falls over Sylvia's face. The thief has played her, though she has yet to understand the extent or the intent of his game.

"Get away from there," a rasping voice calls from the doorway.

Sylvia turns to the sound, her heart in her throat. A squat shadow stands at the threshold. The face is very pale, visible but ill-defined. Mickey turns and knocks Sylvia aside. His flashlight falls squarely on the intruder, and he says, "Son of a bitch." Sylvia only gets a glimpse of the man in the doorway, and to her shock he resembles Louis Towne. She recognizes chipmunk cheeks and small ears, but the view is momentary, and she is stumbling so she doesn't trust what she has seen.

Rossini lowers the flashlight so that the beam falls on the intruder's feet. He then pulls a gun from his coat pocket and levels his left arm to aim the weapon.

Sylvia remembers the boulevard and the man who killed Louis, remembers his size and his posture and the way he held the gun, and she realizes it was Rossini. All along she has underestimated the thief. His eagerness for the job, his satisfaction with the contents of the safe—this had been his plan all along. He'd only allowed Sylvia to believe it was hers.

Two muzzle flares light up the room. The reports are deafening. A body falls in the hallway and Rossini hisses, "Shit. Enough of this blackout crap." He stomps to the door and turns on the light.

Awash in confusion, Sylvia looks around absently as if waking in a strange place with no understanding of how she's gotten there. Rossini is in the doorway, kneeling beside a body on the floor. Sylvia approaches him and when she sees the face of the intruder, she gasps. It is Louis Towne.

His face is longer and misshapen. Tufts of hair stick out around his ears, but he is otherwise bald. Two ragged wounds show above his ear. He still wears the coffee-grounds stubble, but much of it has been torn away on the right side of his face, revealing a patch of darker skin beneath. His nose is longer and his mouth is circled with odd ridges. His eyes are the worst. They stare at Sylvia, but they are the wrong color. Louis's eyes were blue and these eyes are chocolate brown, and even more unsettling, each eye is framed by two sets of eye lashes. "What happened to him?" she asks.

"Mumbo Jumbo," Rossini says in a dry, earnest tone.

"His face..."

"Yeah," the thief says.

Louis's legs begin to kick and thrash on the carpet. Sylvia screams and leaps back, covering her mouth with a palm.

"Settle down," Rossini says, rising to his feet. "It's just a death dance. Muscle contractions."

"How can you be so calm?" Sylvia wants to know.

"I got word that Louis's body went missing from the funeral home. Considering the weird shit he was into, I kept my mind open. Now I think we need to get what we came for and get the hell out of here."

"Is he really dead this time?"

"Don't know and don't care. I've got a full clip. That'll keep him down long enough."

"Are those little statues doing this?" Sylvia asks.

"Probably." Rossini casts another glance at the corpse thrashing on the carpet in the hall.

"Asshole there got drunk one night and started bragging about these things. He called them the Pellis Icons, and he'd spent about twenty years hunting them down. He said they helped him master the flesh, whatever the hell that means. I know he used them to tear apart Tocci, because I was sitting with him in this room when he did it. They do something, and I figure I've got plenty of time to figure out exactly what that is."

'How much are they worth?"

Rossini laughs and shakes his head. "By your definition, not a damn thing. There isn't a fence on the continent who would know what to do with them."

He turns away from Sylvia to take another look at the thrashing man. Sylvia pulls her gun and shoots the thief in the shoulder, sending him sprawling against the wall. He drops his gun and slides to his knees and looks at Sylvia, an expression of pained surprise on his face.

"What the fuck, Syl?" he says. He grasps the wound on his shoulder. Blood spills between his fingers in thick rivulets.

She doesn't reply. Instead she keeps the gun aimed on Rossini's face as she crosses to him and retrieves his weapon from the floor. She slips this into her pocket and walks to the safe. On the floor is Rossini's canvas bag. Sylvia retrieves it and waves the sack in the air until it's opened. Without looking at the thief, she pulls the meager amount of cash into the bag and then scoops the Pellis Icons on top of it. The disappointing void of the safe still feels wrong to her, and she convinces herself that Louis must have kept more. She reaches in and presses against the back wall, expecting a panel to pop free. She does this on every shelf, but the back of the safe is solid and hides no additional treasures. She gives the empty shelves a final look and then turns to leave.

In the hall, the dead man's convulsions have stopped, and she is grateful for this, but Rossini has crawled away. He no longer sits by the door. Sylvia approaches the hall cautiously, gun raised, fingers tensed and ready to fire. The weapon trembles in her hand.

When she reaches the threshold, she is shocked to see the condition of the body in the hall.

It isn't Louis at all. Sylvia recognizes the corpse's face, and it belongs to a low level bookie who went by the name of Tap. His cheeks are red as if deeply sunburned. The collar of his dress shirt is laid wide and his tie has been torn away and lies across the expensive carpet like a crimson tongue. Blood continues to seep from the two well-placed holes Rossini shot in the man's chest. Sylvia absorbs this oddity and wonders how she could have mistaken this insignificant creep for Louis Towne.

A crash in the hallway sends her back into the den. Glass shatters and a great weight hits the floor. Sylvia puts the canvas sack and her purse down and holds the gun in both hands, trying unsuccessfully to steady the weapon, which suddenly feels as heavy as a block of lead. A quieter thump comes from the hallway, and Sylvia swallows a moan.

Movement in the doorway causes Sylvia to fire two shots in rapid succession but the flashing motion is too brief like a flag whipping in a sudden breeze. Her bullets punch through the wall.

Then a man steps into view. Sylvia cannot fire her weapon; the abomination in the doorway makes no sense and the sight of it puts a clamp on her mind, rendering her incapable of comprehension or action.

The body is Rossini's. He is unstable, rocking from foot to foot. One broad hand clutches the doorframe for support, the other slaps at a sheathed knife hooked to his belt. He wears Louis Towne's face like a mask. The cheeks are shiny, stretched tightly over the thief's features with tiny ears jutting from the side of the massive head. The rest of Louis's skin, a sheet of bloodless flesh the color of bacon fat, hangs from Rossini's chin like an untied butcher's apron and swings as the thief rocks from side to side. Bony thorns ring the dangling sheet of skin like teeth. The flesh billows and slaps against the thief's body, attempting to gain greater purchase but it seems unable to secure itself to the fabric.

Sylvia takes in every detail of the unnatural union before her and then repeats the process in a futile attempt to understand it.

Louis's lips move and a hoarse mumble escapes Rossini's throat. The attempt is made again. "Put them back," come the words, though Sylvia can't be certain who has made the request.

The thief finally frees the knife from its sheath at his belt, and Sylvia waits breathlessly for him to carve through Louis's flapping skin. Instead, the thief cocks back his arm and hurls the blade at Sylvia.

It strikes her high on the right breast, sending her stumbling back. The air is knocked from her body, and she nearly drops her gun, but the attack brings clarity, supersedes the paralyzing awe. Desperate to keep her footing, Sylvia regains her balance and assumes a firing stance with the gun clamped in her hands, and she squeezes the trigger. A hole punches in the flapping belly of Louis's skin and passes through to rip its way into Rossini's gut. She squeezes again and again, every shot hitting home. The thief stumbles back to the corridor wall and slides to the carpet. Sylvia continues firing and her final bullet pierces Louis Towne's forehead and that of the man who wears him.

She drops to her knees and sobs. Grasping the hilt of the knife, she pulls it from her chest, and it feels like she's ripping a bone from her body. She nearly faints from the sight of so much blood following the blade from the wound, and though she manages to remain conscious, her head spins with sickening speed. She collapses to the side and grinds her teeth against the pain, and she closes her eyes and inhales shallowly because she needs oxygen but the jabbing pain cuts off her respiration in mid-breath. Sweat slathers her brow, chilling it. Her body shivers from the cold. She thinks if she can just rest for a few minutes, she will conquer the pain and make her escape. People had survived worse. A moment to recover from the shock and then downstairs and out the door and into Rossini's car. At the emergency room she will make up a story about muggers, and the doctor will tell her she's lucky to be alive, and she'll thank him before painkillers carry her into comfortable sleep.

But she is not at the hospital yet, and she doesn't feel safe. Sylvia fights to open her eyes. Louis Towne's skin slides over the carpet toward her. His head is raised like the hood of a cobra and Sylvia sees Mickey Rossini's blood stained corpse through the bullet holes and the empty eye sockets of the face.

Sylvia cries out and a burst of adrenaline provides sufficient fuel for her to rise to her knees. The knife is within her reach and she snatches it up, as the mask of Louis's face bears down on her. Sylvia strikes out. The blade slices into Louis's cheek, and she guides the weapon down with all of her force, nailing the flesh to the floor, and refusing to allow Louis to escape again, Sylvia crawls forward and kneels on the spongy sheet. She yanks the blade free, sending bolts of agony across her chest, and begins to slash at the rippling tissues. Chunks of skin come free and wriggle about on the floor like worms dropped on an electrified plate, and Sylvia slices and stabs and tears until Louis Towne's remains amount to nothing more than a confetti of jittering meat.

Sylvia drops the knife and looks around the room alert for any new threat that might target her, and her gaze lands on the canvas sack, and she considers what Rossini has told her about the mastery of flesh, and then she looks to the trembling tissue about her for confirmation. She crawls to the bag and empties its contents. In desperation she gathers up the ugly iron icons and holds them tightly in her hands, clutches them to her breast. She lies down on the carpet and lets her eyes close and falls unconscious. She dies twenty minutes later.

I met Sylvia Newman some hours after her death. Louis had told me about the woman—went on in some detail about their affair—but to the best of my knowledge I'd never set eyes on her before.

Needled by annoyance, I went to his house that morning to pick up the documents his wife had failed to messenger me before leaving for Miami, and upon finding the alarm system deactivated, decided to search the house for signs of burglary. Upstairs I was met by the sight of Mickey Rossini sitting upright with seven holes in his body. Manny "Tap" Tappert lay on his back with two holes in his chest and a startled expression on his face. But the worst sight awaited me in Louis's den. In the center of the room was a shifting mass that resembled a loose congregation of mealworms, writhing excitedly, and next to this grotesque display was a skinless corpse.

Even partially clad in a black jacket and slacks, it seemed too small, too delicate to have been the remains of an adult. Eyes whiter than paper lay nestled in a field of deep red. Here and there ridges of white bone showed through the crimson tissue of muscle and ligament. My stomach clenched, wondering who could perform such an atrocity on another human being and wondering what a victim might do to deserve such a desecration.

Absorbed by the grotesquerie, what I thought was a hood dropped over my head, startling me back, but my reflexes were no match for Sylvia. She must have been waiting on the ceiling, descending upon me as I stood rapt by the repulsive scene. Her face stretched over mine, and the thorny teeth ringing her skin bit into the back of my head like fingernails working their way into an orange rind. As the skin pulled across my brow and chin and those thorns tore their way in, her memories began flooding me, drowning my own thoughts with scenes from this woman's life:

Sylvia Newman strolls along the boulevard.

Sylvia believes her lover is joking, except that he isn't.

Sylvia is dead but alive in her skin, which she feels ripping like fabric, peeling in a single sheet from her muscles and bones.

A thousand such scenes play simultaneously in my mind. Amid this torrent of information I was lost: I was Sylvia.

Overwhelmed, I ceased what little struggles I'd engaged in and resolved myself to this mental infestation, viewing the torments and triumphs and carnal excesses that had molded Sylvia Newman. The skin of her neck stretched tightly around my throat restricting my breath, and the tiny bones punctured the nape of my neck and scraped across my spine, and more information flooded in but the information was so dense it cascaded through my head like photographs printed on raindrops.

When this downpour ceased, I remained standing in Louis Towne's study but my clothes had been removed and Sylvia busied herself, stretching and wrapping and securing her flesh over mine. Her skin buckled my knees, and we stumbled forward and I grasped the drape for support, but fell nonetheless. The curtain rod snapped under my weight bringing the window treatment down in a wave. We scurried back on my hands and knees and then with great effort, we regained our footing and stood, only to be startled by the sight greeting us.

With night as a backdrop, the window had become a perfect mirror. Sylvia's face, still thick with make-up had fused to mine; her full red lips formed a grotesque O around my own mouth. Her breasts sagged emptily against the skin of her stomach, which shined from such tension it looked as though it might rip at any moment, and the tip of my penis showed through the labial lips between her legs. It was this last that so enthralled me. Sylvia must have sensed my fascination because the skin there began to ripple and pull, caressing the head of my cock until it began to grow, and soon a library of erotic images—Towne fucking her and Rossini fucking her and Tocci and a dozen others—crowded my awestruck mind.

The rippling and pulling intensified. The reflection of this unnatural intercourse filled my eyes as I watched her skin creep along my shaft and then drag backwards revealing the entirety of my erection. Soon I became aware of another sensation—I felt what Sylvia felt, an intense tingling in the lips of skin that eagerly stroked my cock. She willed my hands to her nipples, forced them to squeeze and pinch, dragging the empty sacks of her breasts away from our body. Sparks of pleasure shot like dry lightning through a desert, alighting the tissues and skipping off to some equally sensitive destination. The act repulsed me, and it excited me. Climax burst on us so quickly I cried out, or she did.

After, we stood breathless, staring at ourselves in the window. She spoke to me, moving my lips and forcing air from my lungs through the vocal chords and over my tongue.

"We're very good together," she said. "We can accomplish so much."

I asked her what it was she hoped to accomplish, and she showed me the face of a bucktoothed man named Toady. His expression was tense and hateful. He drew back his fist and punched us in the cheek, and Sylvia's loathing of the cretin became mine.

"There are others," she said. "So many others. All we need are the icons."

"And each other," I said.

"Of course."

We stand at the window, observing the crude bumps and tightly stretched plains of skin, and we whisper back and forth—plans and dreams and longings so deep we have never spoken them aloud to another soul. The words spill quietly from my lips and I observe their formation in the pane and in one heart stopping moment we fall silent.

I find us so beautiful I can't speak another word.

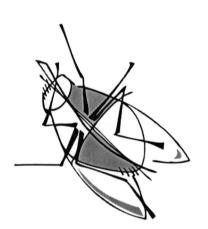

The Butcher's Block

Ian walked through a chill and misty rain, head down with eyes alert for movement. To either side, buildings of eroded and chipped brick rose toward an overcast sky. Glazes of filth covered windows—some whole, some cracked. Other panes were shattered completely leaving black holes in the weathered walls. The warehouses and factories stood long closed in the crumbling ward. The operations had gone bankrupt or company owners had moved manufacturing overseas, their textiles now produced by impoverished women and children.

Alleys, not yet dark, separated the dismal structures. Low creatures scurried in the corridors, raced through the litter and around the trash bins over the wet ground, seeking food or shelter. Maybe they just wanted a mate for the night. They were certainly in the right neighborhood for it: no love to be had, but plenty to fuck.

The area was known as the Butcher's Block, a name likely coined by some irreverent queen, speaking to the volume of meat that cruised the area on any given night. Throughout the dismal district, the lonely sought their hits of flesh. Anonymity implied discretion, but this merely appeased the male ego; indifference was the genuine promise of confidentiality.

As for Ian, he was glad to be on the street and away from his desk. At work, his office had begun to close in on him. The air there was recycled—the atmosphere dead. Late in the day, the numbers on the spreadsheets had blurred and taken on a foreign quality as if he'd been staring at hieroglyphics and not calculable numerals. Even with the drizzle, outside was preferable.

The first man he passed was sitting in a pricey sedan parked at the curb. Ian saw the shadow of the driver through the back window and slowed his pace as he came alongside the car and peered in. The guy wore a crisp pinstriped blue suit. A slick wave of gray hair rolled over his scalp, held in place with glistening oil. A closet case, Ian decided. Just another Suburban John, looking for a spark of fire before returning to the slow burn of his family. The guy was kneading the fabric at his crotch. With his other hand he pointed at the door. An invitation.

Ian kept walking. The man was attractive... for his age. But seeing him brought an uncomfortable ache to Ian's stomach. He couldn't help but see himself in the man. Ian wasn't old, but he felt old wasn't far off. A few years. Hardly a rustle of the calendar. His hair would go white. His skin would crepe like scrunched linen. Negative empathy for the driver fueled his steps and drove him around the nearest corner.

He clipped the shoulder of another man as he took the turn. The guy was leaning against a wall, posing like a tough from a fifties biker film. Three days' stubble covered his jaw. He cast a glance at Ian and then looked away dismissively.

Across the street, two young men in tight jeans and Lycra tops smoked cigarettes and laughed like they were guests at a cocktail party, rather than simply a couple of twinks cruising the block. They were buffed. Muscular arms tested the confines of their snug shirts. Their hair jutted away in calculated tufts. They looked up at Ian and squinted to bring him into focus. One ran a hand through his mist-wet hair. He licked his lips and turned back to his buddy.

Ian continued down the street. Men sat in cars. They stood in doorways, sometimes two or three of them huddled on stoops to get out from under the rain. Most ignored one another in a show of cool detachment. Ian didn't care about a little moisture. In fact, he enjoyed the way it felt on his face after having spent so many hours in the lifeless air of his office. Amid the suits and skirts in the corporate kennel, he'd felt trapped, his mind and body numbed by repetitive tasks and the pretense of good nature he had erected like an electric fence to keep his coworkers at bay.

Usually The Block energized him, brought his system awake with expectation. Tonight though, his insecurities worked against him. More than usual, he noticed the dichotomy of age, seeing no gradations of maturity but rather observing only old men and pretty young boys. And unfortunately, Ian could no longer fit himself into the category of youth.

He was thirty-three years old. In a week, he'd be thirty-four.

Distracted by his thoughts, Ian didn't reply when a man asked, "How's it goin'?" Only when he was several steps farther down the block did he register the question. He paused to look over his shoulder.

The guy was at least ten years older than Ian and not the least bit his type. Cool interest pooled in the man's eyes; his cheeks were ruddy and rough; and the corner of his mouth arced in a fractured smile. In his plaid shirt and snug blue jeans, he looked like a misplaced farmer, who somehow managed to appear completely content amid the urban squalor. Why this middle-aged Jethro thought he could play in Ian's league was beyond him.

This was going nowhere. The only offers of action came from the trolls, and they were out in droves tonight. Ian turned away from the Jethro and continued to the corner. He considered leaving both gray evening and gray men behind and going home. However, what waited for him at his apartment was no better. Rooms brimming with the inanimate miscellany of his life would bring no comfort. He needed skin and spit; these things the Block could provide.

He couldn't even call the tingling urge that drove him lust. That emotion, that need, was mindless and searing. What Ian felt was cold, like a floe of fear, and a litter of mental effluent rode it.

The streetlights flickered on above the sidewalk. At the next intersection, a young man in tight black jeans leaned against the corner of a dilapidated shoe factory. The kid's hair was bleached, stripped white, and his cheeks were as smooth as cream. The face of a growling tiger was tattooed on the rounded muscle of his shoulder. He couldn't have been more than twenty years old. He was hot, this Tiger-Boy, and he knew it, wearing the pride in his splendor like a gold medal. Ian's steps slowed as he approached the kid, who stared at him with ferocious intensity.

He'll want money, Ian thought. *Are you willing to step into that wretched frontier? Do you need to be touched that badly?*

"Hey," Ian said. His throat was sticky with phlegm and his mouth was dry, so the syllable broke in half.

"'Sup?" the Tiger-Boy asked, shifting his position on the wall to give Ian a better view of his crotch.

"Not much. How's it going?"

"I need to get fucked." The kid studied Ian's face, perhaps searching for shock or gratitude. For all Ian knew, the kid found both.

"You work around here?" Ian asked, trying to ascertain if he'd need to spend for the pale young man's company.

"Nah. This is where I play."

The cold disquiet drained from him. Some level of ease returned, and he slipped into a more confident demeanor. He stepped closer to the kid and caught a thin scent of cologne.

"Maybe we should get out of the rain," Ian suggested.

"Cool," the pale kid said, pushing himself away from the wall.

"My name's Ian."

"I don't care," Tiger Boy replied

"Fair enough."

Ian followed the kid around the corner, his gaze tracing a line from the nape of the boy's neck to his rounded ass. There was an entrance to the shoe factory thirty feet down the block. The hasp of the lock had been pried open, so the vast shadowed caverns within were available for brief passions.

He'd been here before. On different nights. With different men.

Further down the block, Ian saw the Suburban John he'd first noticed sitting in a car at the edge of the Butcher's Block. Two men, easily half his age, flanked the distinguished businessman. Both wore smiles on their pretty faces as they led their elder down the sidewalk. Ian's Tiger Boy paused.

"Wait here," Tiger Boy said before running down the sidewalk toward the approaching men.

"What the...?" Ian began, but the question died in his throat as the kid raced away from him.

Shit, he thought. Frustration blossomed as he watched the kid come to a stop before the Suburban John and his escorts. Ian tried to hear what was being said, but he only caught a single word: "Party."

"Hey" Ian called. What the hell was going on? Had this twink just thrown him over for some old fuck?

"Catch you later," Tiger-Boy called back.

"The fuck you will," Ian muttered.

A moment later, the small group, including Suburban John, crossed the street to the far sidewalk. Ian watched the group turn into the darkness and disappear around the front of a deserted warehouse. Furious that he should have been so easily and rudely dismissed, Ian stepped off the sidewalk to follow the group. He walked quickly, dodging the glances of cruising men. Suburban John and his entourage were already well ahead of him, crossing Wilson Drive into the last unlit street of The Butcher's Block. There the road dead ended at a field of jagged earth that climbed to a blunt ridge of dirt. A freeway onramp rose high above it like a great gray sickle, glowing against the plum colored sky. On Ian's side of the street, a single building occupied the entire block.

Once a textiles mill known for its cotton weaves, the enormous structure was now abandoned.

Ian never walked this far down the block. Busted streetlamps provided too many shadows for the truly unwholesome—the junkies, the thieves—and most of the guys out cruising knew better than to cross Wilson Drive.

But curiosity drove Ian forward. Not only did he see Suburban John and his boys turning into the doorway of the cotton mill, but he noticed other young men, emerging from the darkness to converge on the place. One of the boys had said something about a party, but he hadn't meant a private gathering sponsored by the old closet case. No this was something different.

Suddenly, Ian wasn't worried about the snub of his Tiger Boy. From what he could see, the building would soon be swarming with potential tricks.

A hand fell on Ian's shoulder, startling him. He turned quickly, shaking the grip from his shoulder.

"You don't want to go with them." The Jethro in the plaid shirt said.

"How do you know what I want?" Ian countered.

"It's not for you."

"What's not?" Ian asked, increasingly anxious to see what was taking place in the building.

"Just let them go."

Ian was about to protest further when the dark street lit up with the lights of a police car. The sight of the emergency lights startled him, and he pushed his back to the chipped brick of the building. The car raced down the block, painting the grim buildings in a wash of flashing blue.

"Come on," the Jethro said. "It's already started."

"Thanks," Ian said, following the man back to the well-lit portion of the street. He looked over his shoulder and saw two policemen emerging from their cruiser in front of the cotton mill. Their hulking shapes lumbered over the sidewalk and through the mouth of the building.

He'd never heard of raids on the Butcher's Block. Years ago, undercover cops had patrolled the area and occasionally busted a few guys to bump their quotas, but over the years, the police department had decided their manpower could be used in a more productive way. An all out raid was unheard of, but then again, so was a gathering in a deserted cotton mill. The Butcher's Block wasn't known for its social events.

"What was going on back there?" Ian asked.

"The Party. Happens every few months."

"I've never heard of it," Ian admitted.

"You wouldn't have. It isn't for you, or for me."

"But you knew about it."

"Only by reputation. I've never been."

"So what is it? A rave of some kind?"

"It's not what you think, okay? Just leave it at that."

But this mysterious element of a place he knew so well intrigued him. He saw how his interest aggravated the man before him, and Ian said nothing more on the subject.

They stopped walking on the same corner where Ian had met Tiger Boy. "I'm Rob," the man said.

I don't care, Ian thought. "Ian," he said.

"Good to meet you, Ian."

Now what? he wondered. He had no interest in tricking with the guy, so how did he get rid of him? The problem was Ian had let his guard down. A veil of indifference was fine to keep people away. Every guy on The Block wore some facsimile of it, but once that veil was pierced a needling sense of obligation sank inconvenient hooks. Knowing the man's name made it far more difficult to just walk away.

"So what brings you to the Block tonight?" Rob asked.

It was, of course, a stupid question. Rhetorical at best. There was only one thing that brought anyone to this decrepit part of town, and Ian didn't want *it* from this Jethro. His urge to be away from the man intensified. Sure the guy had kept him out of the warehouse before the cops arrived, but it wasn't like Ian owed him a blowjob for it. "Just hanging out," he said, looking at some indistinct point over Rob's shoulder.

"Feel like getting out of the rain for a bit?"

Hearing a variation on the line he'd fed Tiger Boy and thinking it ridiculous, Ian shook his head. "Just got here," he said, as if some undefined period of time needed to pass before he could commit to an assignation.

"Okay."

Rob made as if to leave and then paused. He turned back to Ian and put a hand on his shoulder. The touch annoyed him inordinately.

"Be careful," Rob said. "The Block is changing. Every night there are more and more kids out here."

And that's a bad thing? Ian wondered. "I think you've saved me enough for one night."

"I'm serious, Ian. Youth isn't simple. It has to be tended, and it's cruel."

He had no idea what Rob was talking about, and didn't really give a shit. Ian didn't know what response was expected of him, so he just said, "Okay. Take it easy."

Ian watched Rob's diminishing form, a sad old man amid many wandering filthy streets searching for something that resembled affection. The rain had stopped while the Jethro had been wasting Ian's time, and now, the dark stretch of the Butcher's Block was crawling with men, but this familiar terrain wasn't what interested Ian; it certainly wasn't the cause of his loitering outside the shoe factory. What interested him was the block north of Wilson Drive, the cotton mill and the party within.

He took one last look to make sure Rob was truly gone for the night, then set off. Though rationally he knew the police had aborted the party, Ian thought he might find something—a flyer, a poster, a ticket—outside the building that would offer a clue to the mysterious event. Rob had said it happened every few months, so it was organized and probably had a committee, a website, a newsletter; it must have some established communication loop, and Ian wanted in.

Crossing Wilson Drive onto the darker side of the street, Ian noticed the police car still parked out front. In fact a second cruiser had joined the first at the curb. It too sat quietly. No lights. No commotion.

If they had raided the party wouldn't the cops have been escorting people out by now? Arresting them?

More interesting to Ian was the sight of two slender figures entering the building heedless of the official vehicles. A sliver of anger slid into his chest as he watched the two shadows vanish into the deserted mill, because he realized the Jethro had played him.

The police weren't busting up the party; they were joining it, or at the very least, providing security for the event. What else explained the lack of panic on the sidewalk? Rob had used the appearance of the police cruiser to unsettle Ian, so getting him alone would be easier. Son of a bitch.

Ian walked the remaining distance to the entrance. He opened the door of the mill and paused, listening for music or the telltale cacophony of a police raid. He heard neither, and he stepped over the threshold into a vast warehouse. No lights burned within. On his right, he made out a row of glass walls, likely the mill's business offices. Ahead, large black shapes sat on either side of a concrete walkway like prehistoric giants, squatting in the cavernous space.

Ahead, an excited whisper crept through the gloom. Ian walked forward, his eyes adjusting to the diminished light with each step. He passed towering cylinders of raw, rotting cotton, left behind when the mill closed, and then massive looms with thousands of tiny teeth for weaving. He counted eight rows of the machines. A clicking sound made Ian's heart skip, but when he turned to locate the source of the noise, he saw nothing but oily shadows. At the end of the corridor, Ian found himself amid a series of fifteen-foot tall vats, once used for dyeing fabric, but there were no further sounds or signs of the great event.

He turned to his left to go deeper into the building. Finally noticing a light burning on his right, he passed between two of the
vats and emerged into a vast open area. A doorway across this
clearing glowed with pale yellow light, flickering as if candlelit.

Ian approached the doorway with caution. He pressed himself
to the wall and peered around the edge. There, at the end of a narrow hall he saw the hulking shoulders of two cops, flanking the
distant opening, but it was the movement in the space beyond that
caught his attention. No music played, no lights flashed, nothing
to indicate a party—only flames dancing from tall braziers. Yet
this was the place. Ian saw flashes of exposed skin; naked men
writhed and crawled over the smooth floor.

Ian needed to see more. But how did he get in? Was there a
ticket? A password? He didn't know, but the heat in his balls was
burning away his caution. He considered strolling down the hall,
casually and confidently like he belonged there, but he discarded
the idea immediately. The event organizers had paid cops for security. They weren't going to let just anybody in.

Backing away from the opening with his shoulders pressed to
the wall, Ian went in search of another entrance.

He walked away from the corridor, running his hands along the
dusty wall at his back. He arrived at another hallway and peered
into the gloom. Walking with his arms in front of him, feeling
his way through the darkness, his left hand touched something
cold and metallic. It was a railing, leading up. Having found the
stairs, he climbed to the first landing where a dull light glowed
behind a transom high on his left. Ian reached out and felt along
the wall until his hand slid over the jamb and found a doorknob.
He turned it and pushed.

Across the room a rectangle—once a window, now nothing
but a hole in the wall—pulsed with warm orange light. Through
this opening, low groans and soft whispers played in a sensual
orchestration. Eager now, he hurried across the office. His shin
cracked on a low table, and Ian whispered a curse as pain shot
from his ankle to his knee.

Dangerous shards of glass formed a frame at the window's base like a row of jagged fangs. The atmosphere beyond was alive, dancing with the flickering light of six iron braziers.

The stands formed a rough circle around the periphery of the warehouse space below. Within the pulsing bath of ginger illumination, dozens of naked men writhed and crawled. The majority of the aggregation was young—some extremely so. Their sweaty skin glimmered. Their muscles flexed and relaxed as they struggled for position in the great mound of flesh. Without exception, the boys were aroused, but they showed no interest in one another.

They focused their attention on the other men—the *old* men. Like tide pools, the youth swirled and swarmed around three aged men. Ian saw the Suburban John down on his right. He lay back on the floor, staring euphorically toward the ceiling. Ian's Tiger Boy straddled the man, bucked his hips frantically against the Suburban John's groin. Around them, boys knelt and bent, eager to touch the Suburban John's skin. He was eager too. His hands reached out, stroking chest and ass and cock, drawing boys to him. At one point, half a dozen youth bent over him, covering his hairy torso like the petals of a succulent plant.

Longing broke over Ian like an ocean wave. He wiped at his brow, suddenly wet with perspiration.

To his left, across the room, two police officers gazed on the orgy with blank faces. Their hands were crossed behind their backs as they observed the hedonism layering the warehouse floor, which was purple-black and shimmered where caressed by the brazier's light.

Though his primary interest lie with the tight and glistening forms of the boys, Ian couldn't help but notice the aged three— *How did they warrant such amazing attentions?* The man on his left was bone thin with sagging skin like wet paper. Fine hairs, similar to spider's webbing covered the knobs of his shoulders. He knelt on the concrete, his mouth working furiously on the array of opportunities jutting toward him. Near the center of the room, a fat man with a short brush of white hair, was on all fours being taken from the front and the back. Young hands kneaded the doughy flesh of his back and his ass. They stroked his cheeks and caressed his scalp lovingly.

Ian ached to join this throng. *What must it cost?* he wondered. Obviously "The Party" was no mere free-for-all held in the guts of a desolate mill. If it were, the aged men would surely be spectators of the event, and not its focus. No, the gray men had paid for these miraculous moments. Such attentions must be pricey, and Ian couldn't help but think that any price was justified.

His gaze traced over smooth, rounded buttocks and muscular backs. It lingered on erect cocks. Tight flesh, endless, supple and slicked with sweat. It was all too wondrous.

His view adjusted to the right, where Ian noticed a row of a dozen chairs lining the wall. Sitting in these chairs were more aged men. They wore black suits with white shirts and crimson ties. Like a jury, they observed the writhing piles of flesh with interest. What part did they play in this festival of meat? Were they waiting their turn to wade into the pool of youth, or did they have other interests? Perhaps simply watching? Whatever the case, Ian couldn't help but think their attire suggested ritual.

Turning away from the black suited onlookers, Ian returned his gaze to the dozens of young men. His lust knew no distinction. Every smooth chest and face not burdened with experience was equally beautiful to him. In the same manner, jealousy amplified Ian's hatred for the older men to a uniform loathing. His abhorrence for the Suburban John was no different from his revulsion for the scrawny wrinkled man with the papery skin, who now tried to stand, though the press of bodies made his task tricky.

"Enough," the withered troll shouted, still struggling to get to his feet.

You're crazy, Ian thought, wondering how anyone could possibly call an end to such a incredible occasion. Still, this line of thinking took him to the notion that once the old parties left, there would be nothing left but the spectacle of beautiful boys.

And how do I get down there?

"Really, now. Stop it." The man said, slapping at the boys that tried to keep him down.

"Enough."

The boys turned to face the men in black suits. Those entertaining the other two men did not cease their performance, but for those focused on the protesting man, it was like a whistle had blown, alerting a pack of dogs. Their full attention fell on the twelve men against the wall to Ian's right. He turned as well, curious to know what signal these boys awaited.

It was nothing more than a nod. A massive gentleman with a thick white beard dropped his chin until his whiskers flattened against his crimson tie. Slowly, he raised his head.

A shrill cry rose before the gesture was complete. Ian spun to it, and took a step back from the windowsill.

The kids surrounding the emaciated old man were no longer interested in his pleasure. A red headed muscle boy with freckles stippling his shoulders lunged forward, mouth open, and he bit into the old man's arm, tearing away a chunk of skin and muscle. The old man shrieked as the boy spit the meat to the purple-black floor and lunged forward for another mouthful. Similarly, a dozen other boys, those closest to the geriatric bit into his skin. Their fingers dug into his mouth and eyes, ripping away bits of tissue. The man screamed until he gagged on the fingers probing his throat. He fell backward, disappearing beneath a wave of glistening skin.

The other two men paid no attention to the screams, now muffled by walls of flesh, bone and organ. Gratification occupied their attentions, and all else fell outside their realm of concern. Horrified, Ian put a hand over his mouth, holding back sickness. What he'd mistaken for a heady exchange of pleasure was a fucking sacrifice. His stomach rose higher in his throat, and he swallowed hard. Light headed, Ian dropped his hands to the window ledge to support his weight, nearly slicing the tops of his fingers on the jagged jaw of glass rising from the cracked frame. He gasped deeply to suppress the ill in his belly.

A moment later, the heavy man in the middle of the room, similarly announced his completion. He rocked back on his knees, grinning broadly, wiping spit, sweat and semen from his face. The second company of boys eagerly turned to the jury of men. Again, the beard dipped.

"No," Ian said, but his throat was so tight, what was intended as a warning scream was little more than a high airy whistle.

This man's destruction was even more awful, because it took longer. He was a fighter. He seemed to register what was happening faster than the withered first victim. As soon as one boy latched teeth onto his shoulder, the man swung out, connecting his broad fist with the kid's nose.

Another boy dove in, and the guy drove knuckles into the guy's throat, sending him choking to the floor. But too much weight and exhaustion played against the victim. Though he sprang to his feet quickly, knocking several boys back in the process, he could gain no momentum to extricate himself from the dozens of hands, the hundreds of teeth, coming for him. A boy bit through his ample belly and spat the meat in the man's face. Then fingers dug into the gaping wound, tearing away yellow wads of fat, liberally laced with blood. The man continued his struggle, but a lithe child with blond hair slithered between his legs and bit through his Achilles heel, sending the enormous man face down on the shiny black floor.

The boys swarmed his carcass. Stomping and biting and gouging, flinging bits of bloody skin and greasy fat into the air as they disassembled their so-recent lover.

Youth isn't simple. It has to be tended, and it's cruel.

Ian stared at the windowsill, the sharp serrated line of glass. He breathed deeply, trying to clear the haze of shock from his mind and the sickness from his gut. Hours seemed to pass as he stood there unable to look back into the arena of sex and brutality.

His attention was again drawn to the warehouse floor still teeming with beautiful little monsters when he heard the Suburban John say, "Thank you." The voice carried high up in the chamber, bouncing from one steel girder to the next. "Just give me a minute to rest." Ian looked at the unfortunate man, who lay on the floor staring upward. His ample endowment, still swollen, draped over his thigh. Around him the boys awaited the bearded man's signal; blood lust rolled from their tense bodies in palpable waves.

The bearded chin dipped.

On the floor of the great room, the Suburban John rolled his head. His eyes met Ian's, and there was the slightest moment of recognition before the whole of him fell beneath the swarm of savage boys.

Ian had seen too much. It was time to go, time to find real cops who weren't part of this ghastly event. He fled the window, raced across the unlit room. He stepped over the threshold into the corridor and caught a glimpse of something black tearing through the darkness at him.

His heart flared panic. A sharp pain erupted on his forehead, and then he was falling.

Ian came to slowly, drifting toward light only to sink again into darkness. Finally, he surfaced into consciousness and found himself in the center of the warehouse. Head screaming with a sharp ache, he blinked and winced at the flames rising from the braziers. He tried to sit up and found it required too much effort, so he sank back to the cool, oddly soft floor.

"Help him," a basso voice commanded.

Suddenly, hands slid under his arms and lifted Ian to a sitting position. A boy knelt behind him, supporting Ian's weight with his back as the two boys that had propped him up walked away. They rejoined the mob of young men, who had formed a circle around the center of the room. All of the killing youths were dressed now. To Ian's left, he saw the Tiger Boy, regarding him as if bored. Ahead of him, the circle was open, revealing the twelve suited men, still sitting in their chairs with shadows and firelight playing over their stern features. The man with the white beard tapped his finger against the arm of his chair.

"How's your head?" he asked.

This brought a round of smiles and a few laughs from the other men. A private joke, or just assholes enjoying Ian's pain?

The room seemed to rock to the side. Ian breathed deeply, trying to right himself on the floor, which now felt spongy and uneven.

"I suppose it doesn't matter," the bearded man said. "You were trespassing, spying on events that don't concern you."

"What are you going to do to me?" Ian mumbled, each syllable bringing a clang of agony to his head.

"Such a mercenary attitude," the man replied. His tone was light and unthreatening as if commenting on a piece of décor he couldn't care less about.

"I won't tell anyone," Ian said.

Again, the jury smiled. They laughed. The boys in the circle added their voices to the amused chorus.

"That's very generous of you," the bearded man said around a chuckle.

Ian rolled his head against that of the boy behind him and was again struck by the strange floor covering. It wasn't rubber, but it possessed the shiny supple quality of that material. Further, it was perfectly sleek, polished, and clean. What had become of the fragments of the boys' victims? No tissue littered the black shimmering surface. There weren't even bloodstains. How was that possible? How long had he been unconscious?

"How?" he said.

"How indeed," the bearded man said glibly.

"You murdered them."

"The world will hardly notice. Youth gave them their color; now youth has faded leaving them all but transparent. Only those very near saw them. Family. Friends."

"But you're..." Ian let the sentence end, fearing he would insult this dreadful jury.

"Old? Much older than you think." A minor smile disturbed the edges of the man's mouth. "But we're comfortable in our skins. Youth is a commodity we understand though hardly value. I, for one, find the work of Pollock cold and soulless, but that doesn't mean I won't get a fortune for it at auction. The same can be said for our boys. We accommodate them, and in return, they use their beauty to serve us."

"Serve you?"

"You do go on with your questions, don't you?" the bearded man asked, as if speaking to an inquisitive child. "Yes, they serve. Errands. Chores. Favors. A vast miscellany of minor events that help to shape the days ahead." The bearded man stood from the chair and extended his hands. "Boys, thank you for a wonderful night. We're finished here."

Ian pushed away from the kid at his back and struggled to his feet. The floor beneath him seemed to shift as if he road a raft on gentle surf. Ian turned to the crowd of boys. They ran across the concrete toward the loading bay door. Once they reached its edge they leapt into the beating rain and disappeared—a beautiful nocturnal herd racing toward another night of life.

Murderers, Ian thought, but was unable to see them as anything but lovely.

"They killed those men," he whispered.

"We all serve something," the bearded man told him. "The boys serve us. We serve another."

As if in answer to the man's words, the floor covering crept forward, sending Ian crashing. He hit the sinuous surface and rolled as the purple-black mass shifted and rippled, moving across the concrete toward the shadows beneath the office loft. Ian's bowels turned icy as he rolled and tumbled from the living carpet to land on the cold poured stone.

Ian watched sickened as the grotesque shape rose like a wave. It clutched the overhang above, draping to the floor in a smooth sheet the color of midnight. A ripple rolled across the surface and then another. The skin of this impossible being wrinkled and crested until violent tremors covered it, and in moments it took on the texture of a storm battered ocean. Amid this turmoil a pale shape emerged, pushing through the tortured membrane like the hull of a capsized ship until it was fully disgorged and released to the concrete with a wet slap. A second figure appeared and then a third.

Ian's breath came in short, harsh gasps. The shapes—superficially human yet unfinished—writhed before him. Smooth faces, hardly more defined than porcelain masks crinkled with pain as gaping mouths shrieked through purple viscous discharge. The man with the beard crossed to the squirming things and gently slid his foot beneath one of the quivering heads. The incomplete boy rubbed his cheek against the man's trousers, leaving a trail of glimmering slime on the black fabric; his piercing cries hardly ebbed. Fingers like snaking vines clasped the leg for leverage as the thing climbed to a sitting position, holding the bearded man's thigh tightly like a child clutching its mother for comfort, all the while it continued caressing the pant leg with its cheek. The bearded man reached down to pat the creature's head.

"From transparent to vivid," he said amused.

"Those aren't...?" Ian couldn't finish the impossible speculation.

"We're finished here," the bearded man said again. All of the jury members stood. Three came forward and each collected one of the bawling things from the floor. Then they filed to the back of the warehouse and disappeared through a narrow door. Ian turned and watched the policemen leave their posts at the entrance to the warehouse. Two more officers moved out of the shadows behind the row of chairs where the jury had sat and chatted amongst themselves, as if Ian had already been forgotten.

He backed toward the hallway slowly, his eyes darting between the purple-black creature at the wall and the bearded man, who turned away annoyed. "Get out," he said.

"You're just letting me leave?"

"Of course," the bearded man said. He looked over his shoulder at Ian, eyes shining with intelligence and disdain. "You're irrelevant."

Ian barely noted the cruelty of the dismissal. He fled the warehouse, made his way through the unlighted mill and emerged into the downpour thrashing the pavement of the Butcher's Block. As he raced across Wilson Drive and fell under the street lamp's beam, his tightly knit thoughts began to unravel, revealing moments of violence wrapped around images of glistening skin. The beauty. The perversion. He tried to run faster, knocking a man out of his way, ignoring the man's growling protest as he bolted over the sidewalk.

On the far end of the block, he turned left and was struck by the sight of the Suburban John's car, now abandoned. The empty sedan rose liked a tomb from the curb where it would remain until the police impounded it, the owner's use for the vehicle having now passed. Ian slowed. He approached his own car, digging into his pocket for the keys. He punched the button that unlocked the door and slid inside.

Out of the rain, his frayed thoughts continued to loosen and fall apart. What he'd witnessed in the warehouse was unconscionable. It was evil. He should burn the place to the ground—wait for the next party and ignite the factory, purge it of the seductive boys and the jury they served. That ungodly creature had to burn too; The Party had to end.

Ian slotted his key and started the ignition. He turned on the headlights and the windshield wipers. The glass before him briefly cleared before it was again spattered with heavy raindrops.

Two young men walked through the downpour, oblivious to the weather. Though unfamiliar to Ian, they might have been part of the butchering crowd. They were young enough.

Beautiful enough.

The boys peered in at Ian. Unimpressed with what they saw, both looked away and continued down the sidewalk.

These were the eager faces capable of *shaping the days ahead*, Ian realized. They were nothing more or less than young—the equivalent of being nothing more or less than gold. They mattered...

And...

You are irrelevant.

The bearded juror had understood his meaninglessness. He'd felt no more threatened divulging his knowledge to Ian than he would have in revealing it to a wall, a rock, or a pet. Ian could influence no one, change nothing.

He killed the ignition. The wipers stalled but the headlights remained on, cutting the blur of gray ahead into a static of silvery needles, visible for only a moment before the glass was again streaked, melting any semblance of clarity. He pressed into the seat, and a burst of chills erupted across his back.

Before him was an abhorrent road, smeared and all but impossible to navigate, a road that took him irrevocably forward to erode in miniscule increments from weather and misuse. He would pass through the countryside, but his ability to access the beautiful terrain would dwindle.

He could see it—all of the splendor—but his ability to touch it, to be part of it, would fade with each passing mile, until he was nothing but an impotent voyeur, a prisoner in the vehicle. And what waited at the road's end?

He suddenly envied the butchered old men. Their pain had been terrible, surely, but at least it had been brief, and then they'd found new life—fresh youth; the wonder of it alone would be worth the anguish.

Ian wanted to go back, not tonight and not to destroy, but instead to participate.

Tonight the Party was long done, but he would return to the Block tomorrow night and the night after and every coming night. And on one occasion he would find himself in the company of beautiful young men, and they would escort him through the filthy streets to their party, where he would again meet the jury and their generous monster. The lovely boys would undress him and love him, and he would gratefully endure their attentions, fulfilling small needs until the rending of his flesh brought the bliss of rebirth.

Testify

PATROLMAN JOEL MCCAULEY, AUGUST 19:

Me and my partner, Dekins, were first on the scene. Dispatch got one of those "What's that smell" calls at 9:04 pm, and we were directed to the Travis Apartments in North Central Austin. Even before we opened the door, we knew the news wasn't good. The smell you know? The temperature had been up in the nineties for a couple of days, and the air conditioner wasn't running, so the heat had baked that stench into a simmering whiff of hell.

When I was a kid I belonged to the Boy Scouts. This was in small town East Texas so we were tied into the community good and tight, and once a week a bunch of us made the rounds and did odd jobs for the elderly. One Saturday morning I visited Mrs. Eva Cross. Usually I mowed her lawn and took out her trash; sometimes I'd help her get something off a shelf. That Saturday morning, I found her hanging in her garage. She'd been there for a few days. So I got the scent in my nose real young, and that smell is like a primary color—no mistaking it.

Anyway, the TV was on. You could hear it through the door clear as day, and that stink of rot was creeping out from around the jamb. No one answered the bell—which didn't surprise me or Dekins—and we entered the residence.

The door opened onto a small living room. It looked like a college kid's dorm, right down to the empty pizza box on the floor. To the left was a real nice Sony flat panel jobbie. A foreign flick with subtitles played on the screen. I remember that because the voices seemed unreal—gutteral and harsh, like they spoke in one of those Eastern Block countries. It might have been Russian for all I know. It doesn't matter.

To our right was a relatively new beige sofa—small but not quite a loveseat. We found the victim there. At first he looked like a pile of clothes waiting to be folded, but the truth of it came clear soon enough.

I've never seen anything like it. My daughter cuts these man-shaped dolls out of construction paper. All kids do, I guess. Well the victim looked like one of those dolls if the child had gotten mad at her creation and crumpled it in her fists. Seemed like every bone in the kid's body had been snapped, legs and arms bent at unnatural angles, his torso compressed into a plump sack because his spine and rib cage had been turned to mush.

I didn't know it was that guy from the news.

Louis Dervers—Facebook Post, May 9:

Well kids we've got a new one!!! It seems you can't swing a dead cat without hitting another anti-gay, Christian man-cunt with a taste for cock. This time it's Reverend Robert Wright, seen in the photo with bible in hand and "Angel" (a confirmed male prostitute) close on his heels. The pic was taken by a hotel employee who recognized Wright and said it wasn't the first time the reverend had checked in with a bit of boy candy in tow. I'd like to be surprised, but honestly, the reverend's oh-so-lush, Burt-Reynolds-circa-Smokey-and-the-Bandit mustache clued me in long ago.

STATEMENT FROM XAVIER DUMAS, FORMER CONCIERGE FOR THE HOTEL PALADIN (DALLAS), AUGUST 19:

I'd worked at the hotel for more than eight years and prided myself on excellence in customer service and absolute discretion. These things are important to note, so you understand that posting those pictures wasn't some lark of provocation. Further, I understood from the moment I took those pictures that I stood every chance of losing my job, and I took them anyway, and I made them public. Some things are more important than a paycheck.

Robert Wright has spent his life using his bible as a weapon against the LGBT community. Since his early ministries when he equated homosexuality with bestiality, pedophilia, and incest, he has been an agent of hate. Twenty years ago he formed Family in Front, an organization built on disseminating anti-gay propaganda and establishing those disgusting reformation centers where unbalanced men and women pay thousands of dollars to be "cured" of their homosexuality. He has used his ministry to support conservative candidates across the nation to promote and strengthen the anti-gay agenda. In recent years conservative politicians have adopted him. They call him a spiritual advisor, but he's nothing but a lobbyist for hate legislation. He claims to be compelled to his work, that he "hates" no one; he's doing the will of god. The guards at Auschwitz said they were doing the will of the Führer. It wasn't their fault either.

Just following orders.

On several previous occasions I had seen Robert Wright in the company of young men who seemed to be of a certain type. He made it something of a ritual, visiting the hotel for a day or two before flying down to Austin to wield his influence on the State Legislators. I knew what the hypocrite was doing, but without proof—something absolutely concrete—I refused to make accusations, even against a man who stood for everything I despised. This time I had my cell phone in hand when he entered with the young man, who called himself "Angel." I began taking pictures immediately and kept taking them until the two disappeared into the elevator.

With my suspicions all but confirmed, I waited for the young man to return to the lobby, which he did an hour and a half later. Upon emerging from the elevator I asked him over to the concierge desk. I suggested that I often received requests for men in his line of work from guests in the hotel. I used the common euphemism of "massage" and he informed me that he lived in Austin so clients in Dallas wouldn't be convenient for him, but he could be found at a certain website under the name Angel.

After he left, I visited the website for confirmation.

In the end, I had no choice. I had to expose Wright and his hypocrisy. And yes, I lost my job the day after I posted the pictures on the web. Of course all of the attention immediately fell on "Angel," which would have been fine if he'd shown the slightest integrity.

I was infuriated when the little prick went to the news and denied everything.

JIMMY "ANGEL" ROYCE, QUOTED IN THE *DAILY REGISTER*, MAY 10:

"Mr. Wright hired me as a therapeutic massage technician. That is the extent of my relationship with the man. To my knowledge, Mr. Wright is a devoted family man. Our meetings were in no way sexual in nature."

STATEMENT FROM THE REVEREND ROBERT WRIGHT, MAY 11:

As the ridiculous allegations fly across the internet, I find myself under attack. As such, I will leave this argument to the jackals and return to my home in Nashville. There I intend to pray and reflect surrounded by the love of close friends and family. However, in light of today's news story in the *Daily Register*, I will be retaining the services of a defamation attorney, who will be addressing this matter immediately. Cruel innuendo is one thing, but to pass it off as factual is both reprehensible and illegal.

To be clear, I am not gay. I have never been gay. I've devoted my life to pulling Christian souls back from that abyss and will continue to do so until my dying day.

OFFICIAL STATEMENT (DATED MAY 11) FROM GERALD CHAMBERS, EXECUTIVE DIRECTOR, FAMILY IN FRONT:

Reports have been circulating regarding the Reverend Wright's involvement with a male prostitute. Though the suppositions are genuinely disturbing to all of us here, Revered Wright has not been a guiding force for this organization in over six years. Yes, he was a founder of Family in Front but we have taken his early vision and expanded its reach and efficacy. Our successes speak for themselves. That noted, Family in Front, has neither knowledge of nor connection to the Reverend's current practices, whether they be business related or private in nature.

Should these allegations prove true in any way, it is our sincerest hope that Revered Wright's faith will lead him back to us. Thousands of homosexual men and women have entered our enlightenment facilities to find their way back to Jesus Christ and experience his love and forgiveness, free of the sin and self-loathing it instills. Our prayers go out to Reverend Wright. Our doors are always open to him. We can only sympathize with the pain this incident must be causing him.

STATEMENT FROM MORT HAMMER, CORONER, AUGUST 20:

I remember it well enough. You always remember the ones you can't explain.

I mean, look, it's obvious the kid died from blunt force trauma. The M.E. made it clear that the body hadn't been moved or dumped, so Royce died where he sat. But what killed him? I've seen suicides in better shape after thirty-story dives onto concrete.

Let's see...

All of the major bones in his body were shattered—not just broken—but shattered, yet his skull was untouched. I have never seen a bludgeoning victim that didn't have head wounds. Never. But everything above the neck was intact and unmarred. Then there's the issue of his face. His facial contortions were inconsistent with those of a victim who'd undergone extensive bludgeoning. In such cases we'd expect the victim to pass out from trauma or slip into a comatose state as the internal organs ceased proper function. Granted the lids might retreat to some degree during rigor, but Royce's eyes were wide open. In fact, he looked startled as if death occurred instantaneously.

His organs were pulped and lacerated by bone shards. Most notably were the lungs, which had suffered hundreds of tears from rib fragments. They fell apart in strips when I tried to remove them from the cavity.

So he was beaten to death...except he wasn't.

The condition of his dermis—his skin—was not in keeping with what we expect to find in such cases. We have to suppose that it took some time for Royce to die, particularly since there was no cranial damage involved. So, we would expect to see subtle differences in the bruising patterns of wounds inflicted ante- and postmortem. The first contusions would have necessarily begun swelling, and there would have been some initial coagulation in the subcutaneous tissues in and around the burst blood vessels.

I found no such thing.

To make things all the more what-the-fuck? the skin itself, the outer dermal layer showed no signs of distress, which is to say, the bruising and bleeding were all internal. The skin was only broken in seven places, and all of those wounds were the result of compound bone fractures: three ribs through the chest and back, both femurs, a fibula and an ulna. So it looks like the kid was beaten to shit from the inside out, which is impossible.

Officially, I wrote it up as blunt force trauma by weapon or weapons unknown. Unofficially, it looks like someone wrung the kid out like a sponge.

STATEMENT FROM ESTHER BOUTTE, PARISHIONER AT SACRED CALLING CHURCH, MAY 10:

I don't believe a word of it. The Revered Wright has been graced by our Lord, and we have bathed together in Christ's glory. He is a good man, and the greatest spiritual leader our country has known since the Reverend Billy Graham first took the pulpit.

The good reverend's devotion to Christ has guided him through advanced studies in the world's religions. He didn't just accept his calling; he committed himself to it, studied it and compared it to the ramblings of the Muslims, the Jews, the Orientals, and the Africans, so he understood how dark and flawed those faiths were when compared to the perfect light of Christianity. He even studied many occult practices to better understand the challenges of being a Christian soldier.

"Know thy enemy," he used to say. He knew, and I know, too.

The purveyors of sin are devious and deceptive. But they showed their true colors this time. The homosexuals know good and well that nothing is so disgusting and unnatural to our Lord as their sickness. They know it! That's why they have tried to stain the Reverend's good name in this way. Every demon below is willing to call a holy man brother if it will mislead his flock and send them wandering into sin unprotected.

We've seen through their tricks this time. Yes sir, we have. Our congregation has already begun a collection to help the Reverend through this soul-sickening time.

Ooops he did it again! Second call boy comes forward to claim he's had "The Wright Stuff."

Follow the link to the hilarity!

STATEMENT FROM JENNY LOWREY, SISTER OF JIMMY ROYCE, AUGUST 10:

Why do you want to know about our childhood? It was what it was, and what it was was crappy.

Fulton wasn't the most progressive city, even by Mississippi's standards, and I think Jimmy and I both understood at a really young age that we didn't belong there. I read a lot and that made me something of an alien to the other kids, who were more interested in rough housing and causing trouble—you know, pranks on neighbors and picking through the town dump for garbage they thought was precious. The girls were hardly different from the boys. They'd shoot their slingshots and b.b. guns, killing squirrels and birds and whatever they could get in their sights. I didn't understand their glee in cruelty, and Jimmy was... he was just different. Mostly he stayed in his room and played an old, broken down guitar. He tried to make friends, but the other kids...

I did what I could to protect him once things at school got bad, but we were in different grades, and I couldn't be everywhere at once, you know?

He had one good friend. Her name was Myrna, and I loved her for taking care of Jimmy, but I didn't like her very much. She wasn't all that smart, and she tried too hard, like she was desperate to hold on to the two of us.

Still, we three played together right up until I started high school. We went to movies and played Monopoly and Go Fish. Our favorite game was called Buffy—because of that television program? It was really just a variation of Hide and Seek. One of us would be "Buffy" and would carry around this piece of foam we'd cut to look like a stake. The other two would be vampires.

We'd hide and if "Buffy" found one of us and could "stab" us with the foam stake, we were dead and had to wait until the other vampire was killed. Jimmy wanted to play that game all the time.

It let him be a kid. Most of the time he didn't get to just be a kid.

We basically had to take care of ourselves, you know? Mama worked a couple of jobs—at the grocery and at the lumberyard—and in between shifts she drank beer and chain smoked, and on her days off, she stayed in bed. Daddy? Who can say? I remember him, like those really early memories where everyone is just a shadow moving through a blur? And I remember, or I tell myself I remember, that he smelled like sawdust. Jimmy was too young to remember anything about him, and maybe that's better. There were no pictures of him, none that I could find anyway, and Mama never talked about him. The only men around the house were the guys Mama met at work—most of them married. They came and went before we really got to know them very well. Maybe that's why I got married too young and why Jimmy...

Don't misunderstand. I don't think that's what made him queer. No one knows how that happens, but I do think it taught him to keep people at a distance, and I think that...well it kind of helped him when he... I think it made his job easier.

Dude X—A source close to the victim, August 17:

Oh hell no, Jimmy didn't know his husband du jour was Robert Wright. No way, not until later. I mean it's not like the dark queen of the fundie movement gave him a business card or invited him to prayer meetings. I'm pretty sure Bottom-Boy Bob wanted Jimmy on his knees, but it had nothing to do with repentance. Right? We get these closet cases all the time in our line of work—married guys, politicians, priests—and part of the job is being discreet. The client is paying you to keep your mouth shut until he wants it open. Right? Ha!

I totally understand why Jimmy flipped on Wright, though—I think any one of us would have—because I'm not gay for pay, you know what I mean? Once I get my acting career off the ground, I'm done with buyaboy.com like forever. It's good money and the work is easy, but the glamour wore off fast, you know what I mean? After that, I'm still gonna be queer, and I have to live in the world assholes like Wright are fucking up.

I mean he's like the spiritual leader to half the fuckers in congress? You keep hearing about separating church and state but they go together like lube and anal beads, you know what I mean?

I absolutely think Wright and his Wrongs are behind Jimmy's death. If Wright didn't hire the job out, then one of his freaktastic fundie followers did it to save the Reverend's good name. Whatever, man. It's fucked up, and Jimmy's still dead.

Remember, I don't want you using my name. This is totally anonymous. Call me Dude X. Right? That sounds fucking rad. Dude X. Ha.

JIMMY "ANGEL" ROYCE, QUOTED IN THE *DAILY REGISTER*, MAY 15:

"Mr. Wright hired my services through the buyaboy.com website. At that time he inquired about my rates for a variety of sexual acts. We came to an arrangement and met. I will not go into details, but I can say that our meetings were sexual in nature."

"Yes, we did have sex."

STATEMENT FROM REPORTER YVONNE VALDEZ, JUNE 14:

As a professional courtesy, I'll say...do your own fucking work. I've been on this story for weeks, and every piece of relevant information has already appeared in one of my articles. So read them! Or if you can't be bothered, I'll give you the highlights. Anti-gay Christian Celeb slams nasties with rent boy in Dallas hotel. They get caught. Rent boy tries to protect his client and says things never got hard and moist. Rent boy finds out exactly who his trick was and decides to come clean. He gives me an exclusive interview and is murdered later that same night while laying low in the apartment of a friend who was out of town. The cops have suspects falling out of their asses but not a bit of evidence.

There, now you know what about sixty million other people know. Fucking amateurs.

Quotes drawn from a variety of social media sites:

May 15:

"OMG!!!"

"Like there was any doubt. Wright was just another self-hater who punished the LGBT community for living the life he wanted for himself."

"Up is down. Black is white. Wright is wrong! So fucking wrong."

"Wright served the church and let them drain his humanity, because he believed it when they called him abomination. Self-loathing. Vicious. Disgusting. Bravo Jimmy Royce for dragging this piece of shit kicking and screaming into the light of day."

"Bravo, Angel [Jimmy]! You're our hero!"

"This is heroic? He was forced by the media to say SOMETHING. He was either going to align himself with Wright, who's on his way down or with the gay community, who will put his face on magazine covers and support his ass for the rest of his life. Was the decision that difficult? That heroic? Reach higher people."

"I <3 Jimmy!"

MAY 16:

"If we lose, Satan wins. Send your donations today."

"Wright's church is actually raising money for his de-queerification! WTF?!?!"

"We've all swallowed a load here and there, but those poor dumb fuckers have to be drowning by now."

MAY 17:

"Rest in Peace, Jimmy. My heart holds you."

"Another Angel in heaven."

"One more fag in the fire. Ha. Ha. Ha."

STATEMENT FROM THE REVEREND ROBERT WRIGHT, MAY 26:

Never before have I so well understood the weakness of man. I thought I was beyond temptation, far from the whispered invitations of sin. That was my pride, and this is my fall.

Without delving into the unwholesome details, I am issuing this statement to confirm that the well-publicized allegations against me are, to some minor extent, true. I admit this knowing that the only path to Our Lord is one of honesty, and though this path often winds through brutal and unforgiving terrain, I will travel it, guided by love and light.

I have embarrassed my family, my friends, my church and the countless devoted who have looked to me for guidance all these long years. I can only say that I'm sorry. I'm unwell, and with the help of Our Lord I will fight my way back to grace.

Placing myself in the hands of my brothers and sisters, I will undergo counseling at one of the excellent Family in Front facilities. I prefer to leave the location unspecified so that my personal shame and the notoriety it has fostered will not interfere with the enlightenment of myself or any other Christian seeking clarity and grace.

STATEMENT FROM MYRNA JONES, AUGUST 17:

Jimmy and I were best friends. We've been friends since grade school. We came to Austin together last year because he'd heard all about the music scene, but mostly we came to Austin because we both wanted to get the heck out of Fulton, Mississippi.

We talked about everything, and yeah, he told me about Wright. I mean, he didn't know the guy was a reverend, certainly didn't know he was famous, but he told me about a guy—I figured it was Wright because of the timing, you know? Anyway, Jimmy told me about this client—Jimmy always called them clients—and this one had hired him off the website and paid Jimmy to drive up to Dallas. He did it in February and then again in May when...well, you know.

Jimmy said the guy was into role-playing, which happens all the time I guess, but Wright was a strange one. He didn't want to be a naughty schoolboy or a prison inmate getting worked over by a guard. He wanted Jimmy to stick a doll with needles while he was fu...while they were conducting business. Jimmy told me the guy howled like a snake-bit dog when one of those needles slid into the doll's body. Like voodoo you know?

Jimmy laughed his ass off about it after the first time they met, telling me all about the nut job with his dollies. The second time he didn't think it was so funny. See, Jimmy and Wright had finished their business and Wright was in the bathroom cleaning up. The door was closed and Jimmy heard the water running, and he was kind of bored so he picked up the doll and for laughs, he jabbed a needle through the thing's chest.

Well, the next thing he knows Wright is screaming like a stuck pig—which is about right if you ask me—and Jimmy yanks the needle out of the doll. Wright comes screaming out of the bathroom, and he snatches the doll from Jimmy's hand and tells him to get out of the room.

The whole thing freaked Jimmy bad. Then those pictures hit the web and suddenly reporters and weirdos were everywhere. It just got worse after...after he di...was killed.

You saw what happened at his funeral. All those a-holes with their "God Hates Fags" signs, and the gays were there and the two groups were screaming at each other across the street, and there were all of those cameras and news crews and I kept thinking, why are you people here? You didn't love him. You didn't even know him. He's just a thing to you. A doll for stupid, greedy children to tear apart.

STATEMENT FROM ESTHER BOUTTE, PARISHIONER AT SACRED CALLING CHURCH, MAY 10:

The Reverend was married, you know. His wife, Evelyn, was a beautiful Christian woman. They were a blessed couple. When she died he was absolutely devastated, as anyone would be after losing a true and pure love. I'm not surprised he never married again. The whole thing was so tragic. She fell down the stairs of their home in Nashville. Broke her neck. What made it all the more heartbreaking was that Reverend Wright was talking to her on the phone the very moment it happened. He called Evelyn from his hotel in New York as he did every night when his calling took him away from home, and they were having a pleasant as you please conversation. And then she lost her footing. He had to listen to her fall. Can you imagine anything so horrible?

NOTE FROM KIM VANDERHOOF, PROFESSOR OF RELIGIOUS STUDIES, ST. PAUL'S UNIVERSITY (DALLAS):

I'm afraid you're the victim of lurid horror films and the machinations of the Caribbean and New Orleans tourism boards. In actuality "voodoo doll" is, at best, a misnomer. Firstly, the use of sympathetic magic is more in line with the practices of Hoodoo, a bastardization of Vodou (note the spelling) that became popular in the Southern United States centuries ago. Of course, the practice of jabbing pins in representational figures has an extensive history in folk magic and has examples in nearly every primitive culture. This is not unexpected when considered in the context of a population of immature intellect. For instance, when a child plays with a doll, she gives the toy attributes—whether of herself or others—essentially creating a kind of reality for the plaything. In an environment of pervasive superstition and limited intellectual growth, it is easy to see how this function of childhood imagination could evolve into a facet of an overarching mystical belief system. The doll not only represents the subject, but is also magically connected to the subject. Once this belief is established in a receptive population, it is easy enough to manipulate and propagate.

This is not to say that dolls are completely foreign to Vodou practitioners. Often, they will nail effigies—called poppets—with an old shoe to trees. They generally do this near cemeteries, with the dolls acting as symbolic messengers to the afterlife. And the dolls of babies may be placed on altars and other objects designed to honor spirits, but only in the lowest of folk religions do we see the use of sympathetic representations—i.e. dolls, photographs, etchings—in rituals meant to curse or bless an individual.

That noted, I can provide you an extensive list of resource materials if you are interested in pursuing a detailed study of Vodou as a religion and its cultural impact.

STATEMENT FROM THE REVEREND ROBERT WRIGHT, AUGUST 21:

I cannot thank my brothers and sisters in Christ enough for their support during this difficult time. After succumbing to weakness and confusion, straying far from the path our Lord has designed for me, I can now return to my teachings and my calling, feeling embraced and emboldened by the Word of God.

When I was first instrumental in creating Family in Front, I never thought that I would one day walk through those doors, low and shamed and seeking the warmth and light of their charity.

Perhaps it was always God's plan that I should save myself by first seeking to save others. I thank Him every moment of every day for guiding me home.

I leave this facility a stronger, yet humbled man, who is truer to himself and closer to his Lord.

PATROLMAN JOEL MCCAULEY, AUGUST 19:

The Jimmy Royce investigation is ongoing

The Dodd Contrivance

Imagine looking into a raindrop and seeing an entire world at work—the labor and the joy and the pain of its populace; the celebrations and the battles; the shifting currents of climate traversing miniscule continents and infinitesimal oceans—all encased in a liquid pellet with a volume no greater than that of an inconsequential breadcrumb forgotten between stove and larder. With this as your supposition, it is then necessary to discard the premise or become overwhelmed, because surely if such a world can exist in one drop, others must exist as well, and following this hypothesis it stands to reason that the real world, the one occupied by man and beast, king and servant, is likewise sheathed and similarly fragile.

And what should happen when those drops collide? Could gutter streams and filthy puddles be universes unto themselves, where the many worlds come together to struggle anew with fresh species from neighboring worlds, or merely confluences of destroyed planets with uncounted casualties that had briefly thought themselves immortal as they plummeted from cloud to dirt?

Samuel Beaufort smiled at this whimsical notion, sitting in his favorite chair at the window and listening to the rapping rain. It was a familiar fancy, one he revisited often, though only in his thoughts. In the one instance he'd actually voiced the idea to a small group of colleagues at the club, he'd been summarily excoriated with disdainful glares, so he'd learned to consider the theory a personal entertainment rather than a topic of conversation. Coffee cooled in a china cup resting on the mahogany table beside him, forgotten as he gazed at the precipitation beading on the pane. Rainfall speckled the glass, smearing the light cast by the few lamps still burning in the city beyond. At his feet, the honey-colored hound whimpered and nuzzled his ankle. He looked down into the warm dark eyes and nodded solemnly.

"Of course, it's impossible. It's likely quite insane, but isn't that what makes it such an interesting study?"

The hound responded with a second whimper and a more forceful push at his leg. Then the animal stood, stretched out its front paws and began circling the Persian carpet. The bitch was still quite young, though her exact age Samuel did not know. One afternoon just over a month ago she had joined him on his stroll through the central park and proved fine company, and since he lived alone—his long-passed wife having died in her twenty-second year—he thought to bring a second heartbeat into the too-quiet home. He'd named the animal Ruby after a particularly scandalous aunt, and though she often still bounded with the unrestrained energy of youth, he found her a pleasant companion in an otherwise empty home.

"You're quite right," Samuel told the dog while pushing himself from the chair. "We should take the next step and examine this phenomenon in greater detail. What kind of scientists would we be if we left all things in the realm of theory and speculation?"

After retrieving Ruby's tether, his own topcoat, hat and gloves, Samuel withdrew his umbrella from the stand at the front door and allowed Ruby to lead him into the storm. Samuel had always loved the smell of the rain, reveled in the clatter of a particularly forceful storm. When viewed through the pelting drops the buildings around him took on the texture of raw wool—gray, nebulous, and frayed. A climax of thunder cowered the dog, who pulled back on the lead, now uncertain about taking her constitutional in such dreary weather.

"Ruby," he said, "discovery is a terrifying thing, which is why so few have the heart to accomplish it. Now, let's explore."

Though apparently not convinced of her master's supposition, Ruby took a hesitant step toward him. Soon enough, she fell in at his heel, beneath the cover of the umbrella as Samuel guided her to the south.

The gray static of rain against the black backdrop of night soothed him. Streetlamp flames spluttered, flashing yellow auroras in the gloom. Carriages crossed the boulevard ahead, but the streets were otherwise unoccupied, and Samuel's fascination with worlds within the rain transformed into a new fancy. Turning away to allow Ruby some privacy while she relieved herself beside a stoop, Samuel began to consider what being truly alone might be like. What if the entire city, the entire world, were to be emptied of humanity, leaving only himself and his fine companion to wander smooth roads and grassy dales, seeing the important locations of the earth without the hindrance of a populace? Would such desolation prove soothing or maddening?

Ever since Leslie's death some ten years past, Samuel had been alone. Parents long dead and no siblings, his only remaining family consisted of an Uncle who lived in Charleston and another in Albany, along with a number of cousins with whom he'd socialized extensively in his youth but had seen rarely in recent years. His social circle was quite large, but his friendships few. The men at the club were such rigid creatures, never questioning their status or the social structure that allowed them it, but rather blustering on without a hint of inquisitiveness, reaffirming their position and denigrating those who fell beneath it. Samuel knew they considered him an odd-duck, perhaps even crazy for all of his chatter about what might be rather than extolling the virtues and vices of day-to-day existence. The only member of the club who truly intrigued him, though he could not claim friendship with the man, was one Hubert Dodd, a bearish braggart with a penchant for inappropriate often scandalous humor and the ability to weave gilded lies that engaged with their sheer brazenness. Though not close to the man, Samuel admired Dodd's imagination and listened intently whenever the man regaled the salon with one of his outlandish tales.

Often, Samuel had thought to invite Hubert Dodd to his home for a meal. He found the man at turns overbearing and standoffish, yet always fascinating. He'd thought to question the man in some detail about the adventures he'd recounted, perhaps even catch Dodd in a lie, though not to embarrass the man, but rather to show that Samuel thought the stories remarkable, regardless of their veracity. He felt a kinship with Dodd. They both had suffered the hushed derision of their conservative peers, yet both were established enough in the society to remain on the guest lists for all of the right gatherings. But he'd never managed a proper introduction, let alone extended a social invitation.

Ruby's pleading whine and her wet haunches against his trousers alerted Samuel to her desire to leave his fanciful experiment behind and return to the warmth of the fire. He was about to acquiesce when a great bolt of lightning ripped the sky above them and a cannon-shot of thunder peeled.

His terrified hound backed away, ducking low to the ground, and before Samuel could calm her skittish nerves, Ruby had escaped her tether. The honey-colored hound barked furiously at the sky. Whimpered. Then she set off in a blinding tear, leaving Samuel with a damp leather strap and a look of surprise on his face. A gust of wind pulled hard against the bowl of his umbrella, sending him back a step, but this concession to motion proved to be a necessary goading. He ran after his dog, into the storm, through dim, empty streets, lit only by flickering lamps and flashes of lightning.

In the distance he heard the muffled yaps of his companion, and they guided him, but the clatter of the weather muddled his sense of direction. He turned right, certain Ruby's voice had risen from that direction, only to have the familiar bark rise at a great distance to his back. The poor creature was obviously traumatized by the storm, running aimlessly for someplace warm and dry, a place she would perceive as safe. If she were a rational animal she'd return home, flee to the north where an old soup bone and the roar on Samuel's hearth would assure her comfort, but for all of her fine companionship, Ruby was not a great thinker and instead had to rely on inaccurate instinct for guidance.

Samuel followed her on a winding path beneath tall brick homes. Caught sight of her twice, dashing like she had a fox in her nose, ignoring his calls and vanishing around a distant corner.

Finally he came upon his dear hound in an alley between two grand structures—a large, fashionable house and another building which, save for its intricate architectural detail, including a cornice of brass about the eaves, he might have taken to be a carriage house or stable. The corridor between them ended in a high stone wall, and rain coursed over the barrier, giving it the appearance of a great perspiring beast. The door to the house stood open, as did the one to the detached building. A dull glow oozed from the opening on his right, providing a trifling illumination to the scene before him.

Ruby crouched facing the corner between the outbuilding and the wall. Her growls were all but eaten by the torrential clatter, but she seemed to have cornered something, perhaps a cat or one of the raccoons that scavenged the city's waste. He hoped it wasn't a rat. Samuel loathed the creatures and a chill ran over his neck and spine as he considered having to face one.

But as he moved closer to the scene, a flash of lightning bathed the alley and Samuel gasped. The bleaching light revealed Ruby's prey in brief, vivid detail. It was no rat. But exactly what this creature *was* he could not say.

Though the size of an average cat, and possessing some feline traits about the head, this beast was hairless and the color of muddy water. It's legs jointed awkwardly, reminding him of sketches he'd seen of the crocodiles said to roam the Nile Valley. The unnaturalness of the animal lodged in Samuel's throat and knitted a web of uncertainty in his mind. His curiosity insisted he carefully observe and catalog this beast; understand something of its composition, but a potent dread kept him at a distance.

He called for Ruby, wanting to keep his precious pet from the mouth and claws of this sinister oddity, but she disregarded his appeals, focusing her full attention on the thing she'd cornered. Seeing no option, Samuel stepped forward, affixing a sliding loop in the tether so that it would secure tightly to the dog's neck unlike the manufactured collar attached at its end, which had proven something less than reliable.

Just as he reached Ruby, her head whipped up as if finally hearing her name being called. Samuel lunged forward, repulsed at the idea of getting too close to the unnamable creature, but instead of managing to slip the lead around the dog's head, the loop passed through wet air. Ruby eluded his attempt at capture and raced to the side disappearing through an open door in the building on his left.

Samuel backed away from the corner, uncertain if its occupant might find him less threatening than his hound had been. He shuffled several steps until he stood inside the threshold. Lantern light glowed at the far end of the hallway, and he saw Ruby at its center. He searched for the panel of the door but found nothing save splintered planks, barely clutching twisted hinges. The state of the door disappointed him as he should have liked a means to lock out the creature in the alley, but since this option had been denied him, he decided to collect Ruby quickly and get her home.

Setting off toward the dog, who sat at the edge of the dim light, Samuel fell under the distinct impression that he walked on a balcony, rather than an expanse of floor. To his left the wall seemed to end at his waist, forming a banister, and though he had no clear sight of the space beyond—merely shapes of gray atop sheets of black—he felt certain it stretched out and down from him. At his club, they had wired one of the studies with electric light in a rare concession to progress, and though this man-made incandescence was neither as soothing nor as dependable as the gas-lit fixtures, he thought it would be nice to bring illumination to this peculiar and unfamiliar space with the simple turning of a knob, but having no such modern novelty, Samuel bolstered himself and made his way toward the muted light ahead.

Yet he was forced to pause, because another shape had joined that of his hound. This form was decidedly human, though quite small.

"There's the pretty Milly," a girl's excited voice cried. "There's my ever-so good girl." Samuel detected a lilt of brogue in the words, likely one of the Irish working as a servant for the owner of the adjacent home. But why was she claiming familiarity with Samuel's pet?

Was it simply the exuberance many youths showed toward domestic animals, or had Ruby once belonged to this girl and gone stray only to find her way back after a month in Samuel's care?

"Excuse me?" he said forcefully, so as to be heard over the marching rain. "Miss?"

He now stood close enough to see the girl, but was surprised to find it wasn't a girl at all, but rather a fully-grown woman, though quite certainly petite. Her hair was the color of carrot soup and her skin as white as bone.

"The dog's mine," the woman snapped, clutching tightly to Ruby's neck. "You piss off home. He don't need you no more."

The vulgarity startled Samuel, and he puffed up with outrage as he was not accustomed to being addressed so harshly from the likes of a servant, but the woman's claim gave him ammunition. "You have no rights to that dog," he charged. "Clearly, you don't even know it's gender. You said 'he' doesn't need me, and it's quite apparent the animal is a female."

"Not the dog you nancy," the girl spat, "Him, the one that sent her to you... *He* don't need you no more. The dog is mine. He had no right giving her away."

"No one gave me that dog," Samuel replied, infuriated with the diminutive woman's impertinence. "The dog was left to stray, and I cared for her."

"You got all the brains of a shite stew," she replied. "That bugger, Mr. Dodd, sent her to you, made it all a game 'cause he thought it would be a fine story to tell." The woman pulled something from her pocket. She held it up and back so that it caught the light. "This here calls my Milly home," the woman said. She put the instrument to her lips and made a great show of blowing, but no sound emerged from the pipe. Still, Ruby's ears pricked, and she shot to her feet, searching the landing as if her name had been called. "You see that there? I don't know how it works, but it does. He trained her to come when this was blowed on. Proves she's mine. Now piss-of home."

"Miss, I will only warn you once about your language."

"Good," she said, swiftly returning the pipe to her pocket. "'Cause I don't give a piss if you like the way I talk or not, and I don't want to hear nothing more about it. I just want my dog."

"And what would your master, Mr. Dodd, have to say about the way you treat his guests?"

"Don't think he'd give a donkey's cock one way or another. He's right out of his fucking skull. Now get out of the way and let me and my Milly go."

Lightning flashed above, and the space to Samuel's left lit up as if it had no ceiling at all. Something large and confounding occupied the center of the space, but he'd only managed to see it from the corner of his eye. Before he could turn to take it all in, the atmosphere was again as black as velvet.

The lightning had a different affect on the woman. She yelped as if it had burned her, and as the thunder rolled through the rafters, rumbling the very walls of the structure, she quickly struggled to lift the dog.

Samuel's heart sank when he thought he might lose Ruby forever. In their brief time together, he'd grown fond of the bitch, liked having her at his feet and lying next to him at night kicking her legs as she scampered over dream landscapes. He loathed the idea of her being kept by this crass and horrible woman.

"I'll pay you for the dog," he said.

"Don't need it. Got my pogue from the bugger when he lost his mind, and after what he done to me, I deserve every penny. You know what it's like to serve a monster? You see what he did to that door? Him's got the luck I come back to board up the other down there," she said throwing her index finger toward the staircase at her back.

"I'll be quite generous. I have grown fond of the animal."

"He said he'd be generous, too. The only thing he ever gave me was this here dog, and then he took her away. The rest I'm taking myself, because he don't need it anymore and the dirty bugger don't deserve none of it no how. He's against God that one. He's the Devil himself. That there," she said, pointing into the vast space on Samuel's left, "that there is Hell, and you can go on down and wait for him in it."

Obviously, the small woman had lost her mind, and it occurred to Samuel that she may have become delusional and murdered the master of the house in her derangement. It happened all the time with the immigrant classes. Samuel bore them no ill will generally, and he certainly didn't believe they were the beasts his friends at the club often claimed, but they were raised harshly by rough hands and their morality—their value of life—differed from that of men like Samuel and Hubert Dodd. Her fixation on Ruby seemed to contest this cold-blooded perception, but Samuel felt an instant chill and wondered if his colleague from the club lay bleeding somewhere in the main house, struck down by a servant who'd succumbed to religious mania.

"Where is Mr. Dodd?" Samuel asked.

"He's in another Hell," the girl replied. Ruby wriggled in her grasp. "He made a Hell here and found one in his own damned head."

Seeing no use in arguing with a lunatic, Samuel decided to change his tack. He gripped the handle of his umbrella quite tightly, should he need to use it in defense, and then he squared his shoulders.

"I can run much faster than you," he announced.

"Who said we was gonna race?"

Ruby whimpered and looked at him with the same pleading expression she used when she needed her constitutional.

"My point being that with the dog in your arms, I can reach a constable and bring him back before you make it to the end of the road. Now, I have offered to pay you generously for the animal. I suggest you allow me to do so. Otherwise, I shall be forced to involve the authorities."

Apparently, Samuel's logic worked on the woman, because the tension left her shoulders and face. "Bugger," she muttered, surrendering to the futility of her situation.

She dropped Ruby, who had only a short distance to fall. Immediately the dog raced to Samuel, taking a seated position next to his leg. Samuel presented the servant with an ample number of bills, enough to make her eyes light.

"Take care of Milly," she said, tucking the bills into her boot. "She's a good dog. The only good thing to come out of this place."

A moment later, the dreadful little woman was gone, tromping through the mud in the alley toward whatever destination summoned such people. Samuel bent low to scratch Ruby behind an ear.

"I hope I wasn't being presumptuous," he told her. "If you'd rather accompany that foul woman, I should quite understand, though I think remaining with me will provide you a more comfortable future."

In response, Ruby opened her mouth as if to yawn, but instead gave a weak yap, which Samuel took as acceptance of his decision. Ruby pressed close to his woolen trousers, and Samuel was finally able to slip the tether around her neck without incident.

An explosion sounded at his back, startling both man and dog as a cloud of brilliant white erupted around them. Unlike the previous flash of lightning, this one did not come and go.

Rather the light, shocking after so much gloom, remained. Samuel spun, his heart lodged in his throat. Surely, lightning had struck the building and the persistent illumination suggested fire, but what Samuel saw upon completing his turn was no natural element.

The ceiling of the building was made of glass. Hundreds of small panes captured in an intricate steel web partitioned the dark sky beyond into a grimly colored grid. A great metal pole descended from this ceiling, ending at an immense platform, which while no taller than a steamer trunk spanned a good thirty feet. From this suspended panel a series of tubes and wires and rods dropped to a great apparatus of gears the smallest being no larger than Samuel's head, while the largest being the size of a respectable carriage. Burnished wood, perhaps mahogany, and tarnished metal were used to fashion the complex series of cogs, all of which now groaned and cranked. The distance from Samuel's location on the walkway to the floor was no less than forty feet. There he saw the base of this grand mechanism: a thick glass column, wide enough for Samuel to stand within and stretch his arms. The tube rose into the heart of the complex works, which creaked and turned like the heart of a great watch. Within the clear tower, dozens of coils glowed, throbbing energy as if they had captured the lightning itself.

Samuel gazed on astounded by the intricacies of the contrivance before him. It was impossible and amazing. His gaze ran from ceiling to floor and then back skyward to the mesh of metal above. As he drew his attention downward again, he noticed a series of flat metal plates beneath the wooden platform, a detail eclipsed by the magnificence of the whole.

The plates, two dozen in all, pushed forward and back along narrow tracks like finely fitted drawers. A great ratcheting suddenly filled the hall. Only when it happened again did Samuel notice that the plates were locking into positions along the base of the platform. This seemed to cause the complexity of gears to become sluggish. One by one, the metal sheets came to a snapping rest, and though this technical marvel thoroughly intrigued Samuel, his gaze was soon drawn away.

A dark form moved across the far wall. Perhaps it had only been a shadow cast by one of the revolving gears, but the sudden motion caught Samuel's eye. He followed it over the wall with his gaze, and reared back from the banister when it came to a stop.

The floor and back wall of the chamber below the walkway were alive with motion. Hundreds of unidentifiable forms in a spectrum of unsavory colors—cheese mould green, rotten beef gray, the filthy yellow of infection's discharge—swarmed the lower room to create a foul bestiary in the heart of the city.

Among these insectile and reptilian specimens, another species stalked. This trio of creatures bore a resemblance to man, in that they traveled on two legs and swung two arms, but there was nothing human about them. Their skin seemed to be the color of porridge and it stretched tightly over twig-thin appendages punctuated by knotty, grotesque joints. Tufts of beet-red hair jutted from their scalps. Exhibitions of their savagery proved many, even in the momentary viewing. They beat and tore the others creatures. They stomped them beneath clawed feet. And from all of their adversaries, they took a taste.

Samuel rushed away from the banister, yanking Ruby along as he made his way to the door. So horrible had been the vision, he instantly wiped it from his mind, which proved to be a transient comfort at best, because he forced himself to turn back to see what his mind wanted him to never see again.

In the room below, the coils within the glass tube faded. Two more plates clicked into place, sounding like pistol reports in the vast chamber. And in the dying light, Samuel saw the writhing bodies of the unholy menagerie scrabbling for their places along the floor and the walls. He ran back into the rain, following his eager hound, without opening his umbrella. Cold water drenched him and brought a little of his sense back, and he stopped in the muddy road, though Ruby struggled with the tether, attempting to drag him away from the perverse scene behind them. Hubert Dodd had risen in his thoughts to cancel his retreat.

No, they were not friends. Perhaps civil acquaintances, but certainly not friends. Surely the device and the monstrous creatures that guarded it were in some manner of Dodd's manufacture, but if this were the case, Hubert Dodd would certainly be the most brilliant man alive. And hadn't the terrible woman told Samuel that Dodd had arranged for them to meet through his discovery of Ruby? Something about a joke? A story?

Drenched to the bone, Samuel turned, taking great care to pull Ruby to his side so as not to add to the dog's ill ease. He took a step toward Hubert Dodd's home. Ruby complained, digging her paws into the mud and barking a frightened tune.

"Of course, you're right," he told her. "It's a foolish thing to do, but think of what we might learn should Dodd be alive to tell us it?"

Indeed Hubert Dodd was alive, but just barely. They found him in the front parlor of his home, lying amid a clutter of discarded papers and strewn books, and Samuel believed the man had been attacked by the foul-mouthed servant girl with whom he'd bargained for Ruby's ownership. Dodd sprawled naked as a jay. His once hearty face now appeared gaunt and his intimidating bulk seemed deflated, with sallow skin creped at his joints and creased below the navel. On closer inspection however, Samuel found no cuts from a guttersnipe's blade, nor any indication Dodd had been accosted about the head. Rather, he seemed to be under the influence of a powerful opiate. The man moaned solemnly, then burst forth with a startling round of giggles.

The condition of the man and his surroundings appalled Samuel. Bodily waste had settled into the carpet and clotted on Dodd's skin in long stinking scabs. Further whatever intoxicant the man had consumed seemed to be acting as aphrodisiac as the sickly gentleman's penis remained in a state of erection.

Still not convinced that the servant girl was free of liability, Samuel considered the very real possibility that Dodd had been poisoned, perhaps with some exotic toxin he'd procured on one of his great adventures. Or Dodd may have been feverish from an illness given him by one of the strange specimens he kept in the adjacent building. Thoughts of disease caused Samuel to pause and wonder on his own well-being. Still, if he were going to be infected it would have already happened, and he couldn't leave Dodd to thrash and die in his own filth.

Only upon closer inspection of the man did Samuel believe he found the cause of Dodd's hysteria. Inside the man's thigh, very near his scrotal sack, a pale wormlike creature, long and thin like the lace of a boot, clutched the wrinkled skin. Samuel instantly thought of leeches. He had seen a jar of the black, slime-coated creatures at his physician's office, and though this parasite bore little resemblance to those horrible slugs, he imagined it was of the same genus. Without hesitation he reached down and tugged at the worm, which was dry and scaly, and not slick with vile ex-cretion as he'd imagined, and while the central thread of it easily peeled away from the skin, it held firm on either end.

"Leave it be," Dodd bellowed.

But Samuel ignored the delusional command and grabbed firmly to the worm and yanked with all of his force, separating the worm from Dodd's thigh and discarding the dreadful thing to the carpet where he ground it into the filth and fibre with the heel of his boot.

Dodd appeared infuriated for a moment, then he closed his eyes and sank unconscious.

With no chance of carrying Dodd up to his rooms—even withered, the man bore a tremendous heft well beyond Samuel's physical abilities—he located a large library on the first floor with a broad leather sofa and dragged the unconscious man along the hall atop a carpet. He hoisted Dodd onto the sofa and then set about matters of practicality. Certainly he would need to call a physician, but no servants remained to send about this task, and Samuel feared leaving the stricken man alone. He stoked the hearth in the library and did the same with the stove in the kitchen, on which he placed an ample stockpot that he set about filling with water from a ceramic pitcher. Ruby followed at his heels from library to kitchen and then up the stairs where Samuel came upon a guest suite. He removed pillows and blankets from the mattress and carried them back to the library. They remained piled on the floor while Samuel used warm water to clean Dodd's reeking skin. Then he wrapped the man in blankets and pushed a pillow beneath his broad head.

He thought to leave then. In part, his concern was for Dodd, thinking to hurry back into the storm to fetch a physician who might competently treat the man; but he also felt a profound disquiet as he considered the creatures occupying the building next door. Surely, he'd seen some of them scrabbling about the walls. Even if the door were locked as the servant girl had suggested, some might climb from the room and spill over the banister. He thought about the catlike species he'd encountered in the alley, and his resolve to leave this place heightened. Upon making the decision to depart, the sickly man stirred and came awake. Confusion and exhaustion worked on Dodd's face. He looked like a drunk who'd woken to find himself in strange rooms. "Samuel," he muttered, using the familiar name as if they were dear old friends. The name caught in his throat though, and he coughed violently.

"What have you done to yourself?" Samuel asked.

"The parasite?" Dodd asked, suddenly concerned. A great scramble beneath the blankets indicated he sought the thing out on his thigh.

"I've done away with it."

"Good man," Dodd said. "I was unable to do it myself. Its gifts were beyond my refusal."

"Gifts?" Samuel asked, confounded.

"Some manner of opiate," Dodd said before another racking flurry of coughs convulsed him. When the fit passed he continued, "Even when I first discovered it latched to me, I knew it was trading the blood it drew with an euphoric substance. I thought to document the effects of the creature before removing it, a clear indication that the opiate worked with an initial subtlety on my reason, and as the hours passed, I drew deeper into its thrall, until I was its prisoner."

"Where did you find such an odious specimen?" Samuel wanted to know.

"Dear, Samuel," Dodd whispered as if to a dense child, "I did not find it. It found me."

"Because of that contraption?"

"You've seen it?" Dodd asked, seeming pleased with the information. "I dare say, it's a wonder."

"But what is it?"

"The contrivance is an accumulation of knowledge," Dodd said. "*Some* of that knowledge emerged from my own tinkering and experimentation, and some of it I quite simply stole, at the time not being aware of the comprehensive design. That came when I discovered the particular property of lightning."

"And what property is that?" Samuel asked.

"Do you remember regaling the men at the club with your theories about raindrop worlds? How you believed that each drop contained the possibility of realms and what might happen when those varied worlds puddled together?"

"Yes, but..."

"You were not incorrect, at least not in the broadest sense. That was one of the reasons I thought to bring you to me. Many worlds run adjacent to our own. They bump and caress and gather. Like the raindrops, these other realms are innumerable, shifting and fluid all part of the collecting puddle you imagined, but they are segregated by sheer membranes, which is to say the drops heap without dilution. But the lightning... the lightning creates a momentary tear between realms. It is a double-edged sword that slices the veils, and my device holds those lips of fabric open, making it possible to cross realms as easily as stepping over a threshold into a new and astounding room."

"You've made these journeys?" Samuel asked, dumbfounded.

Dodd snuffled a laugh and leaned his head back, letting it sink into the pillow. "I am not that brave," he said. "Were it not for the specimen you so kindly removed from my leg and that odd bird-thing I keep in the laboratory cage, I wouldn't have even known of the experiment's success, but it is apparent that if these creatures can slink into our world, then we could just as easily cross into theirs."

"And what of the others?"

"What others?" Dodd asked.

"The other specimens in the laboratory. It brims with them."

Dodd smirked as if having been made the butt of a joke, but then his eyes cleared and he pushed himself upward. "What day is this?"

"Day?"

"What is the date?"

"It is the Sixteenth of November."

Dodd's face slackened as if the muscles there could no longer sustain the weight of his skin. "November?" he asked.

"Yes."

"For the love of God, I've been in thrall for a fortnight? Maureen must have cared for me until she lost all hope for my recovery."

Samuel thought about the coarse Irish woman and couldn't imagine her caring for anyone, let alone the man she'd described in such callous terms, but perhaps she'd endured so much in the last two weeks that her harsher instincts had surfaced. Still, if her master had been so ill, why had she not summoned a physician for his care?

"What of the weather?" Dodd asked, attempting to drag himself from the bed.

"Is that really relevant?" Samuel replied.

"Has it stormed frequently?" Dodd demanded.

And then Samuel took his meaning. If Dodd's contrivance operated on lightning, nothing could be more important than the weather. The news on that front was quite bad. "Storm most days."

"And lightning?" Dodd asked.

"And lightning," Samuel confirmed.

"God help us. My contrivance lacks only the convenience of predictability. The rifts in fabric shift away from its hold and mend themselves, which is to say that the device may hold back the curtain for a moment or an hour or a day at a time, but cannot do so indefinitely. Had the weather been calm, my worries would be few, but with each fresh bolt that strikes my conductor a new tear occurs."

Dodd struggled to his feet, but his legs were not sufficiently recuperated for the task of sustaining his weight and the bearish man collapsed on the floor amid a great *Whush!* of air. Samuel and Ruby rushed to the fallen man. The dog hoped to soothe the tumble with licks to the man's face, while Samuel took the more practical approach of grabbing him under the arms and assisting Dodd back onto the sofa.

"What can we do?" Samuel asked.

"The device's controls are in the laboratory. If you could get there it is simply a matter of withdrawing the coupling rod from the lightning rod on the roof, or disengaging the coils from the base. Either would take no more than moments, but if the laboratory is as infested as you claim..."

Samuel considered wading into the writhing mass of exotic monstrosities and knew his courage fell well short of the task. The very notion of approaching that building raised gooseflesh on his neck.

"It must be burned," Dodd said. "There's no alternative."

The pronouncement startled Samuel. Much of Dodd's life and a considerable portion of his estate must have gone into the creation of the contrivance, and the sheer miracle of its existence contended a casual approach to its destruction. What might be discovered should the wonder of the device be controlled and utilized in the pursuit of knowledge? What existed beyond these folds? Surely they all didn't contain unsavory beasts. It seemed wrong to do away with such opportunity, and yet, Samuel knew such a dangerous machine could not continue to function unchecked.

A roar of thunder shook the house and Samuel looked to Ruby, who cowered at the edge of the sofa. Then he looked at the weak and sickly man.

"It must be burned," Dodd told him earnestly. "You'll find tins of kerosene in the cellar."

But simply setting fire to Dodd's laboratory proved no easy task. There was the possibility of the fire spreading to the house or to other homes on the block. Considering Dodd's incapacitation, the man would never be able to flee in time, so his evacuation of the property would have to precede Samuel's arson. A carriage had to be summoned, and the debilitated man packed into it. And so he was. Though Dodd continued to refuse the attentions of a physician, Samuel told the carriage driver to help Mr. Dodd into his house on Walnut Street and once having done so, fetch Doctor Meriwether with due haste.

He placed Ruby in the carriage next to a blanket-wrapped Dodd. She whimpered and tried on more than one occasion to leap from the coach, but Samuel was forceful, and though the dog never settled, she ceased her attempts at flight.

"As for you, young miss," Samuel said to his pet, "you keep an eye on our guest until I return. You're the lady of the house, and it's your duty to make visitors feel welcome."

She whined and leaned out to lick his face, tongue swiping and darting with affection. He chuckled, tickled by the wet tongue, and gave her a good scratch behind the ear before closing the carriage door and rapping the back, sending it on its way.

Then Samuel returned to the house. The first order of business was to locate Dodd's stock of kerosene.

He followed the man's directions, found the door to the basement, and after a deep breath, again reminding himself that the wonderful device could not survive, he pulled open the door and was immediately accosted with a stench not unlike sulfur. The foulness of odor clotted in his throat and Samuel removed a handkerchief from his pocket to cover his nose and mouth. With a lantern firmly clutched in the other hand he began down the stairs.

The atmosphere here was cold and damp and worked quickly through the wool and cotton of his garb to latch onto his bones. The meager light of the lantern only revealed four steps at a time, while the rest of the chamber swirled, shadows upon shadows.

A clicking sound deep within the basement startled him. Too fast to be a clock mechanism and too sharp to be dripping water, Samuel felt tremendous unease as he attempted to identify the sound. A number of possibilities occurred to him: a draft sending a bit of wood against a beam or window jamb; a rat gnawing its way into a wooden storage crate; but again he felt the noise was too rapid, too precise to fit into any scenario of which he could conceive. Another sound, like the throaty belch of a toad rose from beneath the stairs.

Samuel froze in place, waiting for the noise to come again, but only the tick-ticking in the corner sounded. Could some of the creatures from Dodd's laboratory have slipped into the house? Made their way to his basement? It struck Samuel as wholly unlikely, as the door above had been secured upon his entry, so he continued his descent until he stood on the hard packed dirt of Dodd's basement. The smell here was dreadful, working through the cloth of his kerchief like maggots digging in flesh.

Dodd had told him the canisters were lined against the wall directly ahead of the staircase. Samuel walked forward and lifted the lantern high. A wall of crates, tattooed with stencils rose to the left, but the light could not reach deeply enough into the room to reveal the casks he sought.

Another great belching filled the chamber. Samuel turned to it, and something skittered across the floor just ahead of his light. His heart leapt into his throat and panic cascaded down his spine like water from a melting glacier. The clicking multiplied until it sounded as if the entire basement were chock-a-block with racing metronomes. Motion displaced the air at his back, and Samuel spun around, swinging the lantern like a club, but it passed through the air harmlessly.

Upon completing this pirouette, Samuel found himself facing a hole in the wall of Dodd's basement. Its diameter spanned a good meter, more than enough room for a small man to have squirmed through, certainly large enough to accommodate any of a number of creatures. The dawning realization brought a fresh stream of icy tingles to his back.

Some faction of the hellish bestiary had managed to escape. A burrowing species had taken the initiative, and now shared the same dismal void in which Samuel found himself. The panic became too much for him to bear. The lantern clacked in his trembling hand. He begged his feet to move, wanting nothing more than to vanish from the hideous gloom and to reappear on the street or even in front of the mantle at his home, and though his mind screamed for his legs to take action, they resoundingly denied his pleas.

Only when the air again felt displaced very near his left ear did Samuel manage to turn away from the gap in the wall of Dodd's cellar. Samuel whipped around in a reflexive jerk. The lantern flew from his fingers, sailing into the darkness like a comet. It glanced off the side of a rapidly fleeing specimen, which was clearly of the same clan as the savage stick-men he'd viewed in the laboratory. Amid a crash of brass and the cracking of glass, a window of flame opened on the far wall, and in this sudden illumination Samuel noticed two things simultaneously: his lantern had made impact above a row of cans he recognized as kerosene containers; the other revelation came in the form of dozens of tiny specs hanging like fireflies about the back wall and ceiling. Moist eyes from innumerable heads reflected the spreading flames, and faces bathed in the orange light cast by the conflagration pushed tightly together like blossoms in an unholy garden.

A scream escaped his lips, and Samuel fled for the stairs. An unknowable appendage reached through the gap between the steps in an attempt to trip him up, but Samuel sprang past the terrible limb with a yelp of terror and continued to scrabble toward the dull light above. He attained the landing and the room beyond and slammed the door. He searched for a lock but finding none, he backed away and quickly surveyed his immediate sur-rounding for something with which to secure the panel. Finding nothing, he chose flight, but instead of racing through the house, he made his way to the kitchen and the door to the alley, which remained open.

Another of the cat-like creatures had joined the first in the dim corridor. They groomed one another, only pausing long enough to eye Samuel curiously before setting their foul tongues back to task.

He thought to flee this block entirely, to run and keep running until he was again secure in his own rooms where the unspeak-able creations of some alien god did not prowl with malicious intent. But his rational mind—sorely tested to be sure—screamed at him to finish the task, to destroy Dodd's device and bring an end to this grotesque invasion. All he need do was cripple the contrivance so that it could no longer brace open the panels of veil separating his world from the others. A single lantern, well-thrown, could fulfill his duty. Perhaps the bulk of the mechanism would go unharmed but it could be disassembled at some future time, just so long as Samuel sabotaged it sufficiently to make it ineffective.

Lightning flashed directly above his head, thunder immediate-ly accompanying the bath of light. He heard its crackle and pop. A brilliant glow of light rose from behind the banister beyond the door, and he knew that Dodd's contraption was again in use.

A small body with skittering claws struck his leg, and Samuel recoiled to the jamb of the laboratory door. He searched for the source of the attack and was shocked to find it came from a fa-miliar face.

Ruby, his fine pet, raced in for another pounce, her tail whip-ping the air and her eyes glittering with happiness, unaware of the horrible spectacle surrounding her. She must have escaped the carriage and sprinted back to him—her unconditional affec-tion drawing her like moth to killing flame.

"Beautiful dog," Samuel said. "Foolish beast."

Scooping her into his arms, he hurried onto the walkway above Dodd's laboratory. He followed it to the place where he'd spoken with the awful Maureen and continued to the stairs where he found the lantern she'd left behind. Balancing Ruby, Samuel lifted the lamp free of its hook, and dashed back to the walkway near the door.

Dodd's contrivance continued to fill the space below with light. The floor positively swarmed with unclean creatures, fleeing from and feeding on one another with abandon. A soft dove-gray animal appeared near the glass column, encasing the glowing coils. Much like a deer but very short and very plump, the animal gazed on in paralytic horror until a creature like a massive limbless scorpion dropped onto its back and buried its stinger in the unfortunate animal's haunches. Then both predator and prey fell beneath the swatting claws of one of the porridge colored stick-men.

Great washes of blood sprayed from the monster's claws, dappling the glass column and misting the surrounding beasts. The stick-man cast aside the stinging creature and fell on the soft body of the plump deer. Its teeth tore away at the pink belly, releasing a cascade of glistening organs and a wash of dark fluids that spread across the floor.

Ruby wriggled and whimpered in his arms, and Samuel attempted comforting words but what might be said to alleviate the terror of the abattoir below?

He considered where to attack the device, and felt certain the glass and gears would prove impervious to the minor threat of his lantern. Instead, he decided his greatest luck would come if he could set alight the wooden platform with its numerous locking plates. If the oil sufficiently set blaze to the structure it would cease function.

With no further thought on the matter, Samuel launched the lantern and waited, breath held, until it cracked open upon the upper deck of the device. Flames dripped down like brilliant wax, showering the menagerie below and causing a chorus of fearful screeches and chirps. "Have that," he said triumphantly, observing the slowly spreading sheet of fire atop the platform. Pride welled in him as he heard wood pop with the burning, knowing it signified the likelihood that once the fire had fed in earnest the planks would collapse and with fortune, completely destroy the mechanisms below.

Confident in his success, Samuel nuzzled Ruby's neck and turned from the laboratory to face the alley...

And the abominations that looked back at him.

Two of the stick-men stood beyond the door, rain pasting their crimson hair to the gleaming skin of their brows. This was Samuel's first unobstructed view of the things' faces, and he wished to have never seen it. Eyes like shattered emeralds, faceted with ridges and fissures, glared hungrily at him, and beneath these horrible ocular configurations three narrow slits rippled like the gills of a fish. But the mouths were worst of all. The stick-man on the left yanked something forcefully from its jaws and tossed the hindquarter of one of the odd cat-like animals to the mud. Then its face opened. Oh that terrible gaping chasm, with hundreds of pin sharp teeth lining the roof and jaw, bits of prey still snagged on the barbs.

Behind Samuel, the laboratory glowed ominously with flame and the device's still radiant coils. Something about the light had changed, but he daren't look back to observe the anomaly. The stick-men came forward cautiously, assessing the strength of their quarry.

A great explosion sounded in Dodd's house. The fire had made its way into the kerosene stock to create a firebomb that blew through the flooring and sent shards of glass flying across the alley amid enormous gouts of flame. Samuel thought he and Ruby's luck had shifted for the better, as the tumult distracted the stick-men, bent them low to cower from the tremendous force behind them. For a moment, as the hot wash of air blew over his face, he even allowed himself to hope the blast would send fragments of ruins at his assailants like shot from a rifle, cutting them down in the mud, but the hope lasted only a moment. Though distracted, the stick-men had not fled from the conflagration; it had simply pushed them over the threshold, blocking any chance for Samuel's escape.

Refusing to serve as repast for these terrible creatures, and horrified that Ruby might meet the same fate, Samuel clutched his dog tightly and backed to the railing. The stick-men recovered and righted themselves at the doorway, and Ruby greeted them with a fierce growl, but Samuel knew she would prove no match for the barbaric and perverse species.

Instead, he closed his eyes, holding the dog so tightly to his chest it made her whine painfully, and Samuel launched them backward over the railing. It was better to break apart on the floor below than to suffer the bloody intentions of the stick-men. Ruby would forgive him this cowardly end.

As they dropped, Ruby turned in his arms, scraping his cheeks and waistcoat with her paws. She yelped in terror and the sound cut clean to Samuel's heart, but this was better for them. Better than teeth. Better than claws. Better than...

Grass bends in the wind along a great plain, pointing at a hillock upon which leafless trees stand as straight as columns, jutting toward the gathering clouds. Amid the trunks is a small shack with refined lines and a tower of stones through which smoke pours, like a daughter of the accumulation above, racing skyward to rejoin her parents. As the storm rolls in, announced by the first rumbles of thunder, a panel opens at the front of the shack and two creatures—no longer strangers to this place—emerge onto the hilltop. One of these odd beasts walks on two legs and the other on four.

Their names are Samuel and Ruby, and today as with all inclement days, they run down the hillside and into the field. They dash through the countryside, calling out to one another excitedly as if playing a game. Both seem to enjoy the rain and the wind, and when the sky splits with jagged light, they race toward the bolt, chasing the lightning as if they could catch it and keep it as a precious souvenir.

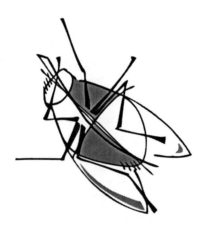

Flicker

All that Kathy knew of love came from images flickering on an old television screen. What came from this screen was fiction, and Kathy had discovered the difference between fiction and reality long ago. Fiction was a house in suburbia, cleaned by a beautiful mother who baked cookies, wore pearls and prepared delicious meals. Fiction was a father who worked a steady job in the city, declared his daughter's beauty to the world and fussed over the men who might date her. Fiction didn't show a little girl, bruised and crying, hiding in a filthy basement terrified of the fuckers she called mom and dad. But reality did. Reality offered a mother who worked out her boredom with vodka and strange men and a father who expressed frustration with his fists and his cock. Reality offered Santa Monica Boulevard on Christmas Day, waiting for one of Keith's friends to pick Kathy up so she'd have her fix and a warm place to sleep. The company she kept was irrelevant. In this, reality's blindness was equal to love's.

And what did it matter? This wasn't a career, just a means to an end. She had ambitions. Early in the mornings as Keith snored next to her, Kathy laid awake imagining herself on the screen with Mark Wahlberg or Tom Cruise. The dream had followed her from childhood. Like Angelina Jolie or Sandra Bullock, Kathy wanted to be a star and see posters bearing her likeness hung on walls by adoring fans and see her name on movie theater signs. Her parents had laughed at her aspiration. They had no time for her "craziness." So, she'd gone into her basement and mimicked whatever movie she'd seen that afternoon, losing herself in a fiction, which effectively filled a vacant childhood—at least for small periods of time. In her basement she became someone admired and loved, became someone strong and heroic, became anyone but Kathy Windman. She'd even played Frankie in her junior high school's production of *The Member of the Wedding*. Of course, her parents had been too busy to attend any of the performances but her teachers and even some of the other parents had congratulated her beautiful performance. Such an exciting feeling it had been for her, being recognized as an actress.

Sadly, she'd never done another play. Her boyfriend in junior high, Larry, had said it was all so stupid. She'd temporarily abandoned her dramatic pursuits at his request, exchanged them for pharmaceutical dreams. The void she'd once filled with acting was soon plugged by blow, blunts, and a six-pack of Bud.

At fifteen, after Larry dumped her, Kathy hitchhiked from Seattle to the city where dreams were everything. One night while watching the dollar movies in a run down theater on Hollywood Boulevard, she'd met Keith. He'd given her a place to stay, a purpose and a new relationship with new dreams. This dream offered needles and a cloudy world where pain was not allowed.

Almost a year had passed since they'd met. And now she waited on a corner for Keith's friend. She couldn't remember his name but he was supposed to pick her up.

She was going to make a movie.

The news had disturbed her at first. Although she wanted nothing more than to see her image on a screen, she didn't want to make porno flicks. She knew what happened to actresses who took the easy way out, who jumped at the money and then got the reputation, an inescapable reputation, as a whore. She didn't want that. She wanted to be a star, with all of the praise and respect that accompanied the title.

But Keith wouldn't hurt her. He loved her. He always told her so. He just had a friend who liked to make home movies. The guy was a voyeur. The movie wouldn't be seen by anybody, especially anyone from Hollywood. It was simply a game that this guy played, and besides Kathy wanted to see herself on the screen, even if the screen were nothing more than that of a high-def flat panel Sony.

As she began wondering where her ride was, a gray Lexus pulled to the curb. Behind the wheel, a well-dressed man with silver hair and a fatherly smile leaned down to look her over. "Are you Kathy?" he asked. His teeth were very white and his skin very tanned. He wore white pants, which were pressed into sharp creases and a crisp cobalt blue dress shirt. The sleeves were rolled up along thick forearms.

She nodded, flipping her hair over her shoulder as she stepped off of the curb. The man pushed open the door. She got in the car and as the door closed, the lock engaged.

"You're Keith's friend?" she asked.

"My name," the man said jovially, "is Desmond Silver. And yes Keith and I have something of a history."

Kathy nodded and stared out the windshield of the sedan as the familiar buildings of her neighborhood pulled behind her. The inside of the car was warm and comfortable after the chill afternoon.

"Merry Christmas," she said uneasily.

"And Merry Christmas to you," he replied.

Light cologne, trapped in the car with them, tickled her nose. It smelled like almonds and reminded her of the movie theater back home. The Marquis, a theater down the street from where she'd lived with her parents, sold really good chocolate covered almonds and if she hadn't spent her lunch money on cigarettes or make-up, she always bought a box of them from the concession stand. They were especially good with a Dr. Pepper.

Wrapping a thin coil of blond hair around her finger, she studied the driver from the corner of her eye. He didn't talk much. That made her uncomfortable, but nothing else about the man seemed threatening. He had a pleasant smile on his round face and really pretty eyes. They were so blue. He didn't look anything like Keith's other friends. Some of them were old, but they looked different. They looked like lizards and when they smiled they looked like hungry lizards. Most of Keith's friends were really creepy.

This guy—Silver—seemed nice, though. She just wished he'd say something. She didn't like the silence. It made her wonder if the man was having second thoughts about her. Maybe she wasn't pretty enough to appear in his movie. People told her she was pretty but she didn't always believe it. She thought her hair was too curly and her nose was too big. It wasn't like Barbra Streisand's or anything, but it seemed pretty big. At least she didn't have a weight problem and she was a natural blonde. A lot of girls were uglier than her—like the girl who lived downstairs from Keith. She had terrible skin and stringy black hair.

"So um," she began, trying to cancel the uncomfortable silence. "You...uh...you like movies?"

"Oh yes. They are the only perfect form of art. What about you?"

"I love them," Kathy said. She was going to mention her ambition of being an actress, but sometimes it sounded stupid when she said it aloud. So she settled for, "Are you going to be my costar?"

The man burst out laughing. The car came alive with its rich, deep sound. As he laughed, his round face constricted, producing dozens of tiny wrinkles around his eyes and mouth. He looked over at Kathy and managed to say, "No, but I'm flattered you'd ask."

"You just like to watch?"

Silver considered this for a moment and then shook his head. "I like to create. Watching is part of that I guess. You see, I choose to expend my energies into the creation of art. Honestly, the thought of anyone actually touching me is nauseating, which is not to say that I am a completely asexual creature." He turned the car and remained silent for a moment before continuing. "The guidance and manipulation of an act, the creation of an impossible scenario is very satisfying to me. Creation and re-creation, fighting over something until it's perfect. That's my passion. I think they call it a God complex."

Damn, Kathy thought. How could you not like being touched?

"Do you have dreams?" he asked in a friendly but stern voice. He took his eyes off the road and fixed her with a crystal blue gaze. "Real dreams?"

"Sure," Kathy replied. *Didn't everybody?*

Silver nodded and tapped the steering wheel once with his thick palm. "Well this place, this world, doesn't care much for dreams, despite what the poets tell us. It makes no accommodation for them. Dreams, prayers, they guide the young, but life's random inequities separate those who succeed from those whose dreams have been little more than inexpensive entertainment. I couldn't accept that." He shrugged his large shoulders and turned the car again. "It doesn't seem fair to only get one chance at a dream."

"No," she said, perhaps too eagerly.

He grinned at her exuberance. "If you make something and it breaks, well...then you've got two choices. If you've got the right tools or the right glue, you can fix it. Otherwise, it's gone. You have to pitch it away. Up until recently, I didn't have the right adhesive. This maddened me. It was like molding a perfect urn only to have the pieces separate in the kiln. But, recently I found a glue that works. I'm very excited about it."

"You make vases?" Kathy asked, uncertain of what Silver was talking about.

"What?" he asked. Then he let his warm chuckle loose to fill the car again. He rocked in the driver's seat obviously pleased by her naiveté. "No," he chuckled. "I was speaking metaphorically. Well, you'll see what I mean. We're here." He turned the wheel one last time and the car left the street.

The Lexus came to a stop in a dead end alley. Buildings loomed on either side of the vehicle casting deep shadows over the dull facades. Moisture crept down the weathered brick as if the stone's cried for solace. A three-story monstrosity stood ahead of them. Condemned and desolate the three structures comprised a melancholy union in the midst of office towers and gleaming condominiums. Filthy plywood covered shattered windows. Obscure, woven symbols accompanied curses and effigies of genitalia on the boards and brick.

"Perfect, isn't it?" Silver asked.

Kathy made a sound in her throat that she hoped sounded positive; she didn't want to insult her host, but the alley and the buildings that formed it were eerie. Once, she'd gone with a friend of Keith's to an old shack behind a seedy apartment complex in Reseda. One guy took her to a deserted warehouse. The strangest place she'd ever partied was with a bunch of musicians. They'd broken into a fire-gutted apartment building in North Hollywood. A friend of theirs had overdosed in the room a few months before it had burned so the place had meant a lot to them. But for the first time, while standing in that dark alley with the kindest looking man she'd ever met, Kathy felt scared.

"It's such a lonely looking place." He sighed. Then his demeanor rapidly changed. He smiled and slapped his hands together before his belly and rubbed them as if to make them warm. "Are you ready?"

Kathy nodded.

Silver set off across the pavement, his feet breaking a path in the litter. Kathy hesitated, put her thumbnail in her mouth, and then took a step forward. She moved slowly, looking around the alley as she crushed trash under her heels. The old man waited by a doorway. At that moment she realized how commanding he was. His frame all but eclipsed the black space beyond. Kathy moved a little faster until she stood before him on the small cement stoop of the structure. A dull, musky odor poured from the building. Daylight was consumed beyond the threshold. Inside, only three steps were visible climbing away at a steep grade.

"Lady's first," Silver said. He stepped aside and waved his arm towards the stairs. He made the motion so gracefully, so slowly, like a magician offering a miraculous illusion to his audience. For a moment, it seemed the gloomy chamber had dissolved his arm at the elbow, but when the arc completed, the man stood before her, whole and grinning.

As she stepped over the threshold into the strange space, a fetid urban perfume climbed along her nostrils and down the back of her throat where it coiled in her windpipe. Refuse, urine and excrement and an underlying odor, an animal odor, coalesced into a rank phantom, a malevolent spirit unwilling to allow her breath, and Kathy choked audibly trying to regain control of her throat. She hesitated, putting a palm over her mouth. What little of the stairway she could see in the dim glow, stretched far above her. At the top, a sickly yellow light fought against a dark siege. Tiny shafts of gray from cracks in the plywood blinds cut the air like minuscule threads woven in raven cloth. They illuminated little, succumbing to the hunger of the darkness.

She turned. Silver stood behind her. His face remained a mask of joviality. He seemed so pleased. She wondered about him. How did he spend his days? What did he do for a living? She assumed he wasn't married because of what he'd said about being touched, but who was he? The boards beneath her feet complained under her weight. Kathy clutched the splintered rail tightly as she led Silver towards the jaundiced glow. Low raspy voices glided in the air above. The words seemed visible, swirling in the thin gray shafts of light. One of the voices burst into laughter, and then the chamber went silent.

She neared the top. Her heart beat rapidly. The struggling light came from a dusty bulb in the hall to the right of the staircase. She saw the graffiti raped walls. To her left, she saw a brightly lit room at the far end of the hall. Then she saw her co-stars. They knelt in a circle around a flickering candle, the light of which extended no more than a foot in either direction. Two were busy with a needle, cooking a familiar dish in a blackened sugar spoon. The sight of the brew made her stomach knot.

Keith had told her to wait until she got to the party, and they'd fix her up. Now she felt the craving in her belly growing, gestating like a child. The hunger kicked. It grew into an unbearable ache. Only seconds after seeing the smoking spoon, Kathy's entire body hurt. The third man, an enormous bald figure with tribal tattoos painting his torso and arms, knelt with his back to the wall. He wore a pair of tattered Levi's and black work boots. He balanced the thin point of a switchblade in his palm. When it dropped, he clutched the handle and retracted the blade. After springing it again, he began to roll the weapon between his fingers as his buddies continued brewing the contents of the spoon.

"Our star has arrived," Desmond Silver announced.

The three men lifted their heads. They regarded Kathy with little interest; their expressions remained flat and bland. The bald man stopped spinning the blade, and it jumped in his hand, landing point down on his palm. His stare caught Kathy's as he executed the move. "Hi," she said. She tried to smile but it collapsed on her lips. "Is that..." she began, "I mean, Keith said... Well, he said I could get fixed up...I mean, did he tell you? Is that cool?"

"You're the star," Silver said, giving himself a wide berth between himself and the girl as he moved into the hallway. "And a star gets whatever she wants. William, will you accommodate the young lady?"

The thin man holding the spoon over the candle's flame nodded slowly. He had long shaggy, brown hair that dropped in ringlets over his ears and framed his emaciated face. The black t-shirt covering his torso hung loosely, dangerously close to the flame. On the hand that held the spoon, he wore a leather glove with the fingers removed.

Silver continued down the hall, leaving her in the company of his friends. The man who was not William, placed a needle into the soupy contents of the spoon and filled the rig. Kathy rolled up the sleeve of her blouse.

She noticed Silver's silhouette in the radiant doorway of the room at the end of the hall, but her eyes were constantly teased back by the sight of her approaching treat. (She and Keith always called it lunch). The man who was not William stood. Distantly she felt the tourniquet applied to her bicep. A finger tapped rhythmically on the crook of her elbow, but she couldn't take her eyes off of the tiny rig floating before her eyes. The bald man chuckled hollowly. The odors of the building receded under the dusty, fungal smell of her treat. William began chuckling along with the bald man, slapping the tattooed shoulder of his friend. The needle penetrated her skin. The garrote loosened. Something fell in the room at the end of the hall and Silver barked his discontent. Kathy hardly noticed.

A warm cascade showered her and the ache of craving retreated under a deluge of pleasure, which touched and then drowned her senses. For all of the familiarity of this sensation, it was a strange high. Her stomach did not cramp. Her flesh did not become clammy. Rather, she slid peacefully into a chemical sanctuary unfettered by ridiculous notions of fear or pain.

Hands grasped her under the arms and lifted, and her mind continued to rise until it felt as if she floated across the ceiling. A soothing current embraced her and then pulled away, only to return a moment later. Fingers touched and tickled, running over her chest and waist. They were undressing her and as each garment was removed, she sighed in pleasure. The tide of euphoria lapped at her neck and her breasts and insinuated itself between her legs, bringing a smile to her lips.

She closed her eyes and then opened them, but the scene before her hardly changed. Soft colors like the melted wax of festive candles pooled and streamed before her, and at their center was an inviting illumination, a thousand-watt heaven to which she was inexplicably drawn. Kathy's mind cleared some, though the rapture remained. Her new friends were carrying her down the bleak corridor, a dismal tunnel that ended in paradise.

They brought her into the welcoming glow. The room was a studio, illuminated by three lights plugged into a low-humming gas generator. Behind the lights, chrome umbrellas reflected harshly over the entire chamber. Dirty, painted walls, like those of the hallway, surrounded her, and she noticed the exceptional darkness of the night beyond the two windows on the north wall. Her clouded and contented mind didn't realize that the panes had been painted black. To her right a video camera stood on three chrome legs and pointed at a stained mattress lying uncovered in the center of the room. Four gleaming eye-bolts were driven into the concrete floor at each corner of the soiled bed. Connected to each of the bolts was a length of chain ending in a cuff-like bracelet. Above the mattress was a flaking iron pipe, and polished silver manacles draped from the rusting tube.

"All right," said Silver as the two men helped Kathy to the mattress. "Let's get started. Kathy, you fine honey?"

"Mmmm?" she mumbled."Good," Silver said. He rubbed his hands together quickly and grinned. "Dallas, William, help her into position. Hurry now."

Her body glided across the chamber. This was so much better than her other highs. She'd never felt so wholly removed from the pains and anxieties of the world. She wondered if she had overdosed, but this felt too wonderful to be an overdose. Kathy closed her eyes. She couldn't really focus on anything anyway, so why fight it? Besides, everything looked so much lovelier with her eyes closed. Then, she was lying down. When had that happened? Why were her wrists and ankles suddenly cold? Distantly she heard a thick voice call, "action."

She drifted in a beautiful stream somewhere between consciousness and heaven, without a single earthbound concern. Oh, she knew what was happening to her body, distantly she could feel the weight, could feel the pressure on her, in her, but that was too far away to worry about. She'd found a pleasant fiction to lose herself in, and she wouldn't mind staying there forever. Here she could have a mother that baked cookies and wore pearls, and she could have a father that loved his little girl without shoving his cock in her, and here Keith kept her to himself, protecting her and loving her with all of the sincerity he claimed but never showed. What they did to her body didn't matter, because it was just a shell, a cell of meat and fluid and bone and a repository for agonies great and minor. She didn't need it—didn't want it.

But now, she was returning to the cell of her flesh because someone wanted her to. She struggled against it, because being away felt so much nicer. Someone slapped her, called her name (Kathy!), called her something else (Bitch!). Ice water drenched her face and pooled against her neck before the dirty mattress drank it away. She forced her lids open. Above her, the bald man knelt. He still played with his knife.

The studio around them was full of people. Women, some dressed in magnificent gowns while others were clad in shabby denim, gazed at her prone body. Men in a similar range of fashion offered glances of appreciation while others looked bored. Couples made love in the shadows behind the glaring lights, their bodies moving as single silhouettes, completely unconcerned with the audience as they writhed in the dark corners. Desmond Silver grinned at her from behind the camera. It looked like his head was part of the device.

"Are we done?" she mumbled. "Can I see it now?" She tried to rise, but something clutched her wrists, weighed on her ankles. Her hands and feet tingled. "Not quite," Silver said. "We still need to get a close-up. Dallas are you ready?"

Discomfort shot along her forearm and Kathy cried out. "Can you take these things off now?"

"The close-up, dear," Silver muttered, leaning close to the viewing screen of his camera."Must...have...a...close...up." He pressed a button on his camera. Shook his head and repeated the gesture. "Dallas?"

"Anytime," the bald man replied.

Suddenly the euphoria retreated. Fear covered her like a blanket of nettles. Dallas knelt beside her, flexing his tattooed arms. Silver continued to fiddle with the video camera. He moved a light closer to the mattress. The audience whispered. Silver returned the light to where it had stood. Kathy saw the blade, opening and closing only inches from her face. It clicked loudly in her ear. William and the other man stopped laughing. Rapt anticipation froze their features. The generator hummed. How odd it seemed that this noise should make her understand the silence in the room.

"If it's a close-up," Kathy whimpered, "you don't..."

"Shhh," Silver hissed.

"But you don't..."

"Shut up!" the director said. "I need to frame this scene."

"Hey," she said. "You can't talk to me like...I mean, you could be nice. You don't have to—"

A dry hand slapped the rest of the words from her mouth.

"'Action," Silver called.

The blade flashed open and stayed open. Dallas slid against her on the mattress. He leaned down to Kathy's cheek, and his tongue, like a bloated leech, violated her ear. Hot breath oozed over her face. Kathy struggled against the binds. "I'm going to kill you now," the man whispered. "So let's see some action, star-child."

But he wasn't serious. This was just a movie. He couldn't be serious. Just a plot or something. The blade was a stage knife— made of rubber—that's why he hadn't cut himself with his tricks. Just a plot. It had to be. But she couldn't stop crying. Her throat felt swollen closed. Her body convulsed from fear. She struggled against the manacles and tore the flesh around her wrists and ankles, fighting to get away from the painted man beside her. She was only sixteen. Keith loved her. Just cinema. Just a movie. Just a plot. It had to be.

The blade caressed her cheek. Dallas grabbed a handful of her hair and yanked her head back, deep into the mattress. She tried to scream but her windpipe suddenly pinched. The chill blade slid over her chin like a steel tear. It traced along her throat, caught on something then continued across. Warmth spilled over her neck and chest, and when Kathy realized the heat must surely have been pouring from her own body, panic clamped down.

She screamed, and the sound filled her head. The warmth pulsed along her throat. She couldn't move. The bald man crawled off the mattress. Silver directed quietly from behind the camera. Kathy kept screaming. The sound filled her ears though it never left her opened neck. Above her, she saw the cracked ceiling swelling and contracting like respiration, as her body convulsed. The generator droned; the camera kept rolling.

Then, she fell. Backwards and down she fell, away from the noisy room and into her screams. The room washed out, bleached of its filth and its threat. And Kathy thought of Keith, thought of stardom, thought of nothing.

She swam in an opalescent pool. Dull gray shapes moved amidst the milky fluid. She recognized each of them despite the fact they had neither feature nor distinct form. Larry was there, telling her she wasn't mature enough for him. Her mother surfaced, screaming and swinging a broom handle, and then sank away as Keith and Desmond Silver drifted by, negotiating her fate. Teachers and friends, lovers and dealers coalesced and dissipated around her. A distant thunder of disco music accompanied the shapes in her head.

Kathy struggled to understand this place, and the more she struggled, the louder the music became. The gray images receded into the pool as its glow intensified.

When she opened her eyes, she stared at the ceiling and wondered where she was. She'd taken a long nap somewhere. A girl about her age knelt over her and smiled. The girl wrung a damp pink cloth into a bucket and reapplied it to Kathy's neck where the cool water bathed a nagging itch, which became apparent only after it had been soothed.

As she thought about her neck, she remembered Desmond Silver and remembered Dallas and his knife. Kathy screamed and rolled away from the girl, thinking that she still lay on the studio mattress. But she'd been moved and Kathy rolled into a wall. She drew her nails across the rough black surface. Screaming and kicking, she tried to escape through an impermeable obstacle. Her nails split and her throat ached.

"Oh don't," the girl said. "Hey. Kathy. Hey. It's all right. Kathy?"

But she kept struggling, desperately trying to escape. She had to escape or they'd really kill her the next time. Her body shuddered as she thought of Dallas' blade, and she fought even harder against the wall.

"Honey," the girl said. "Kathy?"

A strong hand touched her shoulder and rolled her back onto the cot. The girl's face, concerned and friendly hovered inches from hers. A sweet perfume came from the girl, and her eyes were so kind.

"I'm Becky," the girl tried. "I'm from Omaha. Where are you from?"

Kathy's eyes raced in their sockets, fueled by panic and confusion. She couldn't understand what difference it made where she came from? They were going to kill her. But if they wanted her dead, wouldn't she be dead? As she considered this, she also considered the fact that she might have been on a bad trip. Maybe the movie magic had just seemed real. None of it made sense.

"I bet you're from Oregon," the girl said, placing a palm on Kathy's forehead, smoothing back the hair. "Are you?"

"Seattle," Kathy rasped.

"I hear it's beautiful there," Becky said. "I was starting to get worried. You've been asleep for a very long time. All day and most of the night. I know the first time can be traumatic, but..."

"Where am I?" Kathy asked.

"Generally, you're in L.A. Specifically, you're in Desmond's studio." Becky laughed at this, revealing a dreadful smile of swollen gums and broken and missing teeth. She noticed the disgust on Kathy's face, and a cloud passed over her features. She threw a palm to her mouth, hiding the destruction behind her lips. "Sorry, I did a scene yesterday. They haven't grown back yet."

Kathy sobbed.

Becky's face fell into concern again. She leaned into Kathy and hugged her as best she could. "What's wrong honey?"

"They're going to kill us," Kathy sobbed. "Aren't they?"

"Probably," Becky said. She considered for a moment and said, "They've killed me, eight times, but I'm just about done. Desmond said that he's almost got the scene perfect. I'm very excited—you know, about the finished product? I can't wait to see it. He thinks it's going to be brilliant."

What was the girl saying? How could someone be killed eight times? How could someone be killed twice?

"Desmond is bril'," Becky said. "A total genius. Film is his medium."

Kathy sat up slowly, her eyes never leaving the young woman's beside her. "Aren't you afraid?"

Becky laughed and grabbed Kathy's shoulders gently. "There's nothing left to be afraid of...except algebra." The warm, beautiful face smiled lightly. "Let me give you a tour and I'll try to explain."

Kathy stood. She was naked, a light pink sheen covered her upper torso. "I have to get dressed."

"Suit yourself," Becky said. She led Kathy to a door and opened it to expose a rack of clothing. "Something here should fit you."

As Kathy began to dress, the girl started an explanation. "Desmond has been working in this field for years. They used to call them snuff films. Isn't that a terrible name? I hate it. Desmond prefers the term *Film Mort*. Well, when the form was young, he had a lot of trouble.

He couldn't maintain any continuity. After all, once a scene was *finished*, it was finished. No chance for retakes, no chance for artistic expansion. Desmond always likens it to vases."

And he'd said something about glue, Kathy thought, retrieving a beautiful yellow sundress from the costumer's rack.

"That'll go great with your hair," Becky said, nodding at the dress. "Anyhow, Desmond could never glue his vases back together. He could have another brought in, but he could not maintain authenticity. Well, a few years ago, he came across a woman that solved his problems. She had the glue he needed. The first couple of shoots were difficult because he didn't know how to explain himself to his models. A few ran. One even went to the police but nothing ever came from it."

The dress fell over Kathy's head, draping comfortably over her body. A mirror gleamed from the back of the closet door, and she examined herself. A ragged line, red and gnarled ran across her neck from one ear to the other. Her hand went to the wound, felt along the rough edges as the reality of her injury sank in. But there was no pain, no lingering ache. It seemed that the damage was merely skin deep.

"I told you, with your hair..." Becky said, again indicating the dress with a nod. She wrapped a friendly arm around Kathy's shoulder. "Just beautiful." She guided the new girl towards the hall. "Before you, I was the last one to enter the troupe. I guess that's why Desmond asked me to talk to you."

"How long have you known him?"

"Oh about six months now."

"Don't you ever want to leave?" Kathy wanted to leave. She wanted to get to a doctor so he could look at the gash on her throat before it started bleeding again.

"I will soon," Becky said. "I'm going to miss this place. I don't want to go, but the movie is almost finished now, and I'd just be in the way."

"They're not going to let you leave," Kathy said. How stupid could the girl be?

"I keep forgetting you're new. People leave all the time. Let's go," Becky said. The disco music that Kathy associated with her dream pulsed in an adjoining room. She gazed at the door as they passed.

"That's Dallas' room. He loves to dance."

One floor below, Kathy recognized the studio. "Shhhh," the pretty girl hissed, holding a finger to her lips. "They're filming."

The two snuck down the hall and into the studio. The set up was similar to Kathy's first visit—the mattress, the lights, the camera—except a tall white cross occupied the center of the room. A young man, maybe twenty years old, hung from the cross. His arms were bound by thick lengths of hemp. William, with his curly feminine hair, stood at the base of the cross, a cigarette glowing from between his lips. He inhaled deeply, stoking a glowing red ember. Then he applied the searing end to the captive's thigh. The crucified man screamed and rolled his head. Pleading and begging filled the chamber. Another application of the searing cherry. This time the ember disappeared into the soft white flesh of the young man's belly. Then William crushed the cigarette under his heel and walked to the back of the cross. When he returned, he held a fireman's ax.

"Oh God," Kathy moaned. She had to help the man. But no, she had to help herself. She stepped back, into Becky's waiting arms. They snaked around her, crossing at her chest. William lifted the ax and drew the blade slowly across the man's porcelain stomach. The blade did not pierce the skin, but rather caressed it. Still the prisoner screamed, shouted for help and dropped his head to the side. Desperate, pleading eyes caught Kathy's. Then William pulled the weapon back and swung. The blade dug deeply into the crucified body. Blood erupted in splashes and ropes from the wound, quickly pouring down the ivory abdomen to paint the man's pubic hair and genitals. The handle jutted away from the torso like a perverse appendage.

Kathy screamed. Becky shook her and tried to get a hand around her mouth. But it was too late. Desmond and William stared at the girls in the doorway. Whispers of discontent from the audience in the shadows filled the chamber. Kathy fought against Becky's grip, but she was too strong. Then something incomprehensible happened.

"Great," a high voice cried. The man on the cross looked at Kathy, his expression was dark and angry. She stared incredulously. Her stomach knotted and her mind raced. The young man with the ax in his belly gazed down on her. "The shot's ruined. I don't believe this shit," he huffed. "You try and do your best work and some amateur walks in and ruins the whole thing. Desmond," the boy said, "I cannot work under these conditions." He undid himself from the binds and hopped off the cross. The ax remained firmly planted in his gut.

"I know, I know," Desmond said, rushing forward. "I'm sorry. You were perfection, as usual." Silver regarded Becky for a moment. "You should have known better than to bring her here," he said before returning his attention to the disgruntled performer. "Sweetie," he cooed. "The lighting wasn't very good anyway. We'll re-shoot next week as soon as you're up to it."

"Next week? This is going to take at least two to heal," the boy said, pulling the heavy weapon from his belly. He dropped it to the floor, where it hit with a clatter. Blood oozed from the wound, and a purple rope of intestine surfaced in the gash. "We finally had it. What if I can't get the inspiration back? What if the part is cold next time?" The young man looked distraught.

"It finally felt right."

"It'll be okay," Silver said. "You are never less than perfect." He made to put his arm around the man, and then jerked his hand away. Silver whispered accolades in his ear as the two walked out of the studio.

"That was Bobby," Becky said, leading Kathy back to her room. "He's a little temperamental but his style is impeccable. He's been here for about two years now. This is his second film for Desmond. Desmond is a little worried that his clients will feel cheated if they realize he's been used before, but Bobby used to be blonde, and he really does look different now."

Kathy couldn't speak. The horrible images of that bright room still played in her head.

"Don't worry," the girl said. "It doesn't hurt or anything. That's why we have to act. After awhile it's like brushing your hair. It might pull if you catch a tangle, but it doesn't really hurt. You might even get into it." Becky turned to her new friend. The glittering expression that told the world how happy she was to be a part of it had faded. "I do hope you stay. I'd really like somebody to talk to, you know? Somebody to go to the movies with."

The girl smiled at Kathy; the heaviness in her eyes reflected an emotion that Kathy had never been able to define in herself. When Becky left, Kathy felt empty.

Desmond Silver came to her soon after Becky retreated down the hall to study lines for her shoot the following week. His face hung with concern. But it was his eyes, eyes that projected such intense sadness that captured Kathy. He'd changed clothes, opting for a pair of khaki shorts and a black dress shirt.

Kathy felt exhausted. She hadn't even thought of escape. Girls always tried to run in the movies and something horrible always happened. It was better to just rest until her mind cleared. Then she might think of a plan. Right now, she just wanted to sleep.

"Tough day?" Silver asked, sitting on the edge of Kathy's bed. "The first shoot can be rough."

Tears rose in Kathy's eyes. How could he seem so nice? After what she'd seen? After what he'd done to her? How could he seem so kind? Did all monsters have such warm smiles and such fatherly eyes?

"Before," Silver said, "before all of this, I was a doctor, but I had to give it up. I..." He smiled wanly. The corners of his mouth pushed at the tired flesh of his face. "There's a certain attraction for me in the opening of skin. The way it releases under a blade and opens like a waiting kiss, and then the blood comes, constant and warm like affection just waiting to pour over me, and of course in that line of work the beautiful wounds proved distracting. But I saw girls like you every night, trundled through the emergency room because their boyfriends or tricks had gotten tired of them, discarded them after making sure their pretty faces would never land them another man." He shook his head. "They always went back to these men. I used to stay up nights wondering what had become of them. Eventually I had to give up medicine, because of my distraction. Financially comfortable I went into filmmaking. I tried to justify my early films by telling myself that I was saving girls like you from a lifetime of pain. It wasn't very effective. When I found my glue, I found a way of balancing my art with my ideals."

All of Silver's talk about medicine and wounds and glue confused her. He murdered people for movies. He was crazy, and she could care less about hearing the details of his insanity. "I don't care," Kathy said. "I just want to go home."

"Which home is that? The home with the abusive parents or the home with the boyfriend who sold you for a hundred dollars and a bottle of Jack Daniels?"

"Keith loves me," Kathy said. Her voice cracked as tears filled her eyes.

"He doesn't," Silver said. "Kathy, I'm not a good man, but I am an honest one. If you go back to him he will sell you to someone else, and the next man isn't going to have my glue. Any damage done to you will be permanent. Yes, this place is odd, maybe even a little scary, and you will have to endure some terrifying moments, but you will have the support and protection of everyone here—like a family—and when you leave, you will leave whole and ready to make a new life for yourself."

"Can't I just go?" Kathy pleaded.

"If that's what you want," Silver said. "But you need to stay until your neck heels. The glue's efficacy is limited. I'll send William down to give you another shot. We don't want that wound to open."

Silver stood, casting one last smile at Kathy. "I do hope you'll reconsider. I think our film would be stunning." Then he left the room.

The loneliness entered her like frigid air, filling her body and freezing her lungs. She stood hesitantly and walked to the hall. Stepping forward she gripped the door and rubbed the wood with a palm. All that Silver had told her bustled and wrestled in her mind. Her decision should have been easy. Escape. Get as far away from Silver and his freaks as she could go. Run back to Keith. He'd tell her that he loved her, and he'd apologize and kiss her and make love to her and promise he'd never let anyone hurt her again.

Except he wouldn't. She wanted to believe this fantasy, but fantasy was just another word for fiction.

Kathy pressed her cheek against the door, hugged it.

Outside a child picked through a dumpster, hoping that his breakfast wouldn't make him sick before it relieved the foggy exhaustion in his head and the ache in his belly. In the adjacent building, a mother gave birth to a child and sawed through the umbilical cord with a broken bottle before abandoning the screaming bundle in a cardboard box and creeping back into the dawn. A good husband and concerned father opened the door to his silver Honda and let a fourteen-year-old boy back onto the corner he'd taken him from. Cars raced by and the city awoke. It was the day after Christmas and the season for giving had come to an end.

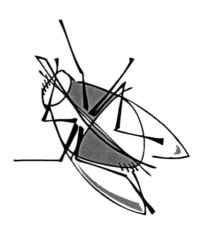

Inside
Where It's Warm

Clouds the colors of rotted meat and tumor spit ashen rain and sleet, and through the pelting downpour, colliding with concrete like the stomping boots of a clumsy army, a scream rises and quickly fades, and I turn to the sound from reflex. Peering between white houses that stare at me like the faces of forlorn ghosts, I see nothing in the gloom and continue my trek down the middle of the road. I am chilled but this is a reaction to the weather, not the fleeting protest of a stranger who is soon enough beyond the fingertips of hope.

My jaw clenches against the cold, knuckles ache from clutching the iron bar, my leg throbs as it has for days, and I think it would have been better to wait until morning to manage my errand, because the early evening is as dimly lit as a waning dusk, except the rain provides cover, masking the sounds of me and the heat of me in icy torrent, and I speculate they do not hunt by sight, or else they would always be at one another. Too little was said about the threat before the newscasts died because too little was known. So I can only guess. I walk down the center of the road, trusting my eyes perhaps more than is wise, and counting on my legs, even the damaged one, to get me far beyond danger should it arise.

I left the city to avoid the problems of a great population, and this decision proved sufficiently warranted, but my preparation was *not* sufficient—all too shortsighted. I accounted for food and drink and warmth, but failed in one important regard, and it is because of this that I expose myself to the wandering threats as I move toward the center of a town no longer thriving—hardly living at all.

She walks across a distant yard, a spirit in a flowing nightdress, and she turns to me and one of her arms raises in a half wave and I think to wave back, but her gait is familiar and in no way inviting, her steps leaden, her knees locked as if bound in braces. She lifts her other arm and moves across the lawn, untended grass a tide of filaments brushing her ankles, and she approaches me like a crippled mother desperately trying to reach a beloved child. I continue along the white line in the street, and she changes course, and soon her bare feet shuffle onto the sidewalk and seem to disappear as if her skin wears an identical shade to the damp concrete. Her hope is to greet me in the middle of the road. I survey the landscape, the lonely, unlit houses, the overgrown lawns, the track of street at my back covered in a screen of sleet, and I see we are alone this woman and I.

Led by chipped and torn nails, guiding her to me, she appears serene. Once, not long ago, she was beautiful, with delicate features, lips plumped by nature or needle, and silky skin, but her eyes, which had certainly been lovely, were now bleached of color, many shades paler than the emerald they'd once been, and a thin cowl of sopping hair frames her too gaunt face in an unflattering way. Amid the weather she seems a black and white image, projected on a screen agitated with static.

The iron bar bites into her scalp and follows her down. I step back and observe her fingers, once crowned with impeccably painted nails, which are now serrated and stripped of polish in unflattering tracks. She lies motionless, and I check over my shoulder to be sure none of her breed has found opportunity in my distraction, and we are still alone this woman and I, only she is beyond concern.

Then I continue on my way.

At the edge of town I see five more like the woman, but they are enrapt with a banquet, crouching over the body of an obese man wearing red canvas sneakers and blue sweat pants, the latter being devoured in great swatches along with the meat and fat beneath. I have come to understand they are never quite so vulnerable as when they eat. The ritual of feeding mesmerizes them, and if it weren't for fear of summoning more, I could draw my pistol and execute each of them without disturbing the others until the bullets ended their trances, but the food distracts and incapacitates them and this is an opportunity, so I cross to the far sidewalk and make my way onto Main Street.

My thoughts wander and I recall a party I attended. Like Poe's *Masque*, the privileged gathered in a penthouse apartment to toast their good fortunes while small fires dotted the city below. The crowd, drunk and jovial, made me uneasy, as crowds often do, so I spent much of the evening at the window, gazing down at the panic and the pockets of flame licking the distant streets. A man approached me, a handsome mannequin draped in Italian wool and arrogance. He suggested we spend the evening in a spare room, naked and together while the city collapsed, because it was his intent to overdose on pain pills and found the idea of being fucked as he drifted into death appealing. I turned away from this offer and again peered through the glass, downward. Men and women ran and cars collided, but the celebratory gathering heard none of the commotion. Screams couldn't travel so high. The next morning, I left the party and convinced that the outbreak was not an incident so much as a movement, I packed a bag and loaded the car and drove to the North while the police and army kept brittle control of the situation.

I found this town and settled in. The supply of medication I brought from the city lasted until this morning.

The glass door of the drug store is smashed. I look into the gloom and take the flashlight from my pocket and shine it over the wreckage within. Shelves are toppled and the floor is littered with boxes and packets and pools of shampoo. That this place has been looted is of no surprise. It offered food for the scavenger, supplies for the wounded and sick, and free dreams for the addict. I step inside and pain flares at my shin. I wince and continue into the shop, stepping over a cardboard display that had once held cheap dog toys. The lantern beam reveals one derelict aisle after another, but nothing moves here save me, and I make my way to the back of the store, picking through the wreckage, cautious so that I don't wound my legs a second time. The Plexiglas shield that once guarded the pharmacist from his patrons wears an enormous black-rimmed hole. A creative junkie burned his way through a barrier he could not smash. On the floor at the foot of the counter, I see the discarded tank of acetylene and note the tremendous streak of blood it lies in. The smear runs like a poorly painted trail along the back aisle and veers right. I pause and listen, though feel no genuine concern.

The afflicted are quiet in their state, but they are clumsy. It would be impossible for one of them to move through the store's debris with any degree of stealth.

I climb onto the counter and work my way through the hole and drop onto the pharmacy's linoleum floor. Then I begin to search. As I expect, the shelves have been picked through, but I'm grateful to see they are not barren. My light falls over each shelf and I examine the labels on the remaining bottles and on a bottom shelf I am grateful to find one labeled: Truvada. The weight of the bottle is a relief. It goes into the backpack brought for this chore and I return to my search, finding labels that read Viramune, Viread, Zerit and Epivir—all names from the dosage chart I keep in my pocket. They too go in the backpack, rattling like muffled maracas as they drop into place.

Though I consider seeking out a pain medication for the ache in my leg, it strikes me as a waste of time. The addicts—those not dragged away by the wandering threat—would have made a priority of the numbing prescriptions, and the safety and the warmth of the house call me. Back through the charred hole. I hit the floor, and like an echo of my soles' impact, I hear the hiss of a box whooshing across the floor at the front of the shop. I secure the backpack over my shoulders and put the flashlight in my left hand, retrieving the iron from my belt loop with the right. I stand perfectly still, listening for more noise, but hear only the rapping downpour on the street outside.

Satisfied that whatever shares this chamber with me is not moving in my direction, I follow the smear of blood across the back of the store and turn right, and then I pause again because the weather's chill is intensified by uncertainty as I peer down the aisle. The murky air, visible through the shattered front door, shifts strangely; indistinct shapes drift and sway as if caught in an ocean tide, and a new sound, this one clearly caused by a bit of metal clacking on the linoleum in a nearby aisle, sends tremors through my chest.

I move toward it, iron bar raised, flashlight beam illuminating the side of an end cap where condoms are displayed. This seems the only product untouched by foragers.

He steps into the back aisle. Not long ago he was someone's young son, with chestnut hair grown long over his ears and brow. A pea coat too large for his youthful frame drapes from his shoulders. His cheeks are full and his eyes shine like bits of brown glass in the disk of light bathing his face. The bar arcs high over my head, and I begin the downward swing, when I'm struck by the color in his eyes—still vibrant—and the boy cringes, throwing an arm above his head to ward off the blow, and the bar stops just short of crushing his elbow.

I tell him I'm sorry and that he's safe, and he tells me he was with his grandfather and lost the old man in town, and he saw my light, and he'd hoped to find the man here, and the grandfather was wearing blue sweatpants and red sneakers, and had I seen the man.

I had seen the man, but the truth of what I'd witnessed wouldn't comfort the boy. I asked him his name, and he hesitates to share it with me but finally says, David.

A number of lies, meant to quell the boy's unease and keep him quiet so we would not follow too closely in his grandfather's steps, rolls through my mind, and I know David will fight all of them. So I tell him that I spoke to his grandfather, and his brown eyes light up hopefully. Then I tell him that I had promised the old man I would take David to a house where the man waited with others.

The boy wants to believe me, but he is reticent and shuffles back a step. He looks about uncertainly and when he gazes into the aisle on his right, his face goes slack.

I step forward and swing the light in that direction, and it falls on four trudging figures. Not long ago, the man leading these wanderers was an executive, with a stout confident face and a wave of white hair. He wears a blue suit that would have been expensive, reminding me of the arrogant partygoer who'd considered fucking an appropriate preface to suicide. This executive's hand is missing three fingers and his suit sleeve is torn at the shoulder. Flanking him, two women of diametrically opposed attractiveness teeter from side to side as if each step is their last before collapse. The person behind is unidentifiable save for a swatch of jutting red hair.

Then more of these broken wanderers appear at the front of the aisle, and more still until it is clear this boy, David, has led an ample contingent into the shop. I dash to the far aisle and see that it too fills like a chute guiding cattle to the trough. As quickly as possible, I race back to the boy and scoop him up in an arm, causing him to squeal a sharp protest. Pain flares along my shin from ankle to knee as I support his added weight, but I carry him to the burned portal above the pharmacy counter. With a clumsy motion I throw him at the hole, and he drops heavily across the lower frame, but manages to scramble inside without further sound. Then I follow, and my backpack catches on the upper edge of the hole. I twist and fight, terribly conscious of the vulnerability of my body's lower extremities. Finally I manage to work my way through the hole and drop onto the linoleum, coming down hard on my elbow. Adrenaline deadens the pain. Again on my feet, I turn to the compromised shield and the breath slips out of my chest. From where I stand it seems that these dreadful wanderers occupy every inch of floor space. To the left I see the former executive, pushing against the back of a man in an open bathrobe. The man's torso is shredded, decimated by teeth and nails, leaving only a great sheet of scab running from his throat to the chasm in his belly, and from this hollow to his devoured crotch.

David pulls on the sleeve of my jacket to get my attention, except I can't turn away from the spectacle before me. The people beyond the barrier—those in shadow and those in my light's cast—move forward and back in unison as if swaying to music pumped over a frequency only they can hear, and for a heartbeat's time, I envy their unity and wish to feel it, regardless of the perverse rite of passage joining them requires. It is an odd notion, one that surely has roots in my life before this town.

Then David is pleading with me and I turn away, uncertain of what he thinks I can accomplish. We are meat in a butcher's window. The boy insists we have to leave, and a chuckle of disbelief rises in my throat, but I kill it on my tongue. Telling him our situation is hopeless will solve nothing. We might wait, hidden behind the shelves, hoping the wanderers lose interest or forget of our existence, but that is foolish. Already an overweight, black-haired girl with blood-stained braces, wearing a T-shirt that reads "Unclean," attempts to climb onto the counter, her eyes focused on the gap as hotly as the acetylene torch that created it.

David again pulls my sleeve and I follow him, wondering what this boy intends. He leads me to the last row of shelves and points into a gloomy alcove beyond. I lift the light and it falls on a door, and I feel a bolt of embarrassment that I should have thought the store possessed a single entrance and exit.

Before approaching it, I check the partition and see the plump girl with the grisly braces wriggling through the hole, one arm extended in full as if reaching for an invisible handle to grasp for leverage. Her jaws snap at the light's beam, which glints off her dental work creating tiny blades of reflection. Then I swing the flashlight back to the door and find that David has already opened it, and the sound of rain crackles in the pharmacy. I follow him outside, into the cold and angry sleet, and a sharp wing of wind beats over my neck. The back alley of the store is empty, only dumpsters holding month-old trash, slowly decomposing in the metal bins.

The narrow corridor amplifies the angry sounds of storm as downpour claps on concrete, steel, brick, and filth. I ask the boy to stand behind me and lead him to the end of the alley, and he asks why I'm limping, and I tell him I hurt myself.

Are you bit?

He delivers the question with such disgust and fear, I think to ask him what he intends to do about it if I am, but I clamp down on the ire, pinning it to my tongue, and tell him the truth. The limp is the result of a poorly fashioned booby trap set in one of the neighborhood houses I'd been scavenging soon after trading the city for this place. Upon arriving in town, I met a group of men and women and stayed with them briefly. On one of the daily gathering excursions, my foot went through a sabotaged stair step, and though sprains and breaks had been avoided, a jutting nail had torn a considerable gash in my pant leg and the shin beneath.

David insists I show him the wound, and I lift my damp pant leg and show him the bandage. When he insists I peel this back, I release the gathered fabric, allowing the cuff to return to its place at my ankle and tell him we have more important things to worry about and I'm not about to risk infection—another infection—to assuage his curiosity.

The exit from the town, along a different street, one not littered by the boy's grandfather, is uneventful. Night closes fast, and the ice and water continue to pelt, dropping furiously from the tumor-hued cumulus. The cold is inside of me now, affixing to muscle, vein, and bone. The threats we see are distant, on side streets, wandering aimlessly in circles, and if they notice us, it is without interest. I lead the boy to my house but do not take him inside. Instead, I continue along the street to the house on the corner where the others live, and he asks if his grandfather is inside and I lie and assure him that the old man is safely wrapped in a blanket, chatting happily with a fine group of people.

After I knock, a sour-faced man who not long ago had been a promising corporate attorney opens the door and points a sleek, silver pistol at my face. His name is Cameron and he wears a blue cotton dress shirt over black slacks. His blond hair droops shapelessly over his brow. He asks what I want and I introduce him to David and ask if he will get Erica for me. Cameron frowns more deeply, the expression comical in its extremity. He waves us in and checks over our shoulders to make sure I have brought no threat upon the house in the way that David invited it to the drug store.

Inside a battery-powered lantern glows weakly from the staircase. The windows of this house have been covered with plywood sheets and reinforced with studs so that little natural light enters. Pockets of shadow float at the top of the stairs and in the room to my left where I feel people are gathered, though I cannot see them.

Where's Granddad?

David's question takes me off guard. I don't want to have to explain the old man's fate to him and wish Erica would appear so she can relieve me of this repugnant obligation. Cameron presents me with bitter eyes and pinched lips, and I repeat my request to see Erica. He looks from me to the boy and back again and then nods. I hold David by the shoulder and tell him that his grandfather is probably napping in one of the bedrooms, and we will wait for Erica to take him. Faces begin to appear in the wells of shadow at David's back. The men and women come forward slowly, holstering their weapons as they approach and all greet us with smiles and ask me how I am feeling, and I tell them I am fine, and I assure them I will be leaving soon, and this casual statement, delivered without a hint of acidity causes them to frown.

I introduce David to the eight men and women, and he tells them he wants to see his grandfather, and questions alight and then vanish from their brows as they understand why I've brought the boy to them.

Mindy offers to get David a blanket.

Chet hurries off to find the boy a cup of tea.

The others comment on the necessity of these tokens of warmth and how much they will soothe the boy, who has yet to understand the extent of his misery.

Erica walks into the foyer of the house. Not long ago she was a caring, full-figured woman with red hair and compassionate eyes. She still is.

I ask Burt to show David into the living room and then lead Erica to the back of the house.

In the kitchen, I explain what has happened to David's grandfather, and that I withheld the information from the boy because I didn't want him to panic, and she tells me I've done the right thing, and she will speak to him immediately. I thank her and open the back door, making to leave.

Erica tells me I can stay. She tells me I should stay. I tell her I can't stay and return to the storm.

Crossing the backyards, through hedges and over low fences, my leg aching with each step, I am barely aware of my surroundings, but no threat approaches and I reach the back door to my house without incident. Inside, I light the lantern. This house has been similarly shielded with boards and studs—a final kindness from the survivors down the street, the men and women who cast me out.

I peel off my wet clothes and retrieve a towel from a stack I keep in the hall closet. Once dry I pull on fresh clothes and wrap myself in a duvet. I take a can of ravioli and a bottle of water to the sofa and sit down for my supper, but the tepid meal slips down my throat like a mudslide landing hard and gritty in my stomach. I retrieve the pill bottles from my backpack and swallow one Truvada and one Viramune, and then I return to the sofa and hike my pant leg to examine the cut on my shin.

It still hasn't healed. The red gash appears wet and fresh in the flat glow of the lantern. Blood has long since stopped seeping from the wound, but it does not scab and it does not close. The skin at the wounds lips carries the same cranberry stain it showed the afternoon of its infliction. It appears neither aggravated nor infected, but it has been two weeks since the nail gouged my leg and it continues to resist amelioration, and though I don't know what this means, I know it must mean something.

I curl up on the sofa, wrapped tightly in the duvet. I think about what I told the boy about my injury. Though not a lie, it wasn't the whole of the truth either.

I entered a home with others, intent on looting supplies, and I did crash through a step that had been worn away with a saw or file. All true. But after freeing myself from the rigged staircase, leg searing with the fresh cut, I returned to the front of the house and found Cameron in a corner of the living room. He had lost his gun or had set it down at some point, leaving himself unarmed. He held his empty hands in front of him as three rotting wanderers closed in. Their focus on him made their deaths easy. I crushed one's head with the iron and the other two didn't even turn my direction. The second was similarly subdued, and all should have been well, except Cameron found his courage and retrieved a bronze obelisk from a tabletop and swung at the third. Its head exploded into a fetid spray of bone and tissue and fluid, covering me from face to foot.

I had not been bitten, but that didn't exempt me from infection.

Upon our return, Erica insisted on treating my wounds and noted the debris covering the wound on my leg. After cleaning and binding the gash, she offered me a distracted smile and excused herself.

They held their arraignment while I dozed on a bed upstairs, and when I woke Erica, Cameron and Burt stood in the room, the two men aiming pistols at my head. I was told that I'd remain under guard to see if my system had been compromised, and I did not argue their logic. That night, while I slept, they held their trial and I woke to find I'd been found guilty. A bite could kill and turn a man in less than twelve hours, and though I had already exceeded this window period the uncommon nature of my wound—its failure to clot—was suspect, and with great sadness and apology they asked that I leave for the safety of the others in the house. It never occurred to me to argue.

In honesty, I had been considering my future with this band of men and women for days before the accident. Already they spoke of repopulation and of building a society devoted to the Bible's word—for certainly this was a Rapture—and who could say which words from this book would soothe them and guide them in the months to come? I would be useless to them in regard to fatherhood, having carried an established infection into this fresh pandemic—to say nothing of my repugnance for the act—and as to their philosophies regarding a future of god-fearing, black-and-white morality...it comforted me little. I also feared that a gathering of their size provided more opportunity for exposure—the safety of numbers outweighed by the necessity for those numbers to eat and move about. Cameron and the other men relied on their guns, each report a siren, calling the rotted vessels to port, and there were the arguments, the affiliations, the jostlings for power, this group already eager to rekindle politics and government—a new society like a fungus growing from the decay of the old.

So I left the house and they helped me secure this place, and they apologized for their decision, which was unnecessary, and I thanked them, and they returned to the house on the corner. I was left alone and found it acceptable.

Chilled now, I pull the duvet closer to my neck and curl into a tighter ball, staring at the plywood sheets intended to keep the world out.

The loneliness is manageable, if only because it was well rehearsed before the outbreak, not that I practiced misanthropy or reveled in the anti-social. If anything I felt unmoved by the cultural touchstones that so greatly occupied the interests of other people. I didn't follow the television programs dissected and analyzed at office gatherings, preferring documentaries and British crime dramas; nor did I read the latest literary phenomenon, because the voices of Monette and White rang truer to my ears; nor did I take joy or offense at anything a pop musician, movie star, or inexplicable celebrity did or said. This disinterest in glittering culture evolved without calculation, never occurring to me that others should include or exclude me based on such fragile and transient bits of interest. I found politics ridiculous, as logic wasn't allowed to bridge the gaps formed by the Right and the Left. Useful discussion was mutilated as it attempted to cross the laser fences separating the two camps. Religions offered similar obstacles and similar intolerance. I found so many things incomprehensible, so many just plain foolish, and it left me outside—out in the cold, as they say—because I could not with any sincerity claim to belong to this group or that.

Similar estrangement marked my intimate life, not only because of the virus that required awkward disclosure but also for my inability to weave another man into my heart and head. It seemed that my partners always required more than I could give them—more attention, more time, more understanding. They would play games to spark a reaction in me, and I never understood the rules of their games, so I always lost, and they always left. I felt like a cog, filed and sanded, with no teeth left to grip the other gears in the machine.

I drift into dreamless sleep, and come morning the pain in my leg bleats me awake as efficiently as an alarm clock. Through a narrow gap in the plywood, I see the empty street outside, still gray though the storm has passed. The pavement and the grass are wet and the bleak scene sends me back to the sofa, where I doze as the morning hours pass. At noon I take my medications and as an afterthought pop four ibuprofen caplets in the hope that the ache below my knee will subside.

Overnight the pain had escalated, and though still tolerable it concerns me. I check the wound and find it has not changed. No swelling, no discharge, no further discoloration. It remains as it was two weeks ago, and certainly this indicates my system has been compromised, but I am alive long after other infected men would have turned to threat, and I consider the pills I take for the first infection and wonder if they have some affect on this new one. The doctor told me it was a control not a cure.

Fatigued, I lie down and rest my eyes, and I think of the boy, David, and hope that he has come to terms with his grandfather's absence. I know that Erica will do all that she can for him, as she did all that she could for me. Meager light—all the plywood allows to enter—comes and goes, and it is again night. Hunger pulls me from the sofa and I eat a can of deviled ham and a packet of crackers and drink a bottle of water. I take my evening dose of pills and more ibuprofen, and then I put the battery-powered lantern on the table behind me and read a poorly translated German mystery found in the home office down the hall. Soon enough, I am sleep. I'm startled awake in the middle of the night by a tremor in my leg. Fingers of electricity turn to lightning in my veins, shooting from the cut below my knee to the base of my skull, but then I realize my mistake. The wound is the destination—one of many—not the source of this electrical disturbance. Shocks erupt in my head and fan out, coursing across my system in tingles that at first terrify me and then soothe. The pain in my leg vanishes, leaving only a tickle on the skin, and I lay there in the soft glow of the lantern, gazing at the lake of shadow pooling across the ceiling, and I feel certain that something has passed, though I am unable to identify it. Come morning, a voice in the street summons me to the window, and I press my face to the plywood and gaze through the narrow opening. In the center of the road, Erica calls my name. My hands form claws against the planks, scratching.

Wanderers close in on her from all sides, shuffling eagerly in a tightening circle. I think she should turn around and run, build up enough momentum to break through the encroaching mass, and I wonder where her people are and why she's alone in the middle of the street. I make it to the door and fumble with the locks, momentarily confused by the knobs and bolts and the chain.

I need to reach her, need to help.

I throw the door open and step onto the porch, moving as quickly as my legs will allow. The wound no longer hurts, but it feels as if I'm walking through a pool of gelatin. Relativity makes each step an eternity. Erica sees me and screams for me to hurry, and I want to hurry. I want to help. I briefly think of an iron bar and how it should have been in my hand, except the crowd closes on her, and there isn't time, and I'm compelled forward.

I reach the back of the mob and without concern wade into its midst, throwing my shoulders from side to side to clear a path. Ahead of me, I see Erica's face, but a decaying hand clutches her hair, and holds her tight by a fistful of carrot-red strands knotted in its palm. She cries out to me. David has run away, and it's too late to help her, and I have to help David, but I continue forward, striking out blindly to clear my path to her.

Then she is gone, dragged to the ground as numerous bodies crouch and bend, ripping at her clothes and her skin, and I feel I am too late, but I continue to her, and at her side I find room between a man who shakes his head furiously to rip away a piece of her thigh, and another man who chews hungrily on her left breast, and I kneel down and run my fingers over her bare belly, reveling in the velvety sensation of her. My nails hook into her skin and lines of red open like hungry lips.

I lean down and sink my teeth into the meat and my mouth fills with sensation not flavor. The flesh sends waves of warmth over my tongue and down my throat and into my nervous system until the chill is gone, and only then do I realize how very long I've suffered the cold. And it occurs to me I am no different from those who crowd me and shove and push for their morsel of heat; we are of a single philosophy, united. Not long ago, I was alive and alone, and now, having shed the detritus of the individual, I find camaraderie in the single-minded horde, and I know each mouthful brings me closer to them.

I tear at the small wound and shovel bits of skin and fat and muscle into my mouth and each grinding of my teeth stokes the fire in my veins. Fingers, painted thickly with blood, gratefully dig, snagging on viscera and shredded tissue, and I want to go deeper, to hollow this thing out, and I want to be small, so I can climb within and swaddle like an infant held by a radiant crib of ribs and flesh, never again to feel the cold, existing forever inside, where it's warm.

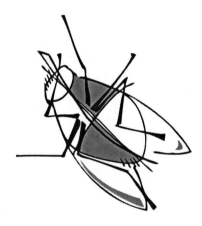

Nothing Forgiven

You drive south on Kingsley. At your back, the funeral of an uncle and the irritation of the family home, chatting uncomfortably with the strangers you call mom and dad and Aunt Lois. Beyond the windshield low buildings approach—shops and restaurants—all pasted against a sky of granite. Like familiar melodies, long unheard and thought forgotten, memories of youth return, rising from the houses, the road and the street signs marking familiar intersections. So much about the city is different, but even more is the same. After thirty-three years, details you thought long eroded emerge in sharp relief, chasing you from one landmark to the next.

Long ago, you made a promise, swore you'd never return to this place. What you did here—what you allowed to happen in order to escape—was just too much to accept. You put the events down to dream, to delusion, to a mind soused with liquor. You saw things that could never be. And for many years, you blocked it out entirely. Jody. Bobby. They were hardly considered over the years. Now though, with your promise broken and the past's topography rising, they return, joining you in the car like phantom passengers.

A pang of guilt cuts your stomach. You search the row of low buildings for a bar, hoping to numb the ache with a shot of single malt. The drive to Newark is long enough without the company of such needling companions. You certainly don't want them sharing the flight back to Dayton, back to Susan.

Your wife is already furious with you. She resented your desertion, reminding you time and again that you couldn't afford such a trip. The house needs a new roof; the toilet leaks, needs replacing; there is mould in the basement. Right up until you left for the airport, she reminded you how many times you claimed to hate the city of your birth. But you know her concern isn't for you. These days, it never is.

You can't blame her. How can you? The accident was such a terrible thing. An evening run, a reckless driver. An active, beautiful woman paralyzed, the prisoner of a wheelchair. Her emotions were bound to be as broken as her spine. And though you can help your wife adapt to the physical limitations of her new condition, you are helpless to stop her depression, her anger, her fits of destructive rage.

After three years, you are as much a captive of the accident as Susan.

You go to work, come home. You try to make her comfortable, endure her irrational outbursts, her phases of black despondence, sometimes weeks long. The settlement is spent.

Your lawyer was lazy, taking an insufficient sum, and the bills keep coming. Month after month, check after check, you never seem to make a dent.

Susan was right; you can't afford this trip, but you need it. You need to experience something beyond her disapproval and the pile of bills on the kitchen table. Yes, you hated this place. Returning was simply an excuse, a location away from the woman you love, because being with her hurts so damned bad that you thought it would kill you.

You tell yourself Susan will be okay. Her sister is taking care of her for a couple of days. They get along well. Susan is likely grateful to be rid of you, despite her protests.

Across the street, its sign glowing in the fading evening light, you see a bar. One drink, you think, just something to sand down the edges.

In the bar, you sit on a stool, watch the bartender shake a martini. You run your drink order over in your mind as if you might forget it, though it hasn't changed in over three decades: scotch, neat.

But when the bartender, a young man with a shag of dark hair, leans on the bar and asks, "'Can I getcha?" you say, "Gin and tonic."

Jody hates the smell of whiskey.

The ache in your belly redoubles, and you squeeze your eyes closed, holding back the memory of a beautiful girl. Jody wants to be remembered, wants *you* to remember her, but you aren't ready. Not yet. Not here.

You drink quickly and order another. The taste of gin is like blood on your tongue, reminding you of pain, but you drink until the second glass is empty.

Head lighter and belly heavier with gin, you walk out of the bar into the fading evening light. It will be night soon, another night on the circuit. But no, the circuit is broken. Your parents railed with age-thin voices against the new buildings—a sewage treatment facility, some other construction—that now rise on Ocean, blocking off the street that was an integral part of the loop. Some of the bars remain, certainly the boardwalk.

You wander to the corner and turn left. There is plenty of time before the flight.

As a kid, you spent weekend evenings walking up and down Ocean, taking energy and joy from the cruising youths and the pulse of rock and roll beating between the ribs of the shore side bars. When you were old enough to drive and owned a car of your own, you joined the thundering parade on The Circuit.

Round and round.

You cross Ocean Avenue, walking with uncertain steps toward the Boardwalk while trying to remember how you felt on those long ago nights. You imagine cars and chrome, conjure crowds of people, their faces blurred and dull. You struggle with the mental film, but it will not focus, and nothing else about those years emerges. Even Jody and Bobby are absent for the moment. Too much time gone. You are a father now, a grandfather. It doesn't seem possible. Your children are older than you were the night you left this place. Your daughter's wonderful son is nearly a year old.

For a while there, only a handful of years, you considered yourself to be on the easy side of life. Your children were educated, had families of their own, and you and Susan still had good money in the bank. The promise of retirement and comfort was already whispered in your ear. Then, Susan was run down, and then the hospital, the therapy, the wheelchair. The endless stack of bills.

Round and round.

On the boardwalk, you stop and look around to see the people, the stands displaying novelties and food, the glowing lights. You hardly remember leaving the bar. The pedestrian crowd is sparse, but you aren't surprised. It is a weeknight, just past dinnertime. An overweight couple in matching bright red Hawaiian shirts eats ice cream, leans on one another affectionately. Two boys count the coins in their palms in front of a booth that sells sunglasses. Groups of people in silhouette wander in the distance. Against the side of a hot dog cart, a young couple embraces, kissing each other with the desperation of juvenile passion.

Oddly, you notice little else. The odors and the sounds of this place elude you, as if you bear witness to the performance of ghosts on a make-believe set. You sniff the air, but receive no olfactory cues. You listen, knowing that there should be voices, music, electronic accolades from the arcade machines. You strain to hear something, so that you can feel a part of this place again. Finally, a rhythmic pulse creeps into your head. It pumps and crashes and hisses. You turn away from the booths. Your steps rap on the boards in time with that distant beat. At a railing, you stop, clutch the banister. Through the darkness a filmy white line breaks on the shore. Then, you understand. The ocean is calling you, leading you back to this dreadful landmark.

And there, only twenty yards away, a familiar face waits. Your heart trips and stutters. You leave your place at the railing, cross to a steep set of wooden stairs and descend to the sand. Jody stands on the beach, hardly changed at all. Her strawberry blond hair drapes over narrow shoulders. At her back, waves pound the shore, crashing and shushing. For a moment it feels as if nothing has changed. More than thirty years crease and fold and slip away. You smile a moment before the fear turns your blood to shattered cutting ice.

She can't be here.

You look back at the Boardwalk, at the lights and the people meandering over the planks. Your mind grows hazy, buzzing with a distant powerful drone. You look back at Jody, standing motionless on the beach.

"Please," you say, taking a step back.

Don't leave. She's why you came back.

You want to run, but something holds you on the sand, facing Jody. Your mind fills with images, one lying over the top of the other so that none are clear. A single voice, like the teller of a story or the singer of a song, accompanies the images. It is your voice, only calm. Its lulling timbre and rhythmic cadence are strange, but what it says is familiar.

You belong here. You belong to the shore, to the waves, to the muscle machines that howl in the night.

For all of your failure to conjure the past only moments before, it comes crashing back. The sand buckles. The cool darkening air shimmers.

You...

You drive north on Ocean, crawling with the highway knights sitting low on their Harleys; checking out the machine-head toughs sporting chrome and revving their Hemis to the heavens. The girls in their bellbottom jeans and broken-zippered boots giggle and wave, then cover their bright angel faces with long fingers tipped in watermelon paint. Streetlight and stars concede to the parade of headlights. Motor perfume, thick and grimy, mingles with the scents of the grilling meat from Boardwalk shacks and the spirits in throat. Clouds of salty mist hang over all. On the left, young rock-and -roll, just hitting puberty and all the more cocksure and wild for it, rages in wooden shacks where the cools gather to fill their heads, their hips and their feet with honky tonk hymns written by low class priests, singing of Gods made in their own image. To the right, past the Boardwalk, off in the darkness, the waves play out a rhythm silenced by the thunder of engine and guitar but felt in the soul and lap of every man and woman on the circuit. Sidewalks team with shag-haired boys and straight-haired girls, each of them half a beast hunting to make themselves whole before daylight. In the street, muscle machines and mom-and-pop coaches crawl along the avenue.

You make a left and then another, down Kingsley. Left again. Round and round. Always chasing the closest horizon, measuring freedom by gas gauge and the remains of a gin bottle.

Night whispers promises, drawing her children to the loop, and their orbit—circles upon circles—is gravitational, pulling the innocent in and keeping them close.

Parked in the lot, your Chevy part of the herd, you pull a bottle from under the seat. You open it, make your wish and release the juniper genie into your mouth. The gin bites. You hate its taste. But the smell of whiskey makes Jody sick, so you drink this. A small sacrifice. One of hundreds. You make another wish, take another hit.

In the arcade, amid the popping squeals of the pinball machines, lights jumping, Richie and Mike plan a drag. They call each other pussy and dork and fag until the deal is set. They wait for their girlfriends to come back from the john, still posturing like gladiators beneath a coliseum crowd. Three little girls, with barely enough rack to support their halters, cheeks slashed pink with mothers' rouge, race by, looking terrified.

Pinballs clang and crack, trying to escape. Their reward is another paddle whack, another bumper shove or a fast descent into darkness.

You stand with a smoke in your mouth, looking hard and bored like it's all just another moment—one of millions—that will come and go with no more meaning than the striking of a match. For some it's a pose, a mask handed out in school for all of the shore boys to wear, but for you it's the way of your face. You *are* hard. You *are* bored. High school is a year gone, the diploma nothing but a piece of paper shoved in a drawer under mom's carton of Pall Malls. The nights come. Round and round. The night dies. You haul sofas for Mr. Lombardo so that the Joneses and the Smiths have comfortable places to sit before going home to your parent's tattered Sears couch. You sit there and wait until one of the Kingsley Boys calls or Jody is finished at the bookshop.

They used to mean the world to you, closer than family. Knowing you'd be with them made you ache with a comfortable lust. Now, that longing is for something different, something distant, something beyond the promise of the night. But Jody is off work, and the night comes. Round and round.

The gladiators Richie and Mike puff out their chests in greeting to their girlfriends now back from the john. Mike drops his smoke on the cold tile floor and crushes it under a boot toe. They will race. One will lose. Neither wins because tomorrow will be the same. These carousel horses can never claim victory.

You leave the arcade and step into the street where the herd of Camaros, Firebirds and Barracudas roll. Tinny music pumps from speakers to greet the growling engines, the shouting voices and the muffled concerts of the shore-side troubadours in an orchestra of soul and steel. Jody waits for you by The Pony. You'll meet her. She'll talk about her day and want you to talk. But it's all been said. Recounting your day is a familiar song, pounding at your ears. All chorus. No verse. You'll hate her for making you sing it. Then, you'll walk back to the lot where your car waits. In the backseat, Jody will open up to you just like she's done every Friday for three years.

She used to be the cure for your disease. Now another symptom.

To the north, a distant and welcoming darkness and you know that if you had once, just once, gone straight instead of turning left, you would be someplace else. For the hundreds and thousands of miles driven, you wonder where you could have gone.

"Please," you say to Night, hoping she'll understand and grant the wish you've whispered so often, the one you tell your pillow with gin-foul breath.

You nearly made it out. Phil lived in Delaware. He had a spare room. Knew about a warehouse that needed hands. Jody wanted to go, wanted to see the rest of the world. But her brother plucked the dream from her. Bobby, with the shore to his back, went face down in the waves, chasing a bottle of Jim Beam with a shot of the Atlantic. Jody used you like a shrink, like a nurse and like a priest, her lips spilling guilt and agony to your shoulder. For her, leaving was forgotten. But still you could go somewhere beyond the circuit where the streets were clean and quiet and life meant a little more than horsepower and neon.

Then you blew a rod, dragging for laughs with Hoyt Decola. Your freedom machine needed repair, so the money you had went up like smoke. The charred dream that remained just more litter for the boardwalk.

Along the crowded sidewalks, you march with concrete boots. People walk and stumble by. Some look at you, recognizing breed, a single face on a hundred bodies. You stop and turn to the wall, check for cold-eyed cops and pull the bottle from your pocket: another miserable shot with the promise of miracles.

Jody waits in front of The Pony. Her hair is strawberry straw hanging like curtains to hide her shoulders. She holds a cigarette to her lips, staring over the line of cars to the sky above the ocean. On her pink t-shirt, your name is written in rainbow-colored letters baked on the fabric. Hip hugger denim caresses her thighs, then erupts into bells that tent her feet. Through the wall behind her, The Jukes beat out a song that makes a man at Jody's back bop.

She wraps her arms around your neck, kisses you. Wants to know where you've been.

You slide an arm around her waist, tell her *something came up.*

Jody wants to know about your day and you shrug. Normally, you'd sing that song just to make her feel better, but tonight you can't bring yourself to it. The night is different. Everything is the same, and you tell yourself that the difference is in your head, but you feel it. Something. It pulls at your gut.

You take her to the boardwalk instead of the car because you don't want to feel her on you; it's too much like a jacket, sleeves wrapped and locked around your chest. The shops with food and sunglasses, the people; a movie that never changes. So, your shoes thump a rhythm on the boards. Jody looks at you like a hero. You look at the planks like a convict. People come and go. Their voices fill your ears, and then fade.

Beneath your arm, you feel Jody pause. Looking up, you notice the empty peanut cart, the railing, the stairs. Fleshy sand fans toward the great black pond that seduced her brother. You know she doesn't like coming here.

You know I don't like coming here.

But there's an answer on the sand. You can't see it, can hardly imagine it. Still, you feel it. Its chain wraps around your heart, pulls tight.

I want to go back to the car.

Before, you would have stopped and changed direction, doing anything for Jody. She was the completion of you as a man. Your jokes were met with her laugh. Your foolishness, her scowl. Her sweet soft body refused you nothing. Once, your dreams were hers, shared and discussed late at night while sweaty stomachs cooled between you. Why did that end? When?

With Bobby?

You look into her frightened eyes. *Baby, it'll be all right.*

She trusts you and offers her hand so you can guide her down to the beach. Sand crumbles beneath your boots. Jody stumbles and yelps. A nervous giggle follows as you pull her tight and hold her steady. Her hair brushes your cheek. You smell the baby shampoo she uses on it. For a moment, the salt, the trash and engine fumes are gone and your head is cleansed by the scent of her and the chain tightens around your heart, pulling you toward the waves.

When you stop, it's because your heart—its slow tic tock—needs winding. So you press your lips to Jody's and taste the bubble gum gloss frosting them. The taste sparks no desire, no pleasure-memory. It's just sweet and sticky.

Jody clutches at you, binding herself to your ribs. Over her head, you see the one that called you standing near the battle of wave and sand.

He is another circuit tough with faded jeans too tight and the sleeves of his t-shirt rolled.

A pack of Lucky's hides beneath the fabric at his shoulder.

This tough is different, though. His threat doesn't grow from muscle or blade. You tell yourself that it's the gin or the trapped beast in your head or the incest of the two breeding dementia.

You know Bobby's face. Around this boy, a billow of smoke as black as the sky curls and dances. Looking closer, you see that he is not resurrected with skin or bone, but rather surf, beach and misty shadow, formed by the wet and the dirt and the air of this place. Night fills the cavities of his eyes and grains of wet sand lay like smooth sheets of brow and cheek. Dry sand weaves his shirt and chutes of seawater form the twin columns of his legs, the cascade an illusion of rippling pale blue cotton. His edges are rough and fray, working outward to become filaments of dark smoke, reaching to the sky. Or perhaps the reverse is true, and Night reached down to sculpt this phantom.

Bobby looks at you. Except for the whirling mist and the fall of his pant legs, he is motionless, staring. Holding Jody closer to your chest, you look on in frightened wonder. Now your heart beats faster, the way you hoped it would with her kiss.

You know what he wants. The knowledge is inside of you like the chain that brought you to this place. He wants you to turn away and leave Jody on the sand with him. The shore ghost wants to share secrets with his sister.

Turn away. Walk back to the avenue where the living go round and round.

You push Jody away, gently and with great care. Her eyes are bright and expectant as if anticipating a compliment or proposal. And you turn away to look at the boardwalk and the wall of light rising behind it from the circuit. Behind you, she speaks your name. She sounds confused and hurt, but you don't turn back. You can never look back. With your next step, you feel her hand on your shoulder but you don't stop walking. The hand is gone, and she speaks another name.

Bobby?

So, you walk over the sand, each step uncertain, earth crumbling underfoot. You climb the stairs toward the boardwalk, up and away from the sand. You walk along Ocean, the motorcade little more than a hum in your ears, a blur from the corner of your eye. Night suffuses the headlights, dulls the neon and blacks out the stars. The faces you've seen too long are now flat and featureless, masks distorted by erosion.

You're behind the wheel of your car, driving north on Ocean but you don't turn left. You keep going, away from the circuit to the great darkness ahead, and you don't look back.

*B*ut now, you are back.
    You let the last of the memories slip away. Jody stands closer now, though still not close. From where you stand you see sand running in smooth sheets over her cheeks and draping long, like hair to her shoulders. The grains mound at her chest, and your name is carved in relief, just empty letters with the night showing through. Bits of captured ocean fill her expressionless eyes and weave the material of her bell-bottom pants.

She drowned the night you left. Just like her brother, Jody walked into the ocean to dream face down. Night demanded a sacrifice, payment for your release from this place, and when it appeared, wearing Bobby's façade, you gave Jody to it and walked away.

You drove for days after that, what little cash you carried fed the gas tank, distance far more important than meat. Then came the jobs, then Susan and the children. Through it all, the numb of that night remained with you like an opiate cloud. You hid culpability behind that mist, kept Jody there for years at a time. When she was able to break through, guilt pecked at your belly, though caused no real damage.

But tonight memory burns away denial's morphine. Looking at Jody's image, guilt claws at your belly and sends acid tears to your eyes.

The easiest thing to do is to step forward, offer Night's sculpture of Jody your hand and let her guide you to peace. She can take you to the water's edge, lead you out and pull you under. A few moments of fear, perhaps panic, but then the pain and guilt will wash away on the salty tide, fear streaming from you like tears, responsibility forever behind.

The prospect of peace soothes.

Your kids are grown and don't need you anymore. Susan will be fine, might prefer to spend the remainder of her life without you. There is insurance, and her sister or one of the kids will take her in. If they sell the house, there will be more money to get them through. It would be so easy, you think, and a scalding desperation fills your chest. It's what you want. What you need. Anything to escape the damned circuit of your life.

Jody reaches out a sandy palm for you. You look at her emotionless face, your chest heaving with sobs. Tears burn lines over cheek and jaw.

"I'm sorry," you say. You are looking at the specter, but Susan fills your thoughts. You can't be sure which woman is meant to receive the apology.

You picture Susan then, screaming at you, throwing a glass at the wall in frustration. She breaks into sobs, and clutches at her face, and you are there, arm around her holding as tightly as you can, hoping to draw the misery from her. Even now, with her thousands of miles away, you feel the emotions burn your chest. You want it to stop, for her and for yourself. You just want the pain to stop.

"I'm so sorry," you whisper, feeling Night's creation pulling, though you refuse to move. "I can't make this mistake again."

But you owe so much.

You wipe at your eyes and turn away. You walk over the sand toward the boardwalk as you did all of those years ago. Night's grip on you tightens, tries to pull you back, but you fight with each step.

Susan is in your mind, and you are no longer swaddled by the lie that she will be okay.

Every time her vehement pain ceased, she reached for you, clutched at your neck, cried apologies into your collar. She needs your warmth, your understanding and your love. If you owe any debt it is to her.

A tendril of sand whips around your face, momentarily blinding with grit. You close your eyes, feel another stinging lash crack across your brow. You keep walking.

When you reach the stairs, you turn and look back. The image of Jody remains on the beach. Around her, long cords of sand whip the air, leaving dusty clouds in their wake. You blink the grit from your eyes, let the last tears wash it away.

Maybe this escape is a reprieve, perhaps punishment. It certainly can't be called justice, but it is right. You will follow the course of your life, carrying the miseries and the joys you are due. Jody will be with you now, no longer obscured by numbing denial. Bobby too. When you reach home, you will hold Susan in your arms. Burdens from the past will find their place among the trials of the present. And in the end, you will gratefully carry them all with nothing forgotten and nothing forgiven.

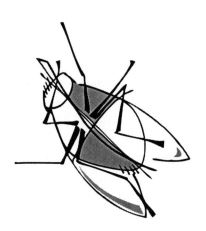

Fine in the Fire

I didn't answer the phone when my brother, Toby, called. His name appeared on the screen of my cell like a bad biopsy result, and instead of answering, I threw back another slug of beer and returned my attention to the television set. The sitcom wasn't particularly interesting, nor was the company of my wife, who'd already decided our marriage was unsalvageable, though it would be another month before she let me in on the fact. She sat on the sofa, frowning. I didn't bother to ask what was wrong. By that point *unhappy* had become a default setting her face hit whenever we shared space, so I barely acknowledged it. What are you going to do? Shit happens, and when enough shit happens you go Pavlovian. Talking to my wife hurt, so I stopped talking to her. I treated my brother with a similar, perhaps greater, level of avoidance. His phone calls invariably included an ample portion of four-alarm crazy and a request for cash. Since I had the routing information for his bank account I could send him money.

Why not cut out the miserable attempts at conversation, and the grief?

When the phone rang again three minutes later, my wife climbed off the sofa and left the room. I closed my eyes and wait-ed for the ringing to stop. If it was important—and it was always important to Toby—he could leave a message. I figured God had created voice mail for just such occasions.

So many months later as the anniversary of that day bears down, I know I should have answered the phone. I get that now. Sometimes when a boy cries wolf, there really are teeth at his neck, but how was I supposed to know? I'd come to think of Toby's head as a scalding pot, and I'd learned to keep my fingers away from it.

Once upon a time, Toby was the golden boy, the Prince of Barnard, Texas. I wish I could ask what happened to him and wonder on the question with genuine naiveté. But I know what happened. The cause. The effect. The whole of it was as clear as an image beaming through a polished projector lens.

Sundays are for church and fried chicken. I sit at the dinner table with Daddy, and I'm thinking about the morning ser-mon. The story of Lot's wife remains vivid and horrible, and I try to imagine what it must feel like to have every speck of my body turned to grains of salt. I see the ceramic saltshaker in the middle of the table. It is in the shape of a white hen with a pink bow, the wife of the peppershaker rooster. And I wonder if I became a pil-lar of salt, would people—maybe my own parents—shave bits of me off to fill their shakers so I could flavor food?

My father smokes a cigarette before the meal and asks me if I've finished all of my weekend homework, and I lie and say, "Yes, sir," and then Toby, who is fifteen years old, opens the kitchen door and stands on the porch, wiping dust from the seat of his Lee jeans. His shirt is torn at the shoulder. Patches of dirt cover his knees and shins. Mussed hair juts away from his scalp in hap-hazard clumps. A bruise blossoms on his jaw, and his left eye is

already good and swollen. Though his appearance could be attributed to any number of accidents, I believe he has been in a
fight.

A yelp of distress flies from my mother's lips, and she rushes to
the door. Slowly, my father rises from his chair and crosses the
room to join her.

Frightened by Toby's face, shocked by the damage, I find myself
more upset to think that someone would dare strike him. Besides
being taller than most boys his age, Toby is an athlete, a star on
the baseball diamond and the football field. Thick muscles cover
his arms and legs; he has our daddy's build. And even without
such physical attributes Toby would have made an unlikely target,
because people liked him. He didn't bully or shove or insult any of
his classmates the way the other football players did. What kind
of fool had the nerve to lay fists on him?

Then the phone rings, and Toby's eyes open wide, and fear
simmers in those eyes. I've never seen my brother afraid before,
except for the pretend fear he acted out when we were little kids,
playing Cops and Robbers. Mama remains with Toby, fussing and
tutting and asking him what happened. Daddy leaves the doorway and goes to answer the phone.

As children Cops and Robbers was our favorite game, and Toby
always played the hero. The games would begin with me
mortally wounded, dying in my brother's arms and Toby vowing
revenge against some "motherless cur"—a phrase he'd picked up
from an old movie.

Then after a spluttering death, worthy of a Shakespearean
royal, I would resurrect as said cur and we'd spend an hour running around the backyard jabbing our plastic guns at each other
and saying, "pow," and "bang," and "eat lead." It was common.
Normal. A cliché enacted by kids all over the world.

It made sense that Toby would play the hero. Not only was
he two and half years older than me, he also embodied the term.
He was just plain good at everything. Give him a baseball bat,

or a math equation, or a guitar and he would figure out how to make them work. People called him, "Brilliant," "Amazing," and "Genius." His best friend, Duke Manheim, used to call Toby, "Flat out impossible," with a tone that revealed the awestruck depths of his admiration. The last few times I visited Toby, he could no longer hold a cigarette between his fingers; they trembled too badly. Instead, he pinched the filter between his teeth and sucked them down in a few desperate puffs.

Daddy answers the phone and at first he smiles. "Hey there, Rick," he says, and I know it's Mr. Manheim, Duke's father and one of Daddy's best friends. The call does not interest me as much as my brother's condition, so I return my attention to Toby, who finishes wiping the dirt from himself and insists Mama leave him be as he steps into the house. Instead of remaining in the kitchen, Toby creeps out of the room without a word. No, "Hey, kid," or "Hey, squirt," for me.

I look to Mama for an explanation, but the concern and confusion on her face matches the gray swirl of chaos in my head. She wipes her hands on her apron and turns to Daddy. I follow her gaze and am surprised to see the expression on my father's suddenly red face. I can't tell if he's about to scream or vomit. He notices us gawking at him and pulls the phone away from his ear.

"Betty, take Peter on out of here." His voice is so quiet and dry it whispers like a desert breeze. Mama opens her mouth with a question, but the words die on her tongue. "Just go on now," he says. "Be sure to get that chicken off the burner. We don't want it scorched."

The phone rang again. I switched the device to vibrate and then stood and passed through the kitchen on the way to my workbench in the garage. Its gouged wooden top was bare—no toys or toasters or bikes needed my attention. The rows of tools on the pegboard were little more than decorative these days. I hadn't had a new project on my bench since my daughter, Jocelyn, had gone off to college.

Above the bench was a small board with a number of keys, each one hung on a hook beneath a neatly printed label. I lifted the set that opened the doors to my parents' house—Toby's house now—and slid them in my pocket. Then I leaned on the bench and tried to remember the last thing I'd fixed there. The lamp from Jocelyn's room? My old ten-speed? I couldn't be certain.

I'd picked up the tinkering bug from my father, and though a good deal of his talent had been lost in the genetic translation that was me, I managed to fix most of the household items that landed on my bench. My father, however, had been truly gifted in this regard. He could repair just about anything, spot the failure in a second flat, and once he identified the problem, he set to fixing it. His days were spent selling heavy equipment at the John Deere facility in Barnard, but on the nights he wasn't bowling at the Longhorn Lanes or swapping stories at the VFW hall he mended, repaired, and even invented. He was the master of broken things. Everything could be fixed, could be improved.

Mama escorts me to the door of the bedroom I share with my older brother and tells me to wait inside while she goes to talk with my father. Toby lies on the bed, staring at the ceiling.

He doesn't look at me when I enter.

"You were in a fight?" I ask.

He doesn't answer. Instead he crosses his arms over his eyes, and I wonder if he's crying. On the shelves above his bed sit his shining trophies—for bowling and basketball, for baseball and football. Thirteen of them. I know because I've counted them a hundred times. My shelves hold books and a single award: a tiny third place trophy for peewee football that has sat without a companion for five years.

"Who'd ya' fight with?"

"Duke." Toby croaks the word but there are no signs my brother is crying, and that reassures me.

"Duke is your best pal," I say, confused.

"No he's not." Toby rolls onto his side, facing away from me.

I know the wounds on his jaw and eye are pressed into the pillow and they must ache, but he doesn't roll back toward me. He doesn't move. I continue to ask questions, but he won't reply, and I persist and I pester, because nothing makes sense to me. Folks admire Toby, they celebrate him, and the only people who weren't his friends were the ones too intimidated to get close, so why had Duke Manheim thrown fists at my brother? At the boy he himself had proclaimed, "Flat out impossible?"

The door opens and Daddy steps inside. He crosses his arms, gazing at me without so much as a glance for my brother.

"You go on down and eat your supper," he says. "I need a word with Toby."

"What did Mr. Manheim say?" I ask.

"Never you mind about that."

And I know it's bad. I can tell by the frown on my father's face. Whatever Duke's father told him was hateful and wrong, but it was more than that. "He lied," I say, though I have no idea what was actually said. My only instinct is to defend my brother from the motherless cur's accusations. "You know he did. Toby didn't do nothing wrong. Duke's a liar and Mr. Manheim's a liar and that's all there is to it."

"Go eat your supper, Peter," is my father's quiet response.

I stretched out on the sofa and listened to my brother's messages. Each word stung like needles passing through my chest, and after listening to the last message—"The machine still works, Petey. It still works." —it felt as if a surgeon were yanking the sutures tight, pulling my ribs together so that my heart had no room to beat.

How could my father have built that thing? He wasn't a bad man, ask anyone. Nearly a hundred people had attended his funeral, and all of them spoke of his kindness, his humor, his helpfulness. He was a Christian, but quietly so, never waving his Bible, never wielding scripture like a weapon. As a father, he was evenhanded and warm. He believed in the belt; he used it infrequently but with great seriousness.

Lying on the sofa, looking at the ceiling and through it, imagining my wife in bed, turned to the wall the way Toby had been turned away, I remembered the sound of my father's belt cracking across my brother's backside as tears fell from my cheeks—more salt for the fried chicken on my plate. My mother said nothing. She ate nothing, merely pushed a fork through her potatoes, creating trenches as if preparing soil for planting.

"**Y**our brother is going to be staying in the workshop for a time," my father says.

I don't understand. "What did he do?"

"He'll be staying in the workshop for a time," my father says as if I hadn't heard him. "Go fetch my army cot from the attic and take it down to the kitchen. Then your mother will take you into town for a cone and a coke."

I grew restless on the sofa. The past and present fell on me like blankets of fiberglass, scratchy and insulating, keeping things in that I'd rather expel. I stood. In the kitchen I took a beer from the fridge. With my tongue and throat soothed, I sat on a barstool at the kitchen island and traced the lines of grout that formed gutters in the tiled countertop. My finger pushed against a pile of mail, scooting the low stack toward the counter's edge.

No one said a word about what my brother had done. At the Dairy Queen my mother revealed nothing about what she knew, if in fact she knew anything. It was very possible my father hadn't shared what Rick Manheim had said with her. You didn't talk about the bad things, and the worse a thing was, the quieter you kept it. It was a practice everyone in Barnard seemed to ascribe to. At school the next day and the day after that, I noticed no changes in the way my schoolmates behaved around me, no whispers of scandal, no sidelong glances of pity or disgust. If Duke Manheim had said anything to his buddies at Beall's High, it had yet to filter down to McNeil Middle School. Whatever had occurred between my brother and Duke was terrible enough that neither they nor their fathers would let the information escape.

As a kid, I wasn't equipped to think in broad terms, so my speculations were laughable. I imagined Toby had called Duke a bad name or maybe he'd stolen one of his friend's toys or record albums.

Again I nudged the stack of mail. A bill lay on top of the pile; it was from Willow House, where Toby lived, had lived for the past eight years. I found it comforting such institutions no longer called themselves asylums.

The beefsteak is tough and the potatoes have been boiled too long and decompose into mush beneath my fork and nothing has flavor no matter how much salt I add. My father sits on my right and smokes a cigarette. His eyes are like Toby's—red and dull. He looks as if he's been awake since Sunday afternoon, since Mr. Manheim's phone call. My mother chats throughout the meal, talking about Mrs. Burlingson's crop of squash and raspberries, and Mrs. Turred's lousy washing machine flooding her basement again, and how Mr. Evans at the grocery told her that he'd caught the Perry boy trying to pilfer candies from the rack by the register. She babbles on and on. It seems she speaks about every family in Barnard except ours. As she clears the dishes, my father stubs out his cigarette and immediately lights another.

"I'm driving on up to Dallas," he says through a cloud of blue-gray smoke.

My mother halts as if someone has put a gun to her back. "The dealership sending you?" she asks.

"I'll be heading out here shortly," he says, not answering her question. "I'll try to be back by supper tomorrow, but no need to wait on me. I'll call if things take longer than expected."

Mama continues on to the sink and gently places the dinner plates in it.

"That's fine," she says. "We're having hot dogs and beans. They'll keep well enough."

I finished my beer, rinsed the bottle, and placed it in the recycling bin. With my ass propped against the counter, I listened to Toby's messages again with the same ache and constriction in my chest. Though very late, after two in the morning, I decided to call him back, but he didn't answer. I left a message so thick with false enthusiasm at hearing from him, I felt ashamed. The performance was as pitifully overblown as my childhood death scenes.

Granted, at that point my brother was no longer able to detect such variances in vocal patterns. He heard what he wanted to hear and inferred the emotions he expected. Oddly enough, in many other ways his condition had improved. His paranoia and the violent outbursts it caused had lessened considerably, and I was grateful for that. Still, they shouldn't have let him out of the home, not without supervision. A guy like my brother couldn't care for himself, not for long, not for days and nights at a time.

After Daddy leaves for Dallas I ask Mama why Toby has to stay outside, and she tells me that Daddy thinks it is best. I persist, because as always, I'm told nothing.

"Don't worry so much about this. Your brother is going to be fine, Petey, just fine. Your father is taking care of him."

I note the oddity of her comment. She speaks as if Toby is sick or injured, rather than being punished for whatever had caused his fight with Duke Manheim. My confusion grows and feeds my frustration, but my mother deflects my questions, tuts them away, smiles at me as if humoring a feeb. After a time, I become convinced she doesn't know what's wrong with Toby. I can tell by the confusion in her eyes and the way she smoothes her hair and the way she smiles, which isn't really a smile at all, and I know that asking her questions is pointless.

My mother accepted my father's silences with the same gravity she'd accepted every word he'd ever spoken. As a boy, I'd thought she had as many answers as my father, an equal on the plain of adulthood with her husband, but that wasn't the case at all. She wasn't a partner quite so much as an appendage, a utensil, an appliance with a good nature and a pleasant face. It wasn't until my father died that I understood the depth of her dependence on the man. Without my father, she turned to me for answers, looked to me to make her decisions. *Should I sell the house, Petey? Should I move in with your Aunt Ruby and Uncle Lou? Isn't it better if I don't go to the hospital? My visits always upset Toby so. If you think I should, I will but...*

I called Willow House's emergency number, but went directly to voice mail. Once the tone sounded I let them know that Toby had slipped out again. I asked that they not involve the authorities, though I know they are bound by law to do so. Leaving my number, I hung up and dig in my pocket for the keys I'd taken from the hook in the garage.

Then I leave the house. In my car, I consider leaving Toby to the professionals at Willow House. All I had to do was call them back and give them the address. There was only one place he could be.

"The machine still works, Petey. It still works."

It's Friday, and I'm walking up the dirt drive to my house. The dust is thick and joins the pollen and both fill the air creating a golden filter for the afternoon sun, which hangs, glaring over the roof. The door to my father's workshop is open, and I see Toby inside. He is holding a small bucket and a brush, and he's covering the window in the door with black paint. He is concentrating on the task, lining up his brush carefully before touching it to the pane and sweeping it across the glass. He is so absorbed in the task that my arrival at the door surprises him.

He flinches and steps back and then his posture relaxes. "Hey, squirt," he says, and the familiarity, the normality of the greeting refreshes like a gulp of sweet tea.

"Hey," I reply. "Whatcha doing?"

"Painting," he says.

"Painting windows?"

"That's what it looks like," he says.

I notice something is missing from my brother's eyes. They are red and the lids are heavy and a dull cast covers them.

"Why?"

"It's a project I'm working on with Daddy," he says. He seems unsure of the words, and he gazes at the concrete floor of the workshop and then back at the black band he has painted on the glass. "It's a secret."

"Are you gonna come back inside?" I ask.

"Not for a while," Toby says. He dips the brush into the bucket and stirs the black paint gravely.

"Why not?" I'm desperate for information, and even though I see my brother pulling into his thoughts, moving away from me as surely as if he were being dragged behind a speeding truck, I persist. "What happened? What did you do?"

"You better go on inside, now," he says.

I look past him into my father's shop. The space was always off limits to us unless we had permission from our father to enter it for a tool or a can of oil. It is large, a converted two-car garage. The floor is clean and cleared except for the army cot, which Toby has made up neatly with sheets and a blanket. The workbenches form a large L in the far corner, and they are similarly devoid of clutter. Neatly organized shelves run floor to ceiling on the right just beyond the cot.

Switching tack I ask, "Can I help?"

Like my father Toby responds as if I've said nothing at all. "You better go on inside."

Then he scrapes his brush along the side of the paint can and presses its bristles to the window. With his customary precision, he coats the glass from frame to frame without getting a speck of paint on the trim.

It is the middle of the night and I can't sleep. I'm still not used to having the room to myself. Toby's absence is a hole I fear I'll be dragged into. I leave my bed and go to the window and stare down on Daddy's workshop, and the dark building with its black windows makes me think of a haunted house, and I think my brother is the phantom prowling it. Daddy's truck is parked only a few feet from the door. He's back from Dallas. I don't remember having heard him come home.

After I tire of looking at the workshop, I leave the window and then leave my room and wander down the hall to the stairs. Though I've made no conscious decision about where I'm going, I creep downstairs and detect a muffled clicking sound that draws me to the kitchen. Daddy sits at the table under the cone of light falling from the hanging brass fixture, bent over a box with a number of colored wires snaking from its side. A brown paper bag rests to his left. Next to this is the slide projector Mama bought at the flea market in Bastrop. She'd never used it so far as I knew, but she'd been very proud of "the deal" she'd found at the time, and I wonder why Daddy has scavenged the device from the hall closet.

He looks up and fixes grim eyes on me. The overhead light casts shadows down his face, and the dark patches beneath his eyes and chin, and the lines around his mouth look like blotches of rot. A stricken quality passes over his face, and he blinks, and I wonder if he recognizes me at all. He puts down his screwdriver and rubs his eyes and I again think he looks as if he hasn't slept since Mr. Mannheim's call all of those days ago. His hair is greasy and flat and the skin on his face hangs as if the muscles beneath have relinquished their grasp.

"Peter," he says quietly. He reaches out and lifts the brown paper bag from the tabletop and lowers it to the floor beside his feet. "You shouldn't be up."

"Did you have a good trip to Dallas?"

"Fine," he says dryly.

I think to ask if he's found anything that will help Toby, but the expression on his face, empty of all but flickers of life, warns me away from the question. So I stand there silently, following the trajectory of the wires poking from the metal box before him, and I look back to the slide projector sitting like a turtle near the edge of the table, and I take in the spools of wire and the cutters and a box with the word "rheostat" stenciled across its oatmeal-colored cardboard box.

"You should be in bed," he says.

"Maybe I could help."

"Get your ass to bed, Peter!"

The following day I see neither Daddy nor Toby, but when I'm outside playing in the yard, kicking a ball across the scrub grass and dirt, I hear evidence of their presence in the workshop. Whispers. The clicking of tools. At one point I kick my ball toward the back wall of the workshop and press my ear close to the blackened window. The glass muffles Daddy's voice, but I recognize his tone, and I realize he is doing all of the talking. I want to hear the words but they are garbled and incomprehensible like prayers spoken under water.

I imagine my father and brother hunched over the slide projector and various electrical wires and components. Daddy might be pointing at a device and a wire and explaining why the two must be joined in a specific way, and I think Toby is lucky to be spending so much time with Daddy. A tickle of jealousy joins my curiosity, and for a time I forget that Toby is being punished, or that he's not well. I still don't understand his condition, but I know I want to join them in the workshop, to be part of the project. Resting my foot on the red ball, I look around the yard, searching for an excuse to knock on the workshop door. But instead of finding a magic key that will justify my intrusion, I see Mama standing at the corner of the house. Her arms are crossed, and she frowns at me.

Later that night, I'm watching television. It is near my bedtime. Mama has given me a plate of two cookies and a small glass of milk to enjoy while Carol Burnett and her costars stumble and mug for the camera.

Just as a skit is about to end, the lights in my house dim and the television screen goes green-black in a hiccup of electric current. I think little of it. Such hiccups are common during storms or high winds. But it isn't storming, and I hear no gusts in the eaves. A roar of laughter, harsh and mocking, pours from the television when it comes back on, and I feel a chill. A minute later, the lights flicker off again.

Vast stretches of darkness gave way to the occasional streetlamp. Driving toward my childhood home, I attempted to shake off the memories, hoping to loosen the tightness in my chest, but the program in my head was nearing an end, and I didn't have a switch to turn it off, not even a rheostat to adjust its power.

What I remembered clearly was that things in our house seemed to return to normal after the night of the flickering lights. The next morning, I found Toby at the breakfast table. He appeared exhausted and confused, but his fatigue didn't seem quite so dire. He wore a clean white t-shirt and a baseball cap, which he'd pulled low on his brow. Mama had fixed pancakes and bacon and Toby tore through them. My father joined us. Unlike Toby, he barely ate. His exhaustion remained, and he smoked cigarettes through the meal, blowing smoke onto his plate, as if in a trance.

Nothing was said about Toby or the workshop or what they had constructed within it, but apparently the experiment had done some good, because for the first time in a week, Toby slept in our room. He went to school on Monday, and when he came home he let himself into the workshop, where he would stay for an hour. And then supper. And then to bed. The spark in his eyes had not returned, and he wore his baseball cap everywhere, somehow eluding Mama's rule about hats at the dining table, which also distressed me because it wasn't usual, but he was back in the house and things had reached a level of normality. And I started to believe the darkness that had tarnished our golden boy was finally being wiped away.

A week before Christmas my father had his first aneurism. It didn't kill him, that would take six more years and two more "cerebral events," but that night, he died some in my eyes, because I saw what he'd built. I discovered his answer to my brother's troubles.

After my mother's tears and my father's expression of perplexed misery, and after the paramedics and the ambulance, and after the red lights vanish over the hill and the front door closes behind me, I trudge to the sofa and fall onto it. Toby is already there, staring at the television; both his face and the appliance screen are dark.

"Do you think Daddy's going to die, Toby?"

"No," he snaps. His gaze doesn't wander from the blank-glass nothing of the TV. "He can't."

"He looked real bad."

"He's a great man, Petey. He's strong. He'll be okay."

And I know Toby is not stating a fact; he is voicing a wish.

"But what if he's not?" I ask.

"Shut up, Petey," Toby says. His command scalds me into silence and I lower my head because I can't look at him anymore. We're silent for a time before he says, "Go on up to bed. I've got things to do."

I do as I am told and I lay in bed, but my eyes are open, and I'm angry at Toby for dismissing me. Abandoning me. The house still stinks of the fish Mama fried for supper. My pillow is as hard as stone and the pillowcase feels scratchy and hot on my neck. My thoughts crackle and pop like damp kindling. I don't understand how my family could crumble, just fall apart like a dirt wall in a hard wind. I don't understand because no one has told me anything that sounds true. *Toby will be okay. Daddy will be okay.* But how can anyone know that? They can't is the answer, but I'm supposed to accept the meaningless phrases as gospel?

Daddy is in the shadows staining my ceiling, and Toby is there, too. They are strangers to me.

I leave the bed and cross to the window and look down on the workshop, and I know Toby is there, and I decide I deserve to know what is happening. So, I walk out of the room, down the stairs, and out the front door, and I cross the walk to the dirt drive and I stare at the workshop door. Toby has done an excellent job and the windows are impenetrably black, but there is a narrow crack beneath the door and I see it is filled with gray light. The light remains for twenty seconds and then goes out, only to reignite after a single beat of my heart. I reach out for the doorknob and pause. The light goes out again; it returns.

Holding my breath, I turn the knob and push the door open. Initially a glaring disc beaming from across the room blinds me. The odors of the place—oil, sawdust, and sour sweat—burrow into my nostrils. A dull hum fills my ears. I lift my hand to shield my eyes from the light and it goes out, but a fog of green covers my vision the way it does after a camera's flash. I close my eyes and the swirling murk remains. The lamp ignites again and before I open my eyes, I turn away.

I am aware of the shelves on the right side of the workshop and that something—One of Mama's sheets?—hangs against the nearest wall. But my gaze lands on my brother and fills with the sight of him.

Toby lies on his cot. He has pushed his hands through leather straps affixed to the metal frame, and they are knotted into fists. His eyes are wide and he's shaking his head frantically. There is something on his head. It is a small cap with metal arms that reach out to press against his temples. Rubber tubing hangs from these shiny appendages and drape the sides of his face where they connect to a wooden dowel wrapped in gauze. Toby clamps the dowel between his teeth like a horse bit. He struggles to get his hands free of the leather straps when the light goes out again.

It comes back on with a click, and the dull hum returns. Toby's back arches and his body goes rigid. His eyes are rolled back and white, and lines of tendon and vein appear on his neck as if he's swallowed a vine plant that is trying to push its way through his skin.

I scream. It does nothing to lessen my dread. I shout my brother's name but he is paralyzed. I step forward and then back up and then forward again. The light dies, and the humming stops, and I turn toward the bench at the back of the room. When the light comes back on, the apparatus atop the wooden surface comes clear. A plug juts from the wall socket; a white cord runs to a junction box, topped by the black knob of the rheostat; two wires, one black and one blue, run like tentacles from the metal box to the cap on my brother's head; another cord, this one yellow, snakes to the slide projector. I can only think of the display as a torture device, imagined and built by my father. But what was it meant to accomplish? I spin toward the image projected on the wall of the workshop and my breath lodges against the stone in my throat. A young woman stands naked in a field, holding a flower to her nose. Her hair, the color of corn silk, frames her beautiful face. She smiles softly. Sweetly. My gaze traces down her throat to her small round breasts and then over her belly to the mound of golden blonde hair between her legs, and then back up again. The room goes black. The picture of the young woman is replaced by that of a muscled man with a dense pelt of hair covering his chest. Beneath his thick mustache his mouth is twisted into a smirk. He is also naked and his hand grasps the shaft of his penis like the hilt of a knife.

The hum has returned to the workshop. Toby is again arched and rigid. And my confusion is momentarily erased as if I understand this perverse experiment, though I'm certain I do not. It seems that Toby is relaxed when pictures of women cover my mama's bed sheet, but voltage and pain accompanies the images of men. I don't know what this is meant to achieve, but I know it has to stop.

I reach across the workbench. Doing so, I lean over the rheostat and notice the switches and the dial on top. Dashes and numbers run in an arc to accommodate the round black knob. Someone, either Daddy or Toby, has run a strip of black electrical tape like a comic eyebrow, blocking out the lines and numbers on the downside of the arc, and above this, written in red ink, is the word, "Danger." I yank the plug from the wall. Despite the pitch darkness I find my way to the light switch on the other side of the shop and flick it on, and then I turn to my brother, who has managed to get one of his hands loose. He frees his other hand, reaches for the bit in his mouth and pulls it away all the while glaring at me.

"Y-you c-can't be in here, Petey," he says. His voice is dry, and he growls savagely to clear his throat.

Only when I try to answer do I realize that I'm crying, and I can't find my voice. Toby removes the device from his head and I see the red marks at his temples, and I know they're the reason he wears his baseball cap in the house, and the sight of them makes me cry harder.

"It's okay," he says. With a tremendous effort, he sits up on the cot and swings his legs off the side. "*I'm* okay."

"No. No. No." I blubber.

"You're too young to understand," Toby says, wiping at his mouth with the back of his hand. "I wasn't right, Petey. I felt things and did things..." His voice trails away. A mask of confusion falls over his face like the darkness between the projector's light. When it passes he says, "Daddy read all about it. He found books in Dallas. He found out what was wrong with me and how to fix it. He had to do something or else he'd have to send me away to an asylum and people would know about me, and they can't know about me. They just can't. Do you want me to go to an asylum, Petey?"

"It's not right," I say between sobs. "It's hurting you."

"It has to," Toby says. His head dips and he observes the floor for a moment. When he looks back at me, the spark I've missed in his eyes has returned, except the light there is hard and cold. A hint of a smile touches the corners of his lips. His expression is hopeful but it's also frightening, because, to me, Toby looks crazy. And when he speaks again I feel certain his mind has come loose, because he says, "It's working, Petey. I'm getting better. Really I am."

I pulled into the drive of Toby's house. My car's headlights swept across the front of the shed like a lighthouse beacon. Black paint still covered the windows. A grey light showed beneath the door and then extinguished. Remaining in the parked car, I peered at the shed with trepidation. I'd thought the machine was gone, dismantled, torn apart, and thrown in the trash. That's what Toby had told me; he'd said it was the first thing to go when he moved in after our mother's death. His lie shouldn't have come as a surprise.

Over the years bits of information came my way. I learned that Toby had made a sexual advance toward his buddy, Duke, which had triggered the fight and the call from Richard Manheim. Of course I'd already figured that out, but Duke himself confirmed it years later. We ran into each other at a bar in Austin, and we got to talking about Toby. He felt bad for my brother.

Such a shame, he'd said. Such a waste.

The grey light flashed and I counted to twenty and then it went dark. Leaving the car, I breathed deeply to calm my sparking nerves. The scene inside the shed would be familiar, I knew, but that didn't make it any more palatable.

In the years before leaving home, Toby had used our father's device regularly. Some days he was the golden hero of my early youth, and other days he appeared crazy, eyes wild and mouth shimmering with spittle as he recounted one moral outrage or another. On those days, he went to the shed and wired himself to the apparatus, as if it were a meditative aid. He marched through the broiling gut of hell all the while insisting he was fine in the fire. *I'm getting better. Really I am.* I begged him to stop. My mother never said a word. My father never looked so proud.

It's easy to blame the old man, but he thought he was helping. In college, I did some research of my own, investigating accepted "cures" of the day, and I found a number of references to electro-shock and aversion therapy. I'm sure this was the kind of information he came across during his trip to Dallas. His life was machines, and each part had to work in a particular way to keep the machine running. It would never occur to him that he didn't understand a part or its function. Its value. My father wasn't a villain; he was just a hick who wanted to save his son from a lifetime of sadness and shame—the only future he could imagine for a broken part in the social machine.

At the door to the shed, I lifted my fist and knocked. The gray light poured from beneath the door and then went out. When my second rap went unanswered I pushed open the door. Toby lay on the cot. He was dead. He'd been gone for a while, maybe since hanging up after leaving me his last message.

The sight of him coiled in my throat along with the odors of urine, burned skin, and singed hair. Deep lines carved in around his mouth and brow; he hadn't even bothered inserting the bit between his teeth. His eyes had poached in the sockets; blood and viscous tears clotted at this temples. He appeared to be smiling, but I had to believe it was the strained rictus of his final shock. For a moment, I thought I could see the golden boy beneath the layers of weight and folds of skin, but it was only my mind playing tricks, an evanescent denial with no more weight than projected light. I choked on a sob and fought an urge to race to the cot, but a loud voice in the back of my head, reason or dread, warned me away from the coursing voltage. Instead of running to Toby's side, I crossed the shed to disconnect the machine.

As I had done on the first night I'd witnessed my father's therapy, I leaned over the rheostat to reach the wall plug. Toby had turned the rheostat to full power. The white dash on the black dial pointed at a peeling corner of tape and the letter *E* in the word "Danger," written in red ink. The ink had faded.

The light went out and then returned with a *shoosh* and a *click*. A deadly hum filled the room. Foolishly, I glanced back at the screen. The image projected there froze me. It was of Toby and our father. The man, younger than I ever remembered him being, stood on a tractor in the parking lot of the John Deere facility. In one hand he held a rag and in the other he held a monstrous wrench. With one foot on the running board and the other on the tractor seat, he looked like a big game hunter, gloating over the carcass of an unfortunate trophy. Toby as a toddler stood on the pavement grinning up at his daddy, clapping his tiny hands together in a display of ecstatic joy.

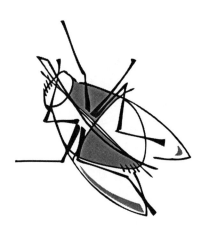

The House
by the Park

The man stood from the concrete bench in his garden and looked at the sky. He saw neither star nor moon, but rather a swirling void. A maelstrom above. Deepest black and steel gray currents shot through with violet and crimson. He breathed deeply, taking in the scent of rose, sage, and freshly mown grass, and then he walked into the house, sat on the floor, and slit his throat with a razor.

It was a chance meeting in a grocery store.

Denis had been at home, gazing into his freezer. There he saw the familiar sight of stacked boxes, an assortment of prepared meals: frozen lasagnas; frozen pizzas; home-style meatloaf with mashed potatoes; batter fried chicken fingers; some Asian thing;

and a lonely Lean Cuisine, a constant reminder of the diet he'd never started. On the nights his friends didn't force him to go out, Denis invariably uncrated one of the plastic trays and listened to the empty hum of the microwave, droning like a monastic chorus—a serenade for the lonely. A requiem. Ever since Benjamin had died—from a congenital heart defect he hadn't thought to share with his partner of six years—Denis had endured the pitiful whirring dirge before most of his evening meals, and he was sick of it.

He wanted a real dinner, and he intended to fix it himself, so he pulled on a t-shirt and stepped into his sandals, and left the house.

He first caught sight of Fred at the end of the produce aisle, turning a green pepper in his hand, studying it as if some mystery were etched into its emerald skin. Fred was dressed in a blue work shirt with a rust-colored tie cinched at his neck. The fabric of the shirt stretched over his barrel chest and belly, but it didn't pinch; it simply looked fitted to the burly form, highlighting the bulk of Fred's chest and the roundness of his shoulders. In many ways, Denis and Fred looked alike. Neither was particularly tall, both were thickly built, both wore full, trimmed beards, but they were not mirror images. Denis had never admired the face his mirror reflected as much as he found himself admiring Fred's. The full cheeks. Smooth, tanned skin. He seemed to be the same type as Denis, only better at it. Denis perfected.

They crossed paths in the meat department—a ribeye for Denis, a cut of salmon for Fred. This time Denis caught Fred's eye. They looked away and then back. Then Fred took a misstep because of his distraction, stumbling a bit. Denis smiled and moved on.

Only later did they actually speak. Denis stood in the frozen foods aisle holding open a glass door as he tried to decide between double mocha fudge and cookies and cream. Another freezer door opened beside him and he checked over his shoulder to find Fred, reaching in for a carton of Rocky Road. He held the cardboard container and seemed to be reading the nutritional information, when his face scrunched.

"Oh fuck this," Fred said, replacing the carton of ice cream on the shelf. He let the freezer door close and leaned against it. "Hey," he said to Dennis. "Do you want to have dinner with me?"

The restaurant was an overpriced joint that pushed soul food to the hipster flock. Later both would agree the place was awful, but the lousy food and atmosphere did not dampen their evening noticeably. If anything, it provided a point of familiarity—something they could share and laugh about.

Over dinner, Denis learned that Fred was the IT manager for a software outfit on the Northside. He liked lifting at Gold's Gym, 70s and 80s rock, low budget horror films, science fiction novels, and long drives in the country. He was, "sorta, kinda, maybe," dating a twink named Eric, but the kid was, "an arrogant little prick, who listens to too much Gaga, and can't fuck."

"Kind of harsh," Denis said.

"I'm being generous," Fred assured him. "He just lies there and poses and coos like he's looking at kittens in a pet shop window."

"Why are you with him?"

"Oh, that's easy," Fred said, "I'm an idiot. My ex had a hard on for the kid, but Eric wanted me, so..."

"Spite fuck."

"I'm not usually like that. Really, I know how it sounds. If you knew my ex it would clear things up, like, a lot. What about you?"

"Single."

And then Denis told Fred about his late partner and the heart condition he'd kept secret, and Fred reached out and put his hand on Denis's. He squeezed. He stroked the back of the hand with his thumb.

After dinner Denis suggested they continue their conversation over coffee. Fred said, "I'll make you coffee."

Three houses separated Fred's modern single story home from the park. Denis loved the sleek façade and upon stepping inside, he found himself further impressed. With its open floor plan, French Doors, pale blue walls, and shocking white moldings, the house looked as if it belonged on The Cape or on a Long Island beach. Denis expected to smell salt air or find wayward grains of sand caught between the polished oak floorboards.

He followed Fred into the kitchen, where his host opened a glass cabinet door and retrieved coffee mugs. These were set on the counter and he turned his attention toward a high-tech brewing system. He hit a button, turned a knob and told Denis it would take a minute for the machine to warm up. Making an obvious joke about heat, Fred leaned forward and kissed him.

In response, Denis wrapped his arms around the man and pushed in close. He felt warmth pouring through Fred's shirt and he wanted it against his skin. He moved his hands to the knot of the tie and pulled it away before working his fingers over the buttons of the blue shirt. His lips only left Fred's for the three seconds it took to pull his own shirt over his head. He dropped it on the floor and then pressed his weight against Fred's torso, feeling the tickle of hair, the density of flesh. They pushed closer. Chest to chest. Belly to belly. Two edges of a wound needing to heal.

Fred led an awkward dance to the sofa, guiding Denis all but blindly around the dining table and a white leather club chair as their mouths remained pressed together. When Fred pulled his lips away, Denis lunged forward for them but Fred put a hand on his chest. He pushed lightly, and bent and lifted the edge of the coffee table, moving it away from the sofa. Then Fred was on his knees. Denis looked down at the rounded shelf of Fred's chest, covered in a carpet of brown hair and then into the clear, green eyes. Their eyes remained locked as Denis's cock disappeared into the beard-framed mouth.

On the sofa, they rubbed and kissed and tasted each other thoroughly before Denis climbed on top of Fred and ground his crotch against the man. Fred locked his legs around Denis's hips. Through it all, Denis's thoughts slid and melted like hot wax, but he always came back to the same words: that chest, those hands, those lips.

Fred directed him to the top drawer of the coffee table, where Denis found a bottle of lube and a haphazard pile of condoms. As he unrolled the condom over his cock, his eyes returned to Fred on the sofa. He had crawled onto all fours, ass out, hands gripping the back of the furniture in preparation. And then he was in the man, and Fred eased back on him. Denis gripped the round cheeks and stroked the light fuzz that covered them. He slid his thumbs up Fred's spine, his fingers appearing pale against the deeply tanned skin. When he reached the thick wings of muscle over Fred's shoulder blades, he drove his hips forward and found his rhythm.

Eventually they did have coffee. Naked, Denis followed Fred back to the kitchen and they again had to wait for the machine to warm up, but this time they talked and touched one another without reticence. They laughed. When they both held full mugs of coffee Fred led Denis to the French doors that opened onto an expansive deck. The clatter of rain greeted the opening of the panels and Fred stepped outside.

"It's raining," Denis said.

"Yeah," Fred said. He smiled. "I'm weird like that."

So they leaned on the redwood railing, shielding their coffees from the misting rain with their upper bodies. Fred wrapped his arm around Denis's waist and pulled him close.

"We're doing this again, right?" he asked.

"Yes," Denis said without hesitation.

Then they were kissing, pressing tightly together. Rain ran down their chests and coursed in rivulets around their compressed bellies. Fred backed him to the railing and his mouth went to Denis's neck.

"Son of a bitch," Fred muttered.

"What's wrong?" Denis asked, following the direction of Fred's gaze.

Blue and white lights flashed against the canopy of trees rising above the neighboring houses. He recognized the color and the pattern of a police unit's bubble lights. In the road out front, a car squealed to a stop.

"Might be serious," Denis said.

"Looks like more than one," Fred said. "Let's check it out."

They dressed and walked out front. Two police cruisers and an ambulance lined the curb in front of the house by the park. Other neighbors had wandered onto the walk, forming a tight group near the back of the nearest police car.

"I'm gonna head up and see if anyone knows what's going on," Fred said. "Be right back."

He padded barefoot along the wet sidewalk and sidled up to the group of gawkers. After chatting with a young blonde woman, who stood with her arms crossed over her chest, Fred nodded and hurried back to where Denis waited.

"Looks like the guy killed himself."

"Seriously?"

"That's what everybody up there is saying."

"Shit," Denis whispered. "Did you know him?"

"Not really. I saw him around. Mowing his lawn. Jogging in the park."

"Should we go back inside?" Denis asked.

"Yeah," Fred said. "I don't think I need to see them wheel a body out."

Denis left Fred's house early the next morning. To his right, an official vehicle, the color of pewter, pulled away from the curb. Instead of going directly to his car, Denis walked down the street to get a better look at the scene. He didn't expect to actually see anything unusual, but he wanted a better look at the house.

Like Fred's it was modern, with sharp edges and a lot of glass, but this house had a second floor and a balcony that overlooked the park on the west side of the roof. Yellow warning tape was used to make a fence across the front porch and an X, blocking the front door. All of the windows were black with interior gloom, and Denis briefly wondered why the police would leave the blinds and curtains of a crime scene open.

Another curious thing caught his eye. A hedge of thigh-high shrubs ran across the bottom edge of the living room picture window. It was lush and well-tended, its top flat and even, but the bush nearest the front door was blackened as if it had been scorched. Denis thought this odd, but there could have been a hundred different explanations for the discoloration. For all he knew, it had been that way for weeks.

He lifted his gaze from the hedge and his breath caught in his throat.

Someone stood in profile in the living room window. The figure was pale. Motionless.

Denis took a step back.

As if in response, the figure lurched forward and scurried out of sight.

Denis spent the next two nights with Fred. Their time together was marked by a relaxed familiarity as if months and not days had passed, but the intensity of their attraction was all new. Fresh. Overwhelming.

Thursday night, as the sweat cooled on their skin and Fred rested his head in Denis's lap, Fred said, "Did you see the news about Old Johnny today?"

Jonathan Lucio was the name of the man who'd killed himself in the house down the block. Fred had taken to calling his late neighbor, "Old Johnny." Denis had skimmed the story at his office over the past couple of days, but found it all too unpleasant to pursue. Apparently Lucio was a lobbyist for a Christian outfit, Soul Safe, that pushed an anti-abortion agenda to state and federal legislators. There had been no word in regard to the manner of his death other than the phrase, "At his own hands."

"No," Denis said.

"He had a Facebook page," Fred said.

"Who doesn't?"

"Yeah, but that's where he posted his suicide note."

"That's crazy."

"You don't know crazy. He put a curse on the world. Said his blood would grease the hinges of the gates of hell."

"Bullshit."

"It was something like that, but he definitely used the words 'gates of hell.' I caught a screenshot of it before they shut it down."

"You snagged a screen shot? That's got sick fascination written all over it."

"Eh," Fred said, nuzzling his ear against Denis's crotch. "A bit of morbid curiosity never hurt anyone. You want to see it?"

"Later."

They remained in silence for several minutes. Denis ran his palm through Fred's close-cropped hair, feeling the ridges of the skull beneath the stubble.

Finally Fred spoke. "I'm going to have to have the talk with Eric. We're going to dinner tomorrow night."

"So I should make other plans?" Denis asked.

"Only for dinner. I should be home by nine—maybe eight if he storms out of the restaurant, which seems highly probable. I mean it's up to you. Do you think we need a night off?"

"No."

"Good." Fred turned his head and kissed the head of Denis's cock. He growled deep in his throat and shifted his position. With his tongue, he drew a line through the trail of hair on Denis's stomach and chest, and then climbed on top of him. "A night off would suck."

Denis stood in his kitchen, drinking a beer. The microwave moaned its pitying dirge as a plastic tray of meatloaf and mashed potatoes turned circles on a glass carousel. Seven minutes. Power setting: High.

He couldn't say he enjoyed the evening, back to eating a frozen dinner, waiting for Fred to finish his date with Eric. Jealousy didn't enter his emotional space, though he kept telling himself it would have been an understandable guest. He didn't know Fred all that well. Maybe the man would decide he needed more twink in his life and postpone the break up. Maybe he'd never intended to break it off with the guy in the first place. But Denis didn't really doubt him. Fred had a casual honesty, revealing traits and actions that weren't always flattering. He didn't present this information with dramatic build-up or hesitance, as if fearing Denis's reaction. He stated things simply, the way he'd told Denis about his dinner with Eric.

He ate in front of the television, watching an episode of some droning sitcom he'd seen half a dozen times before. The food tasted bland. The frozen meals always did. At five minutes to nine, he left his apartment and drove across town to Fred's house.

Several times during the drive, Denis told himself he should have called ahead. He didn't even know if Fred had made it back from dinner, yet. He felt a moment of relief when he saw the man's car parked in the driveway, and then a moment of panic when he considered that Fred might not be alone.

"How'd it go?" Denis asked as he walked through Fred's front door.

"Not well," Fred said. He kissed Denis and pulled away. "Not the way I expected anyway. You want a beer?"

"Sure. What do you mean not well?"

He listened to the explanation while following Fred into the kitchen.

"I don't know," Fred said. "I expected him to be indignant. Figured he'd give me some twink attitude before storming out. But he wanted to talk about it. I mean he actually looked hurt."

"I can understand that," Denis said.

"Yeah but we have something... different. I don't know. I guess I didn't give the kid enough credit for depth." Fred stood in the light of the open refrigerator and handed Denis a bottle. "Anyway, I felt really shitty about the whole thing until he called me old and fat, and then I just felt a *little* shitty about it."

"You're not fat."

Fred looked at him wryly over his own beer bottle. He whipped the refrigerator door closed.

"And you're not *that* old," Denis added.

Fred walked past and slapped him on the ass. "You're on bottom tonight, buddy. I'll show you what old and fat can do."

The tire hissed around the blade of the Boy Scout knife in Eric Morden's hand. He hadn't used the knife in a dozen years, and he hadn't even seen it in two, but as motherfuckers went, this motherfucker was prepared. The tire deflated. The corner of the car sank. He yanked the blade free and snapped it back into the handle.

Eric wasn't used to getting dumped. He was beautiful; everyone told him so. And yet some middle-aged, chunky-assed douchebag had sent him packing? It didn't make sense. It defied Eric's laws of physics, which was to say that a pretty face and tight abs were fucking gravity.

Who the fuck did Fred think he was? (And what kind of geek-ass grandpa name was Fred, anyhow?)

Satisfied with the damage, Eric walked hurriedly back toward the park. As he approached the house on the corner, he noticed a man standing on the edge of the lawn. The guy wore a suit that was black or dark blue and a narrow tie over a white shirt. Eric slowed his pace and considered crossing the street—(Did he see what I did?)—but the man turned away as if he'd seen nothing and walked into the park. There he stopped in the shadows beneath a pine and leaned back against the trunk. Eric could just make out the smudge of paleness that made up the man's face.

He didn't notice the house on his right. There was no reason he should. The police tape had been removed and he never followed the news. The house was just a house, but the man ahead, the guy leaning against the tree, might be something he needed—a hard distraction.

The park had a reputation for cruising; that's probably why fat, old Fred had bought a house so close to it. Eric strolled into the park, fully aware of the man's eyes on him. He paused to get a better look at the guy. Pale, he thought. Kind of scrawny. Not hideous but nowhere near Eric's league.

Still there was something to be said for convenience.

He walked up to the man and said, "Hey."

Without returning the greeting, the man grinned broadly. He reached out and cupped Eric's crotch. His fingers gripped a bit too tightly, but Eric said nothing.

Then the man released his hold and walked away from the tree. He headed at an angle toward the back of the house on the corner, and Eric followed. He wanted to believe the man owned the house, so close to Fred's. Somewhere deep down in the spongy darkness of his mind he imagined hitting it off with the guy, visiting the house a few times; maybe sunning himself on the front lawn just to catch Fred's eye. Make the asshole squirm a little.

On the patio behind the house, the trick fell under a dull cone of light from a fixture beside the door, and Eric thought he looked better than he had in shadows. The suit looked like it was quality, and the gauntness Eric had noted in the gloom of the park was nearly erased by the light.

A plant, maybe it had been a fern, sat on a tall, intricately carved stand beside him. Its fronds and stems were limp and black as pitch.

"You might want to water that," Eric said and laughed.

The man's grin grew wider and he shrugged. Nodded his head.

"This your house?" Eric asked.

The man nodded again.

Doesn't he talk? Was something wrong with his voice? His teeth?

Eric tapped the Boy Scout knife in his pocket for reassurance. He was never comfortable with quick tricks, not until he was done with them. A lot of freaks in the world. The man in the dark suit slid open the back door and stood, grinning like a kid who knew he was getting exactly what he wanted for Christmas. He waved Eric into the house with a flourish of his hand. Eric nodded and stepped over the threshold, took three more steps, and then waited.

The grinning man walked around him, passing out of the reach of the patio light. He continued through the kitchen and crossed into a gloomy area ahead, which Eric assumed was the dining room, or maybe the whole place was wide open like Fred's had been. He could barely see but he heard the click of the man's shoes on hardwood floors.

Eric followed. The closer he got to the space the darker it seemed to be, as if it were a bank of sooty fog waiting to engulf him. A hand gripped his ass and he felt the man's body guide him to the right. And the room continued to darken.

"Hey," he said. "How about some lights?"

The hand left his backside and Eric felt a dislocation from reality as if he were dropping through this darkness, rather than just standing at its center. Further, the black air seemed to have density. It buffeted against him, and he again thought of fog. The sensations were startling and Eric reached out to steady himself as he felt certain he would topple.

"What the hell?" he asked.

A light clicked on. The grinning man in the suit stood before him, arms outstretched like a magician awaiting approbation for a trick well done.

Eric shook his head in annoyance.

Then he saw the bodies on the floor. Three of them. Each one had been crucified face down, pinned by spikes to the hardwood like butterflies on a kid's wall. He had no time to react before the man swung out and punched him in the temple. The world spun and swirled, and then his feet were kicked out from under him and he fell hard, his head cracking against the polished wood. Once the initial daze passed, he screamed and thrashed, slapping his palms and his heels on the flooring. The man in the suit landed in a kneel on his chest, knocking the scream from Eric's lips.

He planted his palms on Eric's shoulders and leaned forward. His lips parted freeing a thick black liquid like tar. The ichor fell in dark bands over Eric's nose and mouth and it slipped through his lips. It was bitter and acidic and it began to pour in gouts from the suited man's mouth. It filled Eric's nostrils. He held his breath as long as he could, but eventually, he had to open his mouth to breathe. He gasped. The perverse fluid drained into his throat like bitter syrup, and Eric coughed, gagging on the rich filth.

A moment later, he was flipped over and slid around on the floor like a doll. Facedown, he continued struggling, digging his nails into the glistening finish. A shoe came down hard on the back of his neck. He tried to scream but couldn't. The black shit had grown thick and dense in his throat and his chest was already heaving for breath. The shoe left his neck. He felt a second of relief before the man dropped onto him, knees digging into Eric's shoulder blades. Hands wrapped around his brow and pulled his head away from the wood. A moment later he was stunned by the concussion of his face on the boards.

Then it was time for the spikes.

They were on the sofa, watching a romantic comedy and drinking beers. Denis leaned against the arm of the couch and Fred curled in front with his head on Denis's bare chest. "Feeling better about Eric?" Denis asked.

"Feeling better about everything," Fred told him. "Better than ever."

"Same," Denis said. He pointed at the television. "Do you know why rich, smart, and gorgeous American women always fall for bumbling, barely articulate British guys in these movies?"

"It's the accent. The accent is a snatch magnet."

Denis slapped the side of Fred's head.

"Too crude?"

"You think?" Denis said. A second later he was laughing uncontrollably over the comment.

"Tomorrow, I think we should have breakfast at Dewey's, that pancake place on the other side of the park, and then maybe drive up to the mountains for the day."

"It's supposed to rain all day," Denis said, running his palm over the fur on Fred's chest.

"I doubt it's going to close the freeways."

Denis pinched Fred's nipple. "Smart ass."

"It's nice up there, even with rain. Maybe we could grab a room at one of the resorts, spend the night out of town?"

"Sounds good to me."

He watched the Englishman's stuttering profession of love on the screen and shifted his weight a bit. "You mind if I order a pizza?"

"Mmm," Fred growled. "Fred's tummy like Denis."

"And Denis like Fred's tummy. Now move your ass so I can reach the phone."

"You're about perfect, you know that?" Fred asked.

Maxine Gordon stood in front of the house by the park, scratching her head. Early morning light surrounded her in a pinkish haze as she regarded John Lucio's yard with disgust. The black stain that had devoured his hedges and grass had moved onto her front yard, sweeping like a pointed wave over the lawn. She'd paid too much for soil and sod, not to mention the pricey service to mow and weed every week, to just watch it blacken and die.

It was bad enough Lucio had killed himself, likely dropping property values in the process, but obviously, he'd set something loose before doing so. Every plant on the man's property was ruined, and now her foliage was under attack as well.

She'd already called the city about the situation, and they'd assured her someone would be out to assess the situation, but knowing the city it would be days before one of their drones got off his fat ass to do something. This was simply unacceptable.

Maxine walked toward the park and noticed the stain had spread in that direction as well. It looked like someone had poured gasoline over the plants and lit them up until they were char, but she'd plucked a blade of her own grass and it hadn't had the texture of having been burned. If anything, the blade seemed more succulent, fatter, only instead of being filled with variances of green, the plants choked on a darker nutrient.

She walked to the side of Lucio's house and then around to the back.

Lucio had taken great pains with his garden. He had been particularly fussy about his roses, she remembered, having seen him on numerous occasions pruning branches and testing the soil. They were black now. Everything in his precious garden was, and the discoloration spread to the far back of his property. It was already climbing the trees of the greenbelt separating the neighborhood from Seventh Street.

Maxine turned back for the front of the house and noticed the glass patio door stood open. She shook her head and marched forward. The police had probably left it open after their investigation of Lucio's suicide. Lazy bastards. The glass wasn't broken, and as she approached, she saw no sign of tampering along the metal frame, so she discounted the likelihood of thieves—at least sloppy ones.

At the open door, Maxine poked her head in. "Hello?" she called, not expecting an answer.

But a sound did come back to her. Not voices. Not someone calling out an explanation for his or her presence in the home of a suicide. Instead, she heard thumps and raps, like someone locked in a distant closet, attempting to escape.

Maxine walked into the house and immediately saw motion ahead, though the gloom made it difficult to identify the details of the shape. She pulled her cell phone out of her pocket and dialed 9-1-1. Her thumb hovered over the send icon on her phone's screen. Cautiously, she made her way across the kitchen.

Ahead, she was startled to see a man lying face down on the floor. At first, she'd thought he was having a seizure. He jerked and spasmed against the hardwood, but just his torso and head. His hands and feet were motionless. Next to him, a woman similarly thrashed. Maxine continued forward until she saw all four of the bodies on the floor of the dining room, each of them in an agitated state. And then she noticed the spikes that secured them to the floor and her skin puckered tightly around muscles suddenly cold.

Remembering the phone she jabbed the send command and put the phone to her ear as she backed away from the horrors in the room.

A shrill squeal like nails on a blackboard erupted from the speaker and Maxine yanked it away from her head. She turned to flee the house and saw with dread John Lucio standing in the opening of the patio door.

D enis woke to an empty bed and his heart skipped.

"Fred?" he muttered. He looked around the room. Found it empty. He repeated the name only louder.

When no answer was forthcoming, he climbed out of bed. He walked through the house calling Fred's name, but there was no response. Getting concerned, he went to the French doors overlooking the patio and peered out, half expecting to see the man standing naked, drinking his coffee at the railing. But he wasn't there either.

A little over seven months earlier he'd made a similar circuit around a different house, only the name he'd been calling was "Benjamin." He'd had no concern back then, just curiosity, wondering where his partner had gotten to so early in the morning.

Eventually, he'd found Benjamin on the floor of the garage. Lips parted. Eyes wide. Motionless.

Only later had Denis learned about his partner's heart condition. Benjamin's mother had told him at the funeral home, where they'd met to discuss arrangements.

"Fred?" Denis called, storming away from the patio doors.

The front door opened. Fred lurched inside and threw the door closed. "Son of a bitch," he said. "The little prick slashed my tire."

Denis, confused, paused by the sofa. "What?"

"I went out to get the paper. Fucking paperboy drops it at the end of the driveway every god damn day, so I gotta walk to the street to get it. And I see my car. The back tire has been slashed."

"Are you sure it isn't just low?"

"No, it's not *just low,*" Fred barked. "There's a gash an inch long."

"And you think Eric did it?"

Fred shot him a look that said, *Duh,* and then stomped toward the bedroom. "I have to call Triple-A."

"And the cops," Denis said.

"No cops. They wouldn't do anything about it—probably *couldn't* do anything about it. I don't have any evidence. Besides, the fucker only did it to get a rise out of me. He doesn't have to know it worked."

Maxine came to slowly. There was a terrible scent in the air that she couldn't identify, and a squealing sound, like rats in the walls. The first time she opened her eyes, she saw nothing but a smudge of light, and then she drifted off again, though she didn't realize it—time simply skipped a beat. She was truly awoken by a louder version of the squealing she'd heard before. Terrified that she shared a room with rats, Maxine opened her eyes.

She sat in a corner of John Lucio's dining room with her hands tied behind her back. A thick wad of cotton had been shoved into her mouth as a gag. To her horror, she saw that she'd been stripped naked. She trembled from both fear and chill, and every muscle in her body ached as if she'd been pummeled from head to foot. Tears filled her eyes, and she sobbed into the cotton gag.

John Lucio knelt on the floor over one of his victims. With his thumb and index finger he wiggled the spike that held a young man face down on the floor. Then Lucio pulled the nail free. It emerged, accompanied by the familiar squeal. Metal against wood.

Behind him, two of his victims, the man and the woman Maxine had first seen, crawled on the floor, heads turning from side to side as if listening to music. She didn't recognize these people, didn't *want* to recognize them. Something was wrong with their skin. It was dry and gray, flaking from the muscle beneath like ancient parchment. Their lips were black. Their eyes were the color of oatmeal, with tiny black holes at their centers. Bones poked through their arms randomly, whether from compound fracture or unnatural growth Maxine didn't know. A third broken person crawled into view; its mouth was open, revealing a jagged fence of sharp, shattered teeth.

She screamed into the wad of cotton, catching the attention of Lucio who was removing another spike, releasing the right foot of the boy sprawled only a yard from Maxine. The man in the suit who was supposed to be dead, stood and observed her. He looked so peaceful. Content. He stepped back and wiped dust from the sleeve of his suit. Then he observed the victims in the room and swept his arm toward Maxine.

The victims responded, crawling toward her like eager infants. She tried to move out of the corner, but Lucio was there. He placed his foot against her shoulder and wedged her against the wall. She struggled against it. She didn't want to die. Not here. Not like this.

The four victims surrounded her. One grabbed her ankle with its destroyed palm. Another leaned close to her chest, sniffing at her skin curiously. It pushed its nose against her breast and she squealed in disgust. When it opened its mouth, Maxine observed the saw-like teeth and shrieked.

It bit, pinching the skin unbearably before it whipped its head back and forth and tore away a piece of her breast. Blood spilled in gouts from the ragged lips of the wound. Maxine lost her breath from the pain. From the sight of a part of her disappearing into the black-lipped mouth. The thing chewed and made a humming sound in its throat as if delighted by the flavor. Turning to the others, the victim nodded his head.

And they all began to eat.

The downpour they'd been expecting started while they were eating a late breakfast at Dewey's. Before going to the restaurant, they'd dealt with Triple A, and Denis had followed Fred to the dealership, so he could drop off his car and get a new tire to replace the one Eric had destroyed. The dealership couldn't make any promises, but they might have the new tire on the rim and the rim on the car before noon.

Denis hated to see Fred's mood sour even more, but he understood, and he remained silent, allowing the man to vent all the way to the restaurant and through most of the meal.

"Now it's raining," Fred said.

"Supposed to go on for a few days."

"Great." Fred dropped his fork and looked out the window. "I'm sorry. I'm going to be lousy company for a while. If you want to drop me off at home, we can try the mountains next week. I'm feeling a heavy sulk coming on."

"I don't mind sulking, but if you want to be alone that's cool."

"What I want is to hurt that prick. But I won't because I'm not twelve-years old and because it'll just give him the jollies he was after all along."

They drove back to Fred's in silence. At the lip of the park, Denis followed the road to the left.

The park was built on a sloped parcel of land, surrounded by dense shrubs and trees. The main lawn sunk into a broad bowl of well-trimmed grass. Roads framed its periphery. Denis drove up the rise on the north side of the park, but when they reached the corner on which John Lucio had built his house, he pulled over and stopped.

"Do you see that?" Fred asked.

"I'm surprised we didn't see it this morning," Denis said.

"We didn't come this way. The dealership is the other direction."

"Still," Denis said.

The black stain covered Lucio's entire property and had drifted well into the park. "It's all the way back to the greenbelt," Fred noted. "What is that shit?"

"Maybe we can ask that guy," Denis said.

He pointed over the steering wheel at a tall man wearing hunter green hip waders and latex gloves. He stood in the middle of

Lucio's lawn, poking the ground with a metal tube. A white van sporting the city's health department decal sat at the curb.

"Don't know," the man, whose name was Steve, said. "Just getting my samples now."

"Have you seen anything like this before?" Denis asked.

"Can't say yes," Steve replied. "Any idea who lives here? No one answered the door."

"He's dead," Denis told the man. "He killed himself earlier in the week."

"Oh," Steve said, looking at a plastic bag holding a divot of black lawn. "I'll have to call it in then. I need documentation before I can enter the house. If I had to guess, I'd say the guy doused everything down with some kind of herbicide before he said goodnight. Maybe he didn't like his neighbors and he wanted them to know."

"Are there herbicides that can do this?"

"I suppose," Steve said with a shrug. "I need to get a few more samples up by the house to see if the concentrations are different. He might have chemicals in the basement leaking all over the place. That'd be real bad. But we'll get it squared away."

Back in the car, Denis said, "I think you should stay at my place for a couple of days until they figure this out."

Fred was looking out the window at the house beside Lucio's. The stain had reached the halfway point in the yard. "I think you're right," he said.

They stopped at Fred's house so he could gather clothes, toiletries, his phone charger and laptop. With his bag packed Fred walked through the house and checked the locks on all of the doors and windows.

"I'm paranoid like that," Fred said with a half-hearted smile.

Instead of going directly to Denis's apartment, they returned to the auto dealership, where Fred picked up his car. At Denis's apartment Fred excused himself to the balcony to make calls.

He needed to touch base with a friend. When Denis checked on him, Fred was standing at the railing, holding his hand out to catch raindrops on his palm. He laughed into the phone. It was good to see him smiling, Denis thought.

Early afternoon, they lay in the bed listening to the rain. Denis spooned Fred, arm wrapped around the man's thick chest. Since he was so silent, only light even breaths, Denis thought his boyfriend was sleeping until Fred said.

"Ivan says you're the gold."

"You have a friend named Ivan? Do we know any of the same people?"

"Maybe," Fred replied. "I don't know."

"What did he mean gold?"

"I have a theory. See I'm convinced there's a cosmic scale and for all the gold on one plate there is an equal weight of shit on the other. Eric and his prank fall squarely on the shit side. Whatever is happening to my neighborhood is also weighing things down. But then there's you."

"I like your theory, though I can't say I buy it."

"You don't have to. I know it's nuts. But think about it. We met on Tuesday, not even a week ago, and we haven't spent a night apart since. I've never done that before. Never wanted to."

"Neither have I."

"And my being in that grocery store was totally random."

"I was going to ask you about that."

"I had a meeting at the coffee shop across the parking lot, and I figured it would be easier to run in there than to look for parking where I normally shop."

"I'm glad."

"Yeah, me too. And I'm not saying this other shit wouldn't have happened if we hadn't met. I had no intention of seeing much more of Eric, so that was already in motion, and I can't imagine Old Johnny was waiting around for me to bring home a hot trick before he offed himself. But I'm glad we met, to keep things balanced."

"Well, it's better than you thinking I jinxed you or cursed you or something."

"No chance of that," Fred said. He pushed his ass back into Denis's crotch and growled deep in his throat.

They lay there quietly. The rain rapped in a soothing rhythm against the window. Denis rubbed his hand over Fred's stomach. It was a good moment, except Denis couldn't shake the word, "curse."

Fred had said something about John Lucio's suicide note. Something about cursing the world.

JOHN LUCIO—

The Book of Wives has told me: Tonight the sky will be wrung of light and I will offer my blood at the Gate of Hell. It will grease the hinges, so that as I enter it will throw wide. I sacrifice my Christian soul and curse this sinners' world. In return I will be given After Life. I will anoint four apostles in the black honey, and they will walk the East, the West, the North and the South, spreading the Word. As the souls of the living pass through the gates, the darkness seeps free. Doubters will know truth.

I will know forever.

"You were right," Denis said. "That's pretty crazy."

"Yeah, right? But check out the left side of the screen."

"What am I looking for?"

"The guy had two thousand 'friends.'"

"And nobody thought to check on him? Some friends."

Fred closed the laptop and leaned back in his chair. "Well, his little show was pretty convincing if you ask me. I mean all of the plants dying after he commits suicide. He put together an intricate hoax, if it is a hoax."

"What else could it be?" Denis asked.

Fred shrugged. "I just can't imagine him spraying chemicals all over the neighborhood like that. Someone would have had to see him."

"So it's more reasonable to believe a Christian activist sacrificed himself to the devil to damn the world?"

"The question isn't whether he would or wouldn't do it. Those whack jobs get some fucked up ideas in their heads. The question is whether it worked or not."

"No more horror movies for you."

"Try and stop me," Fred said. He smiled, leaned forward and gave Denis a kiss. "Just so you know, Ivan has a spare room if you want some time to yourself. I don't want you to feel trapped."

"I don't feel trapped. Besides, the city will probably have figured all of this out by morning and you can go back to your place without worrying about toxic exposure or demon possession."

The next afternoon the steady rain shower intensified. They had gone to an early movie and afterward decided to check on Fred's neighborhood. Denis felt a chill as he navigated up the sloped drive of the park. The terrain was painted in shades of gray from the storm. Pellets of rain smeared the air and made the sprawling lawns and picnic gazebos appear unreal, like ancient photographs with badly scratched surfaces. As they neared the far side of the park, they saw the news vans and the city vehicles surrounding the corner lot. A crowd of people stood in the park watching the scene. They too were gray. None of them held an umbrella. This group—easily forty people—stood unprotected from the downpour as they stared at the house by the park. Away from this aggregation on the other side of the road, two aged men in black stood beneath the semiglobes of umbrellas. They had the white collars that identified them as priests. They too were motionless, but instead of looking at the house, their attention was captured by the group of onlookers across the road.

"Street's blocked," Denis said, pointing to the barricade ahead. Flashing orange lights seemed to be the only color in an otherwise grayscale landscape.

"Hopefully, they're cleaning up whatever Lucio put in the ground."

"Do you want me to head back to Seventh Street and come in from the other direction?"

"Absolutely," Fred said. "Somebody up there must know what's going on."

Denis navigated a three-point turn. His headlights fell over the priests and both men turned toward the car. Their faces were stern, agitated. Their gazes were intense, yet looked weary like pictures of soldiers Denis had seen on the web. One of the men touched the cross hanging from his neck. The other nodded solemnly.

They encountered another roadblock on the opposite end of Fred's street. Another group of onlookers, as unaware of the weather as the congregation in the park, had gathered just outside the barricade, and police officers shouted for them to get back, but the rain-soaked crowd paid them no attention. Oblivious. They remained a motionless pack, staring past the police and through the downpour at the house by the park.

"We're not going to get any answers," Denis said. "I don't even think we can get anybody's attention."

"But that's my house," Fred told him. "Shouldn't I fucking know what's happening to my house? Maybe we can go around to Seventh Street and walk through the greenbelt."

"No," Denis said. The police were getting nowhere with the horde at the barricade. They were clearly beyond frustration and working themselves up for violence. "We don't need to get shot."

"But I'm going to need clothes for work."

"Then we'll go shopping," Denis said.

"This is bullshit," Fred said absently. "Complete bullshit."

"We'll check the web when we get home. There are vans around the corner so the reporters must be up there someplace. The police will have to make a statement to them. My guess is, even you had the chance to talk to one face to face, it would be the same story they're going to tell the press."

"It's my house," Fred said.

"Yeah," Denis said, slipping an arm around his shoulders.

He didn't know what else to say.

The news gave them little information. A video clip showed uniformed police officers and men in white hazmat suits poking around Lucio's black lawn. "Authorities are investigating an event of ecological concern," the anchorwoman said. "We have no details at this time but it has been speculated that unknown, possibly toxic, chemicals have been spilled in the area. The extent of the damage and threat to human life is unknown. For now, the public is being asked to stay away from the area until more information becomes available. Again, the twelve hundred block of..."

"Fuck," Fred said. He slapped the sofa cushion with his palm. "I've been quarantined out of my own fucking house."

"Better out than in," Denis said.

"Don't look for a bright side here, Denis. I appreciate it, and I love that you'd try, but please, not right now. I sank my life savings into that place. It was my home."

"It still is."

"Sure, unless it becomes a toxic waste dump, or is ruined by some other *event of ecological concern*."

Denis knew there was nothing he could say that would help. He might mention insurance or spout some platitude about Fred having his health, but he knew the man wouldn't appreciate any of it. Denis had lost the house he'd shared with Benjamin, and no amount of support or condolence had soothed him.

Once he'd thought his home had actually been *his*, but Home was a brittle term; one wholly dependent on finance. Only a mortgage promptly paid gave a man a home.

"I am going to lose my mind just sitting here," Fred said. "Maybe things have cleared out over there."

"It's only been an hour. Why don't we wait and we'll check again after dinner?"

Fred nodded. "I think I'm going to lie down," he said. "Would it be okay if you didn't come in with me?"

"Sure," Denis told him.

The least he could do was give Fred his privacy. They'd been all but inseparable for days.

So Denis sat on the sofa and watched Fred disappear into the bedroom. Denis turned on the television and let the afternoon pass into evening.

He checked on Fred a little past eight. Easing the door open, he poked his head in and looked at the bed.

"Hey," Fred said.

"You okay?"

"Better."

"I thought I'd see if you wanted some dinner; maybe check your place again."

"Not really hungry," Fred told him. "And I think we both know nothing's changed at the house. Let's not waste the time."

"Okay," Denis said. He leaned out of the room and was closing the door when Fred stopped him.

"Where you going?"

"I don't know."

"Then come to bed. I missed you."

Denis woke to dull gray light. Morning. He went to the window and parted the blinds. The rain continued, but it had become little more than mist. Still the gloom that had covered the city remained. He turned back to the empty bed.

He'd heard Fred slipping out over an hour ago. Instead of saying anything, Denis had closed his eyes and gone back to sleep. But now, he felt a wound of unease open in his chest. He didn't know how to interpret Fred's early departure, nor his own apathy in light of his leaving. Obviously, Fred had thought to get an early start, to reach his house before the crazies gathered for another day of rain-drenched gawking. He might even be able to corner a cop or health department worker to learn about the immediate future of his property.

Fred needed time to himself, Denis knew.

He went about his morning, fixing breakfast and powering up his laptop. He discovered an early morning email from Fred and opened it.

Had to check on the house. Didn't want to wake you. You look amazing when you're sleeping. Back soon. F.

Denis smiled, and the wound in his chest knitted. He drank his coffee and returned to the news page, where he found a number of articles pertaining to the events of the day before. The story hadn't changed, as far as he could tell.

An hour passed, and then another.

Finally, Denis decided that Fred had been gone too long. Even if Fred had been allowed to enter the house to gather more of his belongings it shouldn't have taken this long. Denis called his cell number, but he was sent directly to voice mail.

After another hour and another call, Denis took his umbrella from the closet and left the apartment.

He stood at the barricade looking in disbelief at the street ahead.

He'd driven in from the East to avoid the park, and he'd been forced to park his car in the middle of the road because the curbs were packed tight with vehicles. Cars and trucks blocked drives and alleys. But there were no people. The police cars and health department vehicles remained. Two ambulances with their back doors open wide stood just inside the barricade. Yet the roads and the lawns were empty.

Misting rain shrouded the block. The black stain had reached the west edge of Fred's house, consuming all greenery on the right side of the street for as far as Denis could see. It was a war zone. A minor apocalypse.

Where the hell was Fred?

Denis walked around the barricade and crossed to the door of Fred's house. He knocked lightly, so softly it all but negated the action entirely. Finding the door unlocked, Denis went inside.

"Fred," he whispered.

He listened for movement in the house, but even the hiss of the rain was blocked out. He repeated Fred's name as he passed through the living room. In the bedroom, he found a suitcase open on the bed and three pairs of slacks laid out beside it. He left the room and walked to the French doors at the back of the house and bit down on a gasp. The black stain covered everything in sight, as if a talented artist had done a charcoal sketch of the landscape. Even the potted plant on Fred's railing had gone dark.

Denis backed away from the doors. He called Fred's name a final time, but he knew the place was empty. Abandoned. Fear drove him from the house and back to the bleak yard. An insistent voice told him to leave this neighborhood. Fred was gone, lost to the mystery and no longer attainable. Just get the fuck away from here.

But how could he leave?

Ambivalent about his next move, Denis remained in the yard. He called Fred's phone again, and for a moment he imagined he heard it ringing, distantly, muffled by walls and rain, but the sound had no clear direction. It came from all sides, which was all Denis needed to convince himself he hadn't heard the bell at all.

He couldn't just stand there, but he didn't know what to do.

He turned to his car beyond the barricade and saw a man and a woman circling the vehicle. Something in their movement, in their faces, made him think of feral animals like jackals eyeing prey. The woman whipped her head in his direction, and Denis felt a splinter of ice run through him. He spun toward the park and raced through the front yards, away from the disconcerting couple. When he reached Lucio's house he sprinted across the street to be away from it. All of the dread that clung to his skin and burned his veins like acid, rolled from this place.

He looked quickly across the road at the malevolent house, this mother of misery, and saw dozens of people moving about inside. A man pressed himself to the window—a grinning man in a black suit. He raised a palm in greeting and waved wildly as if the host of a magnificent party he couldn't wait for Denis to join.

Denis bolted, entering the park at the same place he'd seen the somber priests the morning before.

He came over the rise and skidded to a stop on the damp grass. The sight awaiting him punched the breath from his chest.

The stain covered the entirety of the park. Hundreds of people wandered aimlessly over the soiled grounds—on the lanes of road, around stalled and abandoned vehicles, and across the lawns. They moved lethargically through the bushes and trees framing the park. He recognized the familiar uniforms of police officers, paramedics, and the white HAZMAT suits of the city's health workers. Others wore shorts or jeans or dresses. Some wore nothing. To his right, far across the field, he saw one of the black-clad priests moving in a slow circle, head cocked back, eyes fixed on the steel gray sky.

Denis backed away. He turned to flee the neighborhood.

Fred stood halfway down the block, hands in the pockets of his cargo shorts. He wore no shirt and the rain pasted thick hair to the round muscles on his chest. His skin gleamed from moisture. He was grinning as if pleased to see his boyfriend this last time.

Then Fred began to run forward, his bare feet slapping the wet concrete. He spread his arms wide like wings, like a lover wishing to take Denis in his arms. And Denis stood motionless, desolate, watching Fred bear down on him.

In a flash, jagged scratches of energy filled his head. Rational thought vanished amid the static and suddenly he found the gray world around him beautiful. Simple. Unfettered by color.

In the flicker of a moment, his fear turned to acceptance. Anticipation.

The burly stranger Denis had loved for less than a week had never appeared more striking. Strong. Vital. Denis opened his own arms in welcome. And when Fred's lips parted, the grin changing into a cruel smile, Denis told himself the man's teeth were perfect and white, and not the shattered, sharp fangs of a thing fashioned in hell. The eyes were green and startlingly erotic, not gray clots behind pasty lids.

Hurry, Denis thought, eager to feel the press of Fred's body against his.

And those hands. And those lips.

Turtle

"Turtle."

The bearded man delivered the word with a breathy gravitas, as if it actually meant something. Royce figured the old guy was snapping under the pressure, or perhaps Paul Winston had always been crazy. Royce didn't know the restaurateur well enough to speculate on his long-term mental state. Royce hardly knew him at all. He'd eaten at the man's establishment dozens of times over the years, and of course, he'd seen the man there, keeping an eye on his employees and checking with customers to make sure they were enjoying their meals. Beyond that Royce had had no contact with the guy.

Winston was a fit man in his early fifties who looked like he'd been athletic once but whose muscles had softened over the years. Bald with a neatly trimmed white fringe over his ears that blended seamlessly into his beard, Winston reminded Royce of Santa. Royce had always liked Santa; he wasn't as fond of Winston right now, so he kept the pistol pressed to his head.

Royce had been in the man's house for fifteen minutes. He'd surprised the old guy. Winston's face had lit up with recognition upon seeing Royce. Then the bright expression dimmed a second later, the moment he noticed the gun.

Inside the house, Royce had locked the door. The place was decorated for Christmas, smelling heavily of pinesap and cranberry candles. Plastic garland, like snaking fir boughs, ran over the wainscotings. Lights circled the bay window in the living room. Next to this stood the tree.

Once the man had been secured, tied to a wooden rocking chair beside the fireplace, Royce had begun the questioning, but Winston had said nothing of consequence. Obviously distraught by the ordeal, he'd sat silently for several minutes, refusing any communication at all. Then Winston had opened his mouth and the word *turtle* had come forth, like it held the answers to any question Royce might pose.

"I didn't ask about your favorite soup," Royce said through a tight jaw. "I asked what you did to Monica."

The gun felt heavy in Royce's palm, the handle slicked with sweat. He worried about dropping the weapon, worried about it going off. Royce wasn't a thug. He wasn't a private detective or a cop. He was an investment banker with Harly-Mack. He led a respectable, even enviable, life. What was he doing in Winston's home, pressing the muzzle of a gun to the old guy's temple?

Of course Royce knew the answer. His wife, Monica, was dead. The once dynamic woman with a Midas touch for publicity had been reduced to babbling incoherence. She had mumbled and sobbed, and then she'd turned violent against herself. It had all happened quickly and it had all begun the night they'd left Winston's restaurant for the last time.

"Go home, Mr. Royce," Winston said. "I won't call the authorities. This isn't you. You're just in shock."

"What did you do to her? What did you say that night?"

"I asked her if she enjoyed her meal," Winston said evenly. "I wished her a good evening."

"Bullshit. She started losing it about ten minutes after we left your restaurant, and she kept mumbling about something you said."

"I read the papers," Winston replied. "She wasn't exactly stable, now was she?"

"She was fine," Royce countered. He glared down at the bald-head, the full cheeks made red with alarm, and again he thought of Santa.

I'll bet you can't.

Can so.

I dare you.

The remembered voices struck Royce like a sickness. His head grew light and he stepped away from the chair, pulled the gun away from Winston's temple. He looked around the room for something on which he could focus and found the Christmas tree. Metal orbs and quaint wooden miniatures adorned the pine. Simple white lights brought a glow to the ornaments. A single silver cone, like the funnel of a tornado, twisted back and forth on its green thread. Wiping his brow and feeling an unnatural tide of sweat on his fingers, Royce closed his eyes and took deep breaths to regain control of himself.

I dare you.

The old voices were understandable. The memory they belonged to had originated with a Christmas long past. And here he was in Winston's apartment—decorated to the hilt with cheap holiday whimsy—and confronting a man who looked like Santa's healthy younger brother. With the strain of the situation, it was perfectly natural he'd remember that long-ago morning, absolutely normal to be thinking about Wes, but:

"I don't have time for this shit," Royce said. The sound of his own voice brought clarity to his thoughts. He returned to his place by the bound man and held the gun to his head. "What did you say to her?"

"She wasn't well," Winston replied.

"She carved the skin off her fucking hand! I think 'wasn't well' understates the situation, don't you?"

"But you just said she was fine."

"Until she spoke to you."

"Are you suggesting I cast a spell on her? Cursed her?"

"I think you knew something. I think you were going to black-mail her."

"And what could I know?" Winston asked. His soft face grew tight with anger. "You came to the restaurant because it was in your neighborhood and the paper said it was trendy. You barked orders at the staff, complained and whined. You and your wife were no different than a hundred other patrons. None of you stand out. You're a table number—end of story. So please tell me what the fuck am I supposed to know about you?"

I dare you.

I don't wanna.

Because you know you can't.

Royce bit his cheek to silence the ghost voices.

"Look," Winston said from his place in the chair, "I know what you're going through. I've lost someone myself recently. It's never easy."

The restaurateur was talking about his daughter. The story had been all over the papers and the news six months ago. The girl had been a hostess at Winston's restaurant. Royce remembered her as being a plain thing with a charming smile. Monica had found nothing charming in the girl. Royce's wife had always called the girl the Bridge Troll, because they had to get past her before they could cross into the dining room.

The girl had been attacked in the park next to Winston's restaurant. Three men had dragged her into the bushes. The girl had been violated and beaten and left for dead. Monica had refused to go back to the restaurant for months after the incident.

Royce felt a flash of pity for the man, but it was quickly washed away. There was a big difference between what happened to Winston's daughter and what happened to Monica.

"Your daughter didn't die," he said. "She didn't carve herself up, screaming."

"Do you really believe death is the worst thing we can experience? My Carla is gone, Mr. Royce. She lies in a hospital bed day after day. Those men beat her so badly her mind is broken, useless. Carla isn't there anymore, her amazing gifts are gone. She used to have such a beautiful voice, an angel's voice. She was studying opera and was preparing for an audition with the city company. Now, all she can do is grunt like an animal and each of those noises is like glass scraping my ears and my heart."

Tears slid down Winston's round, red cheeks. Each traced a line to his beard where the white hairs captured the moisture. The droplets twinkled in the festive lights strung about the room, giving his beard a silvery cast.

"But she's alive," Royce said. "Monica isn't. I don't give a shit about your daughter. I want to know what you did to my wife."

What did you do to your brother?

Nothing. He just fell down.

"You don't give a shit?" Winston asked. He sniffed back snot and tears and sat up straighter in the chair. "Well, that's the problem, isn't it, Mr. Royce? That's why we're here now isn't it?"

"What are you talking about?"

"Never mind, Mr. Royce. The why of it doesn't matter."

"Tell me." Royce pressed the gun into the skin and moved it back and forth causing ripples in the flesh.

"You and your wife," Winston said, his voice low and measured, "you were in the restaurant the night those men attacked my little girl. You left while it was happening. You heard her cries for help, and you did nothing. You kept walking because you couldn't be bothered to help a meager restaurant hostess."

The accusation sent Royce back a step. It wasn't true. Not exactly.

He remembered the night Winston was talking about. After dinner, he and Monica had left the restaurant. They had been celebrating Monica's recent raise. Both were eager to get home and continue the celebration in bed. Yes, they'd heard a girl shouting for help, but they hadn't known who she was. For all they'd known, it was a trap, some kid trying to lead them into the dark park for her friends to rob or kill. The cries had grown more disturbing, and Royce had gone so far as to suggest calling nine-one-one, but Monica had stopped him.

"Then we'll be up all night giving statements to the police. There could be a trial. I don't have time for a trial. Do you?"

The argument had been convincing at the time. Maybe it was the wine. Maybe it was his anticipation of sex. Whatever the case, they'd wandered down the block and even managed to forget the incident before seeing the news about Winston's daughter. By then, it was too late. The press would make them look like monsters if they came forward after the fact. No. They kept their silence and after a few months, they again forgot the incident entirely.

"My baby girl was begging for her life and you walked away."

Royce thought to deny the claim, then threw the idea out. He was holding the gun. He hadn't attacked the girl and neither had Monica. "She wasn't our responsibility. We aren't the police. We didn't know what was happening."

"You didn't *care* what was happening, because it wasn't happening to you."

"How could you possibly even know we were there?"

"Carla."

"No," Royce said. "The papers said she was all but a vegetable. She couldn't even describe the men who attacked her. Even you just said she couldn't do anything but grunt."

"She's my daughter. I can communicate with her in ways no one else can."

"Well Kreskin, why the hell didn't you tell the police so they could arrest the assholes that attacked her? Why did you decide to punish my wife?"

"Those men were managed," Winston said. "Believe me, no one was forgiven."

And now Royce understood. Winston had threatened to take what he knew to the police. Monica had panicked, fearing what the publicity would do to her career. Others might find it a terribly small thing, but Monica knew the importance of her reputation. Her high profile clients would vanish overnight in the wake of something like this. The public humiliation would have been too much for her.

"You fuck," Royce said. "Monica's dead because your daughter was in the wrong place at the wrong time. We didn't do anything to her. In fact if anyone's to blame, it's you. You're the one that should have kept her out of the park at night. You're the one that should have been watching her."

You should have been watching him. He's your brother.

Royce's head grew light again. He stumbled back from the chair as beads of sweat dripped into his eyes, coating his vision and stinging his corneas. The room tipped, then righted too quickly. He thought he might vomit and reached out to the wall to stable himself until the sensation passed.

His thoughts roiled and melted, blurring like his vision. He smelled turkey and stuffing, cooking in the oven. On the floor, his little brother, Wes, was playing with his newly opened Christmas presents. Their parents had gotten the day's fight out of the way early. Their father was down the street drinking beers with Merle and Lon and Dexter. Their mother was upstairs crying.

Wes bounced a toy on his thigh and spoke in a high-pitched nasal tone, creating a voice for the bit of plastic pinched between his fingers.

The giant's coming to eat me, the toy cried.

Royce hated the little shit. His nose was always bubbling with snot and his lips were constantly shimmering with fresh spit. Wes was a disgusting piece of crap, but he got whatever he wanted because he was the baby.

Yes, I'm going to eeeat yoooou, Wes said trying to make his voice low and threatening, but it still sounded girly to Royce.

You couldn't eat that, he said, taunting his little brother.

Could too.

I'll bet you can't.

Can so.

I dare you.

I don't wanna.

Because you know you can't.

Royce shook his head. The unwanted memory tore loose but it wouldn't go away. He stood in Paul Winston's dining room, but ghosts from another room hung about the place. Winston remained in the chair, eyeing Royce, and at the man's feet, Royce's little brother Wes rolled amid torn boxes and shredded holiday wrap. The child bucked on the floor, clutching his throat.

"It's only going to get worse," Winston said.

"What are you talking about?" Royce asked, looking at the man's face so he wouldn't have to see Wes's desperate thrashing.

"Your wife came to me at the restaurant that night," Winston said. "She told me how much she liked the hostess I hired to replace Carla. Your wife told me she thought the new girl added a touch of class to the place, as if Carla wasn't good enough to lead your pretentious asses to a table. She might as well have spit in my daughter's face."

"She was complimenting the restaurant," Royce said. He barely registered how ridiculous the defense sounded. He was still too disoriented by the bizarre double-vision he was experiencing.

"You people," Winston said in disgust, bobbing his head up and down like a rooster hunting a worm, "everything and everyone that fails to serve you or appeal to your precious aesthetic is distasteful. You wear entitlement like wings, thinking it raises you above anyone who doesn't share your narrow ideals. You didn't help my daughter because you couldn't be bothered, because she wasn't part of your accepted class, because there was no benefit to you."

On the floor, Wes slapped the carpet, crushing a swatch of blue Christmas wrap. Through his claw-curled fingers, Royce saw Santa's face, grinning with good cheer.

"Wes," Royce whispered.

"You want to know what I told your wife that night?" Winston asked. "It was one word. One simple word: Marlboro."

"Marlboro?" Royce said. Suddenly he could concentrate again. His brother's body had stopped moving, making Wes less of a distraction. "What the fuck is that supposed to mean?"

"Ask your wife," Winston said.

"Fuck you," Royce yelled, driving the barrel of the gun into Winston's temple, shoving the old man's head to the side. "What does it mean?"

"I don't know what the word means. I just knew it meant *something* to your wife. For as long as I can remember I've sensed the words. They come to me when I need them. Once spoken, they act like worms, burrowing through your thoughts until they find an emotional core. You may have heard the word a thousand times before, but I make it meaningful."

Royce smelled turkey and stuffing. On the floor, his little brother, Wes, was playing with his newly opened Christmas presents. Their father was down the street drinking beers with his friends. Their mother was upstairs crying.

The ugly memory had rewound and started again.

Royce tried to fight it. "No," he said. He shook his head again and bit the inside of his cheek until he tasted blood.

Marlboro, he thought. What could that have meant to his wife? It was a brand of cigarettes. Maybe it meant something else. Neither he nor Monica were the sort to associate with losers who smoked. In fact, they'd completely cut Monica's aunt Holly out of their lives because the redneck hag had clung to the filthy habit.

No big loss, Royce thought. It just meant they wouldn't be getting anymore of those hideous afghans the woman knitted and passed off as presents.

So what had the word meant?

And why wouldn't his baby brat brother quit arguing with him?

Could too.

I'll bet you can't.

Can so.

A realization fell over him, and Royce tightened his grip on the pistol. For a moment the voices of children ceased.

Oh Jesus, the old fuck did something to me. It's just like Monica. In the end, she couldn't think straight. She kept mumbling about blood on her hands and how they used to do "it" with knitting needles.

Do what?

I don't wanna.

"Shut up, Wes! Just do it or I'll take it away, and you'll never see it again."

His little brother popped the toy in his mouth. He tried to swallow, but the molded plastic lodged in his windpipe. Royce thought the brat was acting, making a great show of clutching his throat and hopping around the living room. Wes had looked totally stupid and was even more annoying than he had been playing with his toys. By the time Royce realized his brother was in real trouble, the kid was sprawled on the floor, his hands flapping and smacking the carpet like the wings of a wounded bird.

Then the struggle ended.

And Royce's mother came downstairs, her jaw still tight from the argument she'd had with Royce's father that morning. She found Wes on the floor and screamed.

"Make it stop," Royce told the man in the chair, as his mother demanded to know what had happened to her baby boy. "I swear to God, if you don't stop this I'll put a bullet through your head."

Paul Winston said nothing. He lowered his head and gazed over his chest and belly at the floor.

"I'm not joking," Royce said. "If you don't make this stop, I'm going to shoot. Are you listening to me?"

Are you listening to me, young man?

But mom, I...

You should have been watching him. He's your little brother.

"Winston!" Royce cried.

He spun around, to get away from the angry face of his mother. He tried to escape the room but it felt as if the floor was melting beneath each stride, turning thick and cloying, sucking at his feet like mud. The gun hung in his hand like a brick of lead. He felt exhausted and nauseous. The air in the house was stifling.

The odor of turkey and stuffing wrapped around his nose and mouth like a thick filthy rag. His father had punched his mother in the mouth and stormed out of the house. On the floor, his little brother, Wes, played with his newly opened Christmas present, a small plastic turtle that he bounced on his knee.

The turtle spoke in panicked falsetto through his brother's mouth. *Don't eat me. Don't eat me.*

Royce dropped the gun. It fell to the floor amid discarded ribbons, brightly colored bows and wadded gift-wrap. He walked into a wall and dropped to his ass, stunned because there shouldn't have been a wall in the middle of his parents' living room.

"Don't eat me," Wes squealed. Then his voice fell into a lower register, and he said "Yes, I'm going to eeeat yoooou."

"You shouldn't eat that," Royce said.

"Can too."

"I know you *can*, Wes. Just don't."

"Can so," Wes replied. He lifted the plastic turtle to his lips and slipped it through.

"Don't, Wes," Royce cried. "Please don't."

But it was too late. His brother moved around the living room, hands clutching at his throat. His chest heaved in spasm, but air couldn't reach his desperate lungs. Wes fell to the floor. His hands slapped.

Through the clutched fingers, Royce saw a bit of wrapping paper. It was blue and it had a picture of Santa on it. Then Wes's hand seized up and the bit of paper crumpled in his grasp.

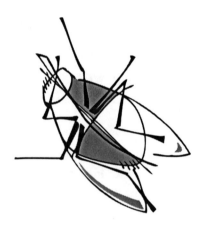

Landfall '35

So much had already been lost. The prosperity of the post-war years had been stacked too high, too thin, and it all came crashing down in what they were calling a great depression. I was comparatively fortunate. A veteran of the Great War, the government felt obliged to put me to work. While old friends stood in bread lines, holding their tattered clothing together with filthy fingers, I worked in a camp by the ocean on a sliver of land framed by sandy beach. For all of the hardship of the last half-decade, many of us on the highway project believed we had reached a place of security. It seemed the entire country had stepped over the edge of a cliff, but we had landed on a ledge of stone, relatively unharmed and ready to begin the steady climb upward. We still felt hope, and we called the camp home.

The camp, one of three established by the Federal Emergency Relief Administration in 1933, sat on the southern edge of Lower Matecumbe Key, dead center between Key West and Miami. The men assigned to the camp came from diverse backgrounds, from pencil pushing accountants and bankrupted shop owners to construction workers and athletes, long past their glory days. Many of us were in our forties, but some white haired and world-weathered geezers traipsed the sand with us, taking the jobs that required no real exertion, like driving the supply trucks and serving meals on the grub line. We were there to build a road, part of the Overseas Highway Project. It was hard work, but it was work, and since employment had become rare and precious, we took our duties seriously and felt grateful for them.

As a group, the war was the common thread between us, so we fell into informal military practices, saying, "Yes, sir," and "No, sir," to our superiors, and every morning we fell in for roll call. We marched to the worksite in units. Many of the men had come to the camp in rags, but they'd brought their old uniforms, clean and pressed and folded neatly in their bags. We called the camp manager "Captain," as he'd carried the rank in Europe, and we came to attention when he entered a room. We needed order amidst the chaos of crumbling fortune and uncertain future, and many of us embraced the regimentation. Our shirts were tucked and our temporary homes were kept tidy, floors swept free of sand every night before lights out.

Sixty shacks, laid in a precise grid like the blocks of a fastidious child, stood just above the sand on wood pilings and stone foundations. Along with considerably more permanent structures—the post office, the school, and the hotel—these cabins made up the camp. They were rickety but new, and they gave us a dry place to sleep and a bit of privacy. The cabins were no protection at all.

The day before the storm I stood on a stretch of beach. A small boy—the child of a friend—danced with the waves, skipping back as the ocean licked at the sand. Then he dashed forward to chase the retreating surf while lines of white foam hissed and vanished as if boiled away. Three gulls, searching for supper in the shallows, drifted on the evening air currents farther down the shore. Behind them rose a dense stand of Mangrove trees and a wall of somber gray clouds.

The boy's name was Robby McMahon, eight years old with carrot red hair and skin the color of milk. A rash of freckles covered his nose and cheeks. His daddy, Chester, waited back at the camp for the chow bell.

I avoided the camp food whenever I could, choosing to fish or snatch crab and shrimp from the tangles of Mangrove roots to choking down the rations slopped into our tin bowls. The food reminded me of war rations, all grit and paste and salt and gristle, and it seemed to expand into monstrous things once it hit my stomach. The nightmares were always worse after a camp supper. But I didn't just fish for myself. My pal, Graham, had taken sick, and I knew the salty, sloppy grub Eric and Baxter spooned out would do him no favors. So I held a length of stick with a twine line and a bent piece of metal on which I'd skewered some flounder gut. The leaden waves were high and hard and drove my unburdened line back to me before the foul scrap of chum could entice a suitable meal to my hook. Behind me the chow bell rang, and I told Robby McMahon to head on back to his daddy so they didn't miss their supper, and he asked if I would be coming along right soon, and I told him I would. The sun should have been high still, and perhaps it was, but clouds, so thick and dark as to remind me of blood-soaked mud, obscured it. Lightning broke above the ocean, and the furious waves rejected my cast line repeatedly until the futility of my endeavor finally sank in.

I wrapped the line around the stick and held it to my shoulder like a rifle and strolled southerly toward the stand of Mangroves down the beach. The air, rich with the scent of salt and fouled by the reek of landed seaweed, felt heavy about my shoulders and thick in my lungs. Voices came up on my right and I turned. A group of six men marched slowly from the south. Other than the constant chatter, their demeanor was military with backs straight, steps precise, moving in unison with eyes forward.

The search party. Apparently, they'd found nothing.

The day before we had received word that workers from the camps to the north—Camp 1 and Camp 5—had gone missing. Seven total so far.

Though many of us had speculated that they'd simply skipped out on the hard, sweaty work, their captains felt certain that these were not the kind of men who shirked responsibility. Good men. Good workers. Fine veterans. Gone. No word from the ferry captains or train station agents in Key West or Homestead about them. So a search party had been formed in the morning and the crew had been instructed to sweep up and down the train tracks and the highway, looking for temporary encampments or other evidence of the men's passing. I waved at the crew and two sergeants at the rear lifted their hands in response, their steps never faltering.

Eventually the sand gave way to a slight rise, and I climbed into a field of beach grass as high as my knee and heavily browned from the long summer. The gentle whoosh of blades against my legs played to the crashing ocean waves and the call of the carrion birds. The field recalled memories of my boyhood home and my sister, Marjorie.

As children my sister and I had tied the tops of wheat stalks together, creating thatch tunnels and shelters in the pasture behind our parents' home. Fragile Marjorie, always nervous, would have worried herself sick over the angry clouds and the coming storm.

I paused and pulled a cigarette from the tin in my breast pocket and a box of matches from my trousers. Marjorie remained in my thoughts as I drew deeply and felt the smoke grate the tissue of my throat before becoming smooth and calming in my lungs as if its edges were worn away on its journey through my chest. My mother had given birth to six children. Marjorie was the oldest and I the youngest. The four in between—all girls—had each succumbed to illness and been buried before their first birthdays, and as a boy, I'd thought Marjorie and I were somehow blessed, chosen among the six to live and thrive and build important lives. Foolish I know, but children look for reason in everything. It's only through enduring the passing of years that we discover the truth: Fate is a blind giant stumbling through the world indifferent to the misery staining the soles of its feet.

At the edge of the mangrove thicket, I put down my pole and opened up the canvas sack I carried to store my day's catch. There was no art or skill to snatching critters from beneath the arched fingers of the mangrove roots, at least none I'd ever reasoned out. Either the fish and crabs were there for the grabbing or they weren't. Still I usually managed to haul something up from the salty water, even if I didn't recognize the fish I'd caught.

I walked into the thicket to a place where the grassy land reached into the ocean a bit, which gave me access to the caged waters on either side. Kneeling down, I immediately saw a shape in the shadowed surf, and I crawled forward, applauding my good luck, but as I drew closer, it became apparent that I had not stumbled on a convenient delicacy.

The man's face was bloated and torn with strips of skin waving in the tide like a paper mask, white and shredded. Black holes had replaced his eyes and the surrounding lids had been gnawed into frayed flaps. An open mouth showed me rotted teeth and diseased gums, but his tongue had been stripped by bottom feeders or plucked out by a tenacious gull. Half a dozen tiny crabs—no longer an appetizing prospect—worked over the man's throat and chest.

I'd seen more horrible things in war, but the sight of the drowned man, so viciously consumed, worked into my skin and clamped around the nape of my neck. I backed away on hands and knees, and then found my feet. Leaving the canvas sack and my fishing rod where they lay, I raced back to the camp to share my discovery.

On the edge of the camp I caught up with the search party. They'd stopped to gab before joining the other men on the grub line. With great care, I explained what I had found, and the six-man party followed me back to the mangrove thicket.

Pulling the dead man free proved difficult as none of us wanted to hold him too tightly. Michael Bainbridge leaned between two thick roots and with his knife, flicked the crabs away from their supper, and then he and two other men reached in and took the collar of the man's jacket. They hauled him upward, but his swollen bulk proved too great to fit between the roots. Eventually, I and another man waded out and around the tree and found a wider opening on the other side.

The dead man's cheek rested on the back of my hand, feeling like cold dough against my skin. I fought an overwhelming disgust to keep hold of him.

We put the body on a tarp and hauled it over the darkening beach. Mercer had been sent to alert the Captain, and Steve ran ahead to find Dr. Mathias, not that the man swinging in the canvas cradle could benefit from a doctor's help. He was beyond pills and draughts and bandages. Well beyond. But the doctor was the only medical authority in the camp, and his official duties had just been expanded to include those of coroner.

"Looks like he got himself tore up under a boat," Gunnar Blake noted.

"No," Michael Bainbridge said. Bainbridge was one of the few men I'd met in the camp that relied on books for entertainment, forsaking card games and trips into Miami for quiet afternoons with a novel. "He hasn't been broken, just ripped up a bit where his clothes weren't covering. The ocean did that to him. Fish and crabs can take a good amount of meat off a man if he isn't fighting back."

"They got his eyes," Dee Dee Macaby said at my back.

"First thing to go," Bainbridge said knowingly. "Fish have a taste for a man's eyes."

We carried the body down the beach, struggling with the shifting weight and the unpredictable sand, sinking to erratic depths with each step. We waited for Dr. Mathias on the north side of camp at the entrance of the infirmary. The doctor and his nurse, who was also his wife, locked the place up tight unless they had a patient inside. If the infirmary was empty they stayed out to the hotel with the Captain and the other swells, but if even a single man lay on a cot, the doctor and his wife moved house to the small room behind the hospital to keep an eye on their patient. Of course calling the wooden shack a hospital was a bit grand, but it's where we put our sick and injured, and it's where we came for sodium bicarbonate when our bellies went sour.

The doctor, a wiry little guy with black hair and small ears, strolled around the motor pool tent, his lantern swinging before him like a teasing faerie. He made no concession to speed, which made perfect sense. A corpse could be patient.

"Steve said you found him under a mangrove down the beach," Dr. Mathias commented, producing a key and opening the door of the infirmary.

"Yes, sir," I replied. "I was crabbing or about to start anyway, and I saw this here fella."

The doctor made a sound deep in his throat and bobbed his head once. We crowded into the infirmary, the four of us jostling back and forth and sideways to get through the door, carrying our morbid load. "Put him on the desk," Dr. Mathias instructed. "No point in fouling bed clothes. I'm sure he's as comfortable as he's going to get."

"Yes, sir," the four of us said in unison.

The doctor pulled a few books off the wooden tabletop and then stepped back, allowing us to position ourselves at the corners of the desk and gently lower the body. We released the canvas tarp and stepped back as the fabric fell like a drape to cover the table's wooden legs. The doctor lifted his lantern to get a better look at the corpse and winced.

"One of the men from the other camps?" Dr. Mathias asked.

"He's wearing a uniform, looks to be a Lieutenant," Dee Dee said. "So I reckon he is."

"Well, the tide wouldn't bring him down the coast like that," Bainbridge said—always so sure of his thoughts. "He must have worked his way down the keys from Camp One or Camp Five and took shelter 'neath them Mang-gers. Maybe he got himself drunk and fell in and drowned."

"That's a fine theory," Dr. Mathias said, making Bainbridge smile and shrug as if it were all very obvious. "I'll keep it in mind while I do my examination, which I should be getting to, so if you gentleman would excuse us."

The word *us* stuck with me for a second. Who else did he mean? He hadn't brought his wife to the infirmary with him—no need to expose the woman to such a sight, though as a nurse she'd likely seen worse—and I soon realized the plurality he implied consisted of himself and a dead man. It was an act of compassion, I thought. The doctor refused to deny the Lieutenant's humanity and presence though his soul had moved on. He was a good man, our doctor.

As the four of us retreated, Dr. Mathias called me back.

"Lonnie, if you have a second."

"Sure," I told him.

I joined the doctor on the far side of the table, my back to its terrible setting.

"Have you checked in on Graham Rowe today?" he asked, placing a hand on my shoulder.

"Yes, sir," I said. "After the shift ended and before I set out to the beach. I was hoping to find him some fresh fish to eat instead of the camp rations. Thought it might sit better with him."

"It might have done at that," the doctor said. "How did he look?"

"Better. He still has the rash and his eyes are cloudy, but his fever's broke and he's got a grip like a vice. He'll likely be up and around in no time."

"Well that's fine," Dr. Mathias said. "I'm pleased to hear it. Never seen anything like it before."

"Me neither."

"That noted, I wish he'd have kept himself here to the infirmary for a spell longer. Never seen a sick man want to be alone so much."

"That's just Graham's way."

"I'll swing by in the morning and pay a visit."

"Much appreciated," I said.

"You're a good friend to him. A lot of folks would have kept their distance what with us not knowing the cause of his ailment. Might have been contagious."

"You help your pals," I said.

"Indeed," Dr. Mathias agreed. He clapped my shoulder and gave me a bit of a shove, turning me toward the door. "You head on back to your room and get some rest. I'm sure the Captain will want a word once I get him my report."

"Yes, sir."

But I didn't go back to my shack. Instead, I followed an alley between the shacks to the center of the camp and turned to the left, heading toward the ocean. It was still early and if it weren't for the scab of clouds covering the sky, the beach and camp would have been bathed in sunlight. Wind gusted between the buildings, moaning horribly like a legion of lost souls, and it carried the tangy scent of electricity on its currents. A drop of rain plopped onto my brow and slid down the side of my nose, running like a tear across my cheek. Our crew leader had complained about his knees and had assured us it meant a storm was on the way, and I'd taken him at his word.

At Graham's shack, I stopped and lifted myself to toe tips to peer through the window. Gray on gray shapes filled the gloom, and when I finally took in Graham's form, my heart skipped mightily in my chest.

He lay naked across his bed, facing me. He appeared as dead as the Lieutenant on the doctor's table. Graham's strong round face now seemed flat like a mask carved of stone. It was the color of bread dough, eyes wide and lips parted. Motionless. A knot of sorrow lodged in my throat and two more drops of rain rapped on my head. I let myself into the shack and crossed to the cot and took up one of his cold hands in mine, and I placed my other palm against his cheek. I was startled to see him blink.

"Lon?" he asked.

Relief came over me and I squeezed his hand gently. "I'm here, Pal," I said.

"It's so dark. Did I sleep all day?"

"Nah. It's just overcast. Storm is coming, Graham. Should be a real corker."

Rain began to rap heavily on the roof to confirm what I'd said. Graham looked toward the ceiling and blinked several times as if uncertain what the sounds might mean. He rolled his head on the pillow and gazed beyond me to the window.

"I guess the storm's here," he said. Then he tried to clear his throat and reached up with his free hand to rub his neck. "Thirsty," he said.

I released his hand, and it fell to his side. From the table by the window I lifted the lantern and a moment later had it lit, along with a cigarette, which I clamped firmly between my lips. I poured water from a canteen into a cup. I put the cup to Graham's lips and he gulped the water down.

"That's good," he whispered.

His voice hissed through the air like a static charge and then vanished. So weak. I couldn't help but note the contradiction of his physical appearance and his state. The sickness that had so affected him had no visible effect on his musculature. His chest and shoulders, covered in a fine spray of black hairs, were immense and intimidating, seeming even more pronounced than before the illness had subdued him, and his arms, seemed particularly swollen, though I attributed this to a play of light and shadow on his skin. The red welts, some kind of pox, still covered him head to toe, but their intensity had diminished. They no longer looked inflamed, and I took this as a good sign for my good friend's recovery.

We shared similar histories, Graham Rowe and I. I'd played baseball—third base for the Yankees—prior to the war and for a brief time after the armistice, before the fury at the back of my head broke free. Graham had been a boxer, a heavyweight. He could have been one of the greats, right up there with Dempsey, Louis, Carnera, or Sharkey. But he'd brought integrity into a business that found any such characteristic an obstacle to profit. He'd fought fair and had refused any suggestion to the contrary, and for his ethical stand, a thug with the Irish mob had shot a .38 slug into Graham's right kneecap, sufficiently ending his pugilistic pursuits. He'd been lucky to keep the leg. Maybe the only luck he'd had in the last ten years.

I guess a lot of us at the camp had a good starving for luck.

As for me, my troubles started long before the market crashed; they began in a trench gouged through the French countryside. It was there, amid blossoms of fire and mustard gas and hails of German bullets that my brain went bad. The quick-fire rages and blackouts came later, after I'd returned home, but they had originated there. I know it. My instability was born from the sight of an unclean woman—a woman who could not die—who walked the battlefields clutching some foul offspring to her breast.

Back home after the war, my career went fast, teammates turning their backs on the man who'd returned from Europe with all of his skills intact, but something living in the back of his brain like a coiled snake. I argued with an umpire. I blacked out. I woke up in restraints. In my absent state, I'd broken the umpire's jaw and blinded him in one eye. Marjorie, my sister and only living family, went into an asylum and then into death, having opened her wrists with a bit of broken glass much to the amusement of the two dozen shaved-headed women sharing her ward and much to the disinterest of the matrons who'd left her to bleed out on the wooden floor. My money vanished in twenty-nine, as insubstantial and irretrievable as the souls of Wall Street suicides. I ended up at the veteran's camp on Lower Matecumbe Key as part of the New Deal, and I thought my luck might turn, but that was simply a delusion of hope—being so far down the only place left to look was up.

Something happened to me in the trenches, happened to a lot of men, I imagine. But they died in the mud with it. I carried it home.

"When are you going to quit faking and get out of that bed?" I asked Graham.

He tried to smile. "It's crazy," he said. "Come here."

I did as he asked, and when he lifted his hand toward me, I took it. His wide palm wrapped around mind, and he tightened his grip. In seconds it felt like my hand was trapped in an apple press. I could feel the bones grinding. Finally, I asked him to stop and his hand dropped away again.

"I can barely keep my eyes open," he said. "Can barely breathe. But I bet I could still crush a walnut without half trying. How can that be? How can I be weak as a baby and strong as an ox at the same time?"

"You're getting better," I told him. "Some parts get better faster than others is all. The rest will catch up soon enough."

This seemed to satisfy him and Graham closed his eyes, took a ragged breath, and fell asleep. I pulled up a chair and then remembered the captain would expect a report once he heard from the doctor, so I left Graham to sleep and stepped into the rain, and in the dimming light, through the pelting downpour, I thought I saw movement on the beach.

I stood there for some time, squinting to bring the shapes on the sand into focus, but it wasn't until a bolt of lightning broke the blackness above the ocean that the scene became clear. Five men stood in the surf, a great wave rising at their backs. Three of the men wore the black coats and caps I associated with a ship's crew or longshoremen. The other two wore strips of torn fabric, merely remnants of garments no longer sufficient to protect their wearers from the elements or provide suitably modest coverings. The lightning flash bleached their faces and bodies white. One of the five stared directly at me and in the heartbeat's time of illumination managed to sink to a crouch as if preparing to spring. Then darkness returned.

The sight of the men so startled me that I hurried back into Graham's shack and threw my shoulder to the door. A great weight hit the other side of the plank and the shack rattled as if it might collapse around us. A second collision coaxed a curse from my lips, and from his bed Graham groaned in his sleep. Then the thunder rolled overhead. I braced myself more securely against the door, but no further assault occurred. I thought I heard a shout from farther down the camp, but it could have been nothing more than the wind screaming at the rain.

Another flash of lightning. Thunder exploded over the shack, and I heard screams, and I was back in a trench, an open tunnel of glistening mud. Guns fired all around me. Explosions lit the night like transient bonfires hovering in the dismal air, and I felt their heat. Men screamed. The torrential downpour couldn't wash away the scent of blood and shit and rot.

The fugue played for only a moment, but the agitation it brought stayed with me. Staring at the dark window from my place at Graham's door, my vision grew red at the edges and my heartbeat sounded in my ears like a marching battalion. The anger came over me in a spasm. So quick. So familiar.

I shouldn't have to be afraid, not again, not ever again. What right did the grim sailors have to attack me?

I threw open the door and clenched my fists and stomped into the wet sucking sand, looking for the strange men. But the next flash of lightning, and the next, showed me I was alone on the beach. Monstrous waves rose in the sparking light. The rain doused me. I breathed in great panting bellows as if I'd just run a tremendous distance, and before long the fury passed, leaving me certain that the sailors had not been there at all. They'd been in my mind, like so many other nightmares.

Like the woman I'd seen on a French battlefield: a dead woman who walked across a plain of brilliant explosions, carrying the body of a newborn baby. And like my sister, drawn through the night by long crimson reins emanating from the gashes in her arms to hover over my bed like a portent of bleak tomorrows.

I sat with Graham for a time and even dozed, dreaming about my sister and trenches filling with blood like gutters during a rain storm, eventually waking to find the light coming through the small windows had not changed, and the rap of the rain had taken on an insistence far surpassing the usual afternoon downpour. Once again, I checked Graham's temperature and found him cool to the touch, with no sign of fever. He stirred in his sleep again, and I pulled my hand away. Having no idea how long I'd napped, and uncertain if I should wait in my cabin for the captain to summon me or simply be on hand for his queries at the infirmary, I left my friend and made a stop at my cabin to retrieve a slicker before setting off once again to see the doctor. Along the way, a man named Horrocks, shouted my name, which I barely heard over the rain. I found him standing in the open doorway of his cabin, and I slogged through the muddy sand to greet him.

Horrock's wasn't an easy man to like, and I can't say we were exactly friends. He was a foul looking man with pendulous jowls and a perpetual stubble on his cheeks that looked as if his face had been smeared with coffee grounds, and though I didn't keep track of his visits to the showers, they had to be infrequent due to the often overpowering reek that rolled from him. Further he was crude in ways that seemed to go beyond a poor upbringing, as he often grinned at the shock his words could bring to the eyes of those with whom he spoke.

"You see that cocksucker Reynolds out there?" Horrocks asked.

I told him I hadn't. The only other men I'd seen in the storm were those my uncertain mind had placed there.

"Damndest thing," he said, drawing the last bit of life from a cigarette, the paper burned down right to his lips. "We were walking back from the mess tent, talking about this bastard storm, and the son of a bitch just disappeared. I figured he made a dash for the latrine because the food is always giving him the shits, or maybe forgot that he'd left something burning in his cabin, but one second he was there trying to tell me the storm would blow over soon enough, even though he knew full well what the report out of Miami said, and then poof...gone. Damnedest thing."

"Did you check his cabin?"

"Nah," said Horrocks, "didn't want my supper getting any wetter. Just thought I'd ask if you seen him. Trying to scrape together a few bastards for a card game tonight. Reynolds can't play worth a shit and I could use the scratch."

"I'll keep an eye out."

This seemed good enough for Horrocks, and he nodded his head before lighting up another smoke.

"What did Miami say?" I asked.

"Come again?"

"You said you were talking to Reynolds about a weather report out of Miami."

"Oh sure, right," Horrocks said as if having to search many months or years through his memory before landing on the bit of information.

"Well?"

"Just a storm," he said. "gonna be with us for a while. Maybe through tomorrow or more. Nothing to worry about they said. If it gets bad the hurricane flags will go up and they'll blow the horn. Looks like you'll get a day off the road."

"Thanks," I said.

"If you see Reynolds, you send him on over. I'd like to take a bit of his money home with me tonight."

"Will do," I replied.

Then I left Horrocks in his cabin. At the infirmary, I found the doctor sliding a notebook into his breast pocket. He'd folded the thick canvas over the dead man on the table. It looked like a giant cocoon from which some hideous creature might emerge.

"Ah Lon," Mathias said, "I'm sorry you came all the way back in this squall."

"You said the captain would want a report."

"Indeed, but he sent word that he wouldn't be leaving the hotel tonight, so I'll be meeting with him there. You are welcome to come, but it's probably a waste of your time. I have your statement, and I've made a good number of notes about our unfortunate friend there. Nothing seems to be amiss—no weapon wounds or broken bones. His skull was perfectly intact. So we'll have this one put down to an accident, likely not dissimilar to the explanation Bainbridge had for it. If you'd like to accompany me, please do, but you'd probably be better served returning to your cabin and drying off. We don't need you coming down with a cold or some other crud."

I agreed with the doctor and waited for him to finish gathering his things—his bag, the brass lantern—and led him into the storm.

"Nasty one," he said, indicating the weather with a wave of his lantern.

"Yes, it is," I replied.

We wished each other a good night and the doctor hurried off toward the road, rounding the motor pool tent, his lamplight guiding him through the scratchy murk. Once he disappeared into the storm, I set off for my cabin, but a shrill squeal stopped me. It sounded like tin being torn, but the shriek lasted only a second and then faded away like the echo of a coin dropping on a church floor. I turned toward the motor pool, where I believed the sound had come from and saw a dot of light drop from the sky, like a falling star. The scene confused me because no flame could burn in this weather, certainly not the entire distance I had seen it drop.

Quickly, I jogged toward the motor pool and ran around it, chasing the fire I believed I'd seen falling from the storm battered sky. The canvas tent, covering the automobiles and trucks, whipped angrily in the wind, popping and cracking like the offspring of the thunder above. I searched the gloom for the strange light but saw nothing save the pale strip of highway ahead. Throwing my gaze up and down the road, there was no sign of a light. I walked forward and after a dozen steps the toe of my boot rattled a metal casing. At first I thought I'd kicked an old can or perhaps one of the tin bowls we took our grub on, but the clanging complaint came from a brass lantern lying on the sand. Though there was no way to be certain, it looked like the lamp Doctor Mathias had been carrying. I bent down and picked it up. The glass was smashed and the scent of kerosene wafted from the dripping wick. And I looked upward, judging the distance I'd seen the light falling from and quickly determined it had originated too high to have been merely tossed, and even if it had been thrown into the air, why in the world would anyone discard the thing in that way?

I called for Doctor Mathias, but received no reply.

Then I thought about bonfires, hovering above the ground, shattering the men they touched into ragged, fragmented pieces.

Lightning crashed, sending blue-white light across the camp and down the unfinished highway. No one. Empty. Deserted.

The lamp had probably been there all day. It couldn't have been the source of the falling light I'd witnessed, unless a biplane had soared through the tortured air and dropped it.

That night the dreams were particularly awful, and I'm certain I didn't sleep for more than twenty minutes at any given time. Too many explosions. Too many pops of rifle fire. Too many screams and all of these underscored by the marching beat of the falling rain.

Four men were reported missing the next morning, including Vic Reynolds and Doctor Irvin Mathias. The news spread through the camp like the plague. I was incredibly troubled by these disappearances, but it wasn't the worst news I got on the morning of the storm. Not nearly the worst.

A fist pounded on my door drawing me from my bed. Outside, amid the continued downpour Arthur Horrocks stood holding a sheet of tin over his head to deflect the worst of the rain.

"Fucking camp is on alert," he said. "We got four sons of bitches missing and the storm flags are going up all along the coast. Might have us a hurricane blowing in."

The news unsettled me greatly. I'd heard about hurricanes before, heard they made a good gulley washer look like mist, heard the wind came on so strong it could launch a piece of wood with enough force to pierce a tree trunk like an arrow. Bad things, hurricanes. I didn't want to meet one. But I was equally concerned about the other bit of news Horrrocks had passed on.

"Who's gone?"

"The doc never made it back to the hotel last night. His wife and the captain are pitching fits. I went in to cover the radio this morning, and they sent me away, telling me to get some men together to search the camp for him. Along the way, we found out Oliver Wertz went out to use the latrine last night and never came back, and I still ain't seen hide nor hair of Reynolds."

"That's three," I said. "Who's the fourth?"

"We checked in on Graham Rowe just after sun up, or what would be sun up if the cocksucking sun ever showed itself, and he didn't answer his door. We checked inside but didn't see him, so we waited a bit, but he didn't come back."

I took the news about Graham like a punch to the breadbasket, even felt a bit of tears in my eyes over it. The men who'd disappeared from the other camps had never showed up—except for the man we'd found in the mangrove roots—and the idea that Graham might have met a similar fate made me ill. I felt bad about the doctor as well, and I considered the fire that had rained down the night before, leading me to discover a broken lantern in the sand. Maybe god himself was reaching down and snatching these men into the sky, lifting them high, only to drop them as an omen of his displeasure—but displeasure for what? We'd all carried our suffering to the lowest place imaginable; how much punishment did any one man deserve?

Horrocks finished by saying that the captain wanted all of the men to round up the women and children and get them situated in the schoolhouse. Then he wanted the men to grab rations from the mess and settle in for the storm. Coffee would be available at the post office all day. If the siren blew that meant the storm was bad and the camp would be evacuated and all the men were to gather at the depot. Safety lines had been run from the post office to the camp. The captain suggested men buddy up so they could keep track of each other in the storm.

Horrocks said all of this as if reading from a notepad. I told him I understood and let him move on to the next cabin.

I decided to visit Graham's cabin myself. Maybe he had been out, feeling better and testing his legs, eager to be moving in the air despite the hellacious weather. I grabbed my slicker and pulled it on and walked across the camp to Graham's shack, and I opened the door to find his bed remained empty. The hole in my chest, one I'd been aware of since Horrocks had suggested Graham was among the missing, flooded with acid and my temper flared.

It wasn't fair. Graham was a good man. He didn't waste his wages on whores or gamble them in an attempt to prove that luck hadn't deserted him completely. He helped the folks in the camp out and despite his bum leg, he more than pulled his weight on the highway crew. What kind of hateful thing would just carry him away? What kind of god would allow it?

Furious, I pounded my fist against the door, relieving only a fraction of my rage. I cursed and shouted and kept hitting the door until the imprint of my fist had been cracked into the thin wood. This proved insufficient to vent my anger, so I stomped across the room and kicked the chair by Graham's cot, and then I kicked the cot itself, sending it hard to the wall.

Graham's hand dropped into view then like a pale dead spider. Something in the night had driven him to the shadows beneath his cot, and his bedclothes had been drawn down like a curtain obscuring him from view. I knelt and pulled the cloth aside and my good friend's empty eyes cut through the gloom to cool the acid in my chest with absolute sorrow. His mouth was frozen in a shallow frown, lips tensed and drawn away from his teeth. His arms curled at the elbows as if Graham had succumbed to a convulsion and death had frozen him in an unnatural and horrific position.

Oddly though, he had gathered a selection of his belongings with him beneath the cot: an old pair of boxing gloves; a photograph of Graham in the ring, arms held high, the referee scowling at his back. My chest tightened upon noticing the cheap straw hat I'd bought him as a joke the last time we'd visited Key West. The items rested against his side as if he'd been clutching them tight before the final spasm of death had overcome him.

I let the bedclothes fall to cover the dreadful scene and my throat constricted around a sob. Pulling the chair I'd so recently kicked to the side of the bed, I sat down and waited for the sadness to pass, but a cheerless souvenir fell loose in my head, adding to my grief.

The telegram from the Orchard Sanitarium, telling me of my sister's suicide, arrived on a Monday afternoon in January as snow fell like confetti outside my apartment's window. I don't remember destroying my furniture or ripping the cabinet doors from their hinges. I remember reading the telegram and the world skipped, and I regained my composure to find myself sitting amid the shards of broken dishes on the floor of my kitchen, my hand broken, two knuckles shattered, blood forming a web on my palm. It was then that I began to believe that neither my sister nor myself had been blessed, but rather, we were cursed, forced to endure life while our siblings escaped the trial completely by dying before the world put them to any real test. I couldn't help but wonder how much a man had to lose before he accepted the fact there was nothing left to fight for.

After a time of pronounced self-pity I brought Graham's body out from under the cot. I took one of his old shirts and held it outside under the rain until it was soaked through and then I wiped his body down, cleaning away the waste that had followed his soul out of his body, and I tossed the shirt back out to the beach before lifting Graham onto the cot. I placed the items he'd selected to carry with him under the bed next to him on the mattress, holding the straw hat for several seconds before adding it to the collection. Then I covered him and his keepsakes with a blanket—it was as close to dignity as I could offer him.

The door blew out of my grasp when I opened it and slammed against the cabin's wall. Rain pelted the grim room, riding gusts of wind. I struggled outside and managed to get the door closed before another gale sent me into the side of the cabin. The ocean rose and fell in great steely swells, capped in a sickly pale foam that crashed to the muddy beach like a great limbless beast struggling to wriggle its way closer to the camp. Again I saw the grim sailors, but this time I knew it was a projection of my mind, a simple memory cast against a gray screen. I made it behind Graham's shack before the next great blast of wind hit, and the shirt I'd discarded to the beach flew past me like a stained spirit.

Unsure of whom to inform about Graham's death, I worked my way from cabin to cabin, clutching close to the thin wooden walls, which offered some minor protection from the storm, and made my way back to the infirmary. From there, I'd radio the hotel to inform the captain that Graham Rowe was not among the missing, but he was with his Lord.

Anumber of men had gathered in the infirmary: Chester McMahon, a strapping Irishman in his mid-forties and the father of Robby McMahon who had kept me company on the beach the evening before; stout and solemn Dee Dee Macaby, a man who craved military order; the always-thinking Michael Bainbridge; and the foul-mouthed Arthur Horrocks. A dozen other men—some of whom I knew by name and others I'd seen in the camp—huddled around a small wooden table and the radio sitting there. A thin voice—belonging most likely to Ricky James who acted as first shift communications officer—trickled and squeaked over the tiny speaker as he updated the weather situation. The rickety building creaked around us, battered by the increasing wind. The gusts moaned and howled. Nails squealed as distressed boards took the full brunt of the gale.

Just to my side lay the body of the dead Lieutenant, still wearing his canvas shroud atop Doctor Mathias's desk. Beyond the gathered men were the ten cots, five to a side, where our injured and ill had spent their days.

"Cocksucker says we're to stay put," Horrocks said. He laid his hand on the table beside the radio, tensed as if ready to beat the machine for having given him unwelcome news. "Got red flags flying from Key West to Camp Number 5, and the mule fucking, shit-stained Captain says we're supposed to hunker down and ride it out."

"That's disappointing," Bainbridge said, scratching his eyebrow.

"I'm about a minute from grabbing Robby and Louise May and taking one of them trucks outside. Get our asses up to Homestead or Miami," said Chester McMahon.

"That's theft of military property," Dee Dee said. "Court martial."

"This ain't the fucking army," Horrocks said with a laugh. "It's a government sponsored chain gang. We pretend it's an infantry unit because it's the only fucking way we can deal with the hard cots, the shit grub, and the lack of pussy."

"Either way, it's theft," Bainbridge noted. He turned to Chester. "You want this to blow through and lose what little you've already got? Are you going to stand with Robby and Louise May on a bread line every day?"

Chester thought this over, and I watched Bainbridge's sharp wisdom deflate his rebelliousness. The man looked around the room, perhaps seeking support from one of the other men, but none of them would meet his gaze. I wouldn't meet it either. The rope the government had given me was thin and burned my hands, but it kept me from falling, and I wasn't about to encourage anyone to take it from me.

"The Captain's never steered us wrong," Dee Dee said. "He says it's gonna pass. It's gonna pass."

"Any word on the missing men?" I asked.

Horrocks twisted his face toward me and shook his head. "We found Wertz's dopp kit wedged in a mound of sand by the latrine. Reynolds, the Doc, and Rowe just plain vanished."

I didn't bother mentioning the lantern I'd found the night before, which might have belonged to the doctor, but I did say, "Graham isn't missing. He's dead."

A hush ran through the infirmary and though a few men dropped their chins as if in prayer, the others turned to me questioningly.

"I went to his cabin after I spoke to Horrocks this morning. He was under his cot."

"Why the good Goddam was he under his cot?" Horrocks asked.

"Must have fallen out of bed," I said. "The fever could have come back, muddled his thoughts. I don't know."

"A few men should go over and retrieve his body, bring it here to be loaded on the train once the storm passes." Bainbridge said this, still gazing at the floor.

"Best leave him be," I said. He was tucked in with the memories he'd considered fond, and that struck me as an okay way to be for a while, better than lying on a desk like the dead lieutenant. Wind slammed into the side of the infirmary, making it groan as if in pain. I waited for one of the men to argue my suggestion, but none of them did. "He's fine enough where he is. The Captain have any orders about how to secure the camp? Sand bags? But-tresses? Anything?"

"No," Chester said through a scowl. "Not a peep. He's all safe and secure in that hotel so it don't make him no never mind."

This complaint brought up a wave of agreement from the room. Men nodded and offered their own words of dissatisfaction. The same men who had refused to support Chester in his plan to steal a truck only minutes before proved more than happy to join in his vitriol. Soon enough, hushed grumblings rose to all out shouts: *What are they doing for us? Where's the evacuation train? I have a family to think about. It ain't right!* Before long angry voices rose so high, I could no longer hear the rain beating the roof or the wind attacking the infirmary walls.

"Enough," Dee Dee shouted, bringing a sudden silence to the room. He began to pace like a colonel before morning roll, throwing hard glances at the men gathered in the shack. A few of the men—whether from reflex or genuine respect—threw their shoulders back and stood at attention. "This may not be a military operation, but the Captain has been appointed by our government, and such a trust is no different than that bestowed upon any military officer. Our government put him in charge because he knows what is best for this project and best for his men, and we have no right to question him as long as there is food in our bellies and roofs over our heads. We could be living under bridges instead of building them. We could waste our days waiting for handouts instead of earning our way and keeping our self-respect. We may not all be soldiers but we are all Americans, and our country needs us. Our government needs us, and it will protect us as it always has."

His impassioned speech, dripping with assurance and patriotism, seemed to inflate several of the men in the infirmary, though McMahon, Horrocks and a handful of others remained stooped and unaffected. I felt similarly unmoved. Dee Dee was trying to rally the troops around the Captain, perhaps sincere in the belief that the man's military rank made him infallible, but I knew that war didn't always bring out the best qualities in a man. In my experience officers were more often than not born into rank—from wealthy, influential fathers who owned banks and corporations—and of the possibly inherited traits, I'd seen far more arrogance than intelligence or bravery. I kept my mouth shut because the Captain seemed to be a good man, one who took his position and its responsibilities seriously, but I did not imbue him with the same infallibility Dee Dee Macaby suggested.

"On a different note, but to the same point," said Bainbridge, "all of our available sandbags are being used to bolster the trestle beams, and the cabins would not benefit from buttressing. The Captain has clearly drawn out a sufficient plan of action. Should we reach hurricane status, we will gather at the sturdier structures away from the beach: the post office and the train depot. The women and children are already safe in the school and will remain there until the storm passes or the hurricane siren is sounded. By that time the evacuation train will have been dispatched from Miami. Right now, since there doesn't seem to be much we can do for our lost companions, except pray, I suggest we take supplies to the three shelters the captain has indicated."

Bainbridge's logic focused the men, gave them something they could unanimously agree upon as a course of action. Horrocks sat back down in front of the radio and twisted a knob, sending a screeching blast of static through the room, and then Ricky James's voice parted the noise.

"Go ahead, Arthur."

"I got a question," a man shouted from the back of the infirmary, interrupting Horrocks' transmission.

I leaned to the side, peering through the crowd to see an unshaven man at least ten years my senior, wearing a tattered gray jacket and matching woolen cap. He sat on one of the infirmary cots, back propped against the wall, arms folded in his lap.

"Hold on a second, Ricky," Horrocks said.

"What's your question?" Bainbridge asked.

"Anybody else gonna talk about those sumsabitches been sneaking around our camp at night?"

The comment startled me, and I took a step back. My hand grazed the canvas tarp enveloping the dead Lieutenant, and I jerked it away as if from a flame. I'd convinced myself that the grim sailors I'd encountered on the beach were no more substantial than dark daydreams, but this man had seen them as well, or at least, he'd seen someone.

"We don't need to hear about your fucking *hants*, Leonard," Horrocks said. The other men in the infirmary laughed mockingly, and I sensed there was a reason the old man's credibility had come under fire. So, I remained silent, waiting to see how the conversation progressed.

"I know what I know," Leonard replied.

"And last spring you saw mermaids by the train trestle."

"We got men missing and the other camps has got men missing," Leonard continued. He pointed at the body on the desk next to me. "And I seen men that don't belong here. Saw one last week, clear as day, talking to Graham Rowe before he took sick and I saw more of 'em last night. Ignore it if you want. I know what I know."

"Bah," said Horrocks waving his hand in the air as if to pat an idiot's head.

"Regardless," Bainbridge said, "I would think the storm is the more pressing issue just now. If you did see interlopers, we can address that situation when the immediate danger has passed, but for now our concern should be for the storm. I would think that even miscreants would have returned to their shelters in this weather."

I should have spoken up, if only to give Leonard piece of mind in his last hours of life, but knowing the truth about those men wouldn't save anyone.

After lugging supplies to the school, the post office and the depot, I returned to the infirmary where I waited by the radio with Horrocks and Bainbridge, both of whom had lost all humor as we overheard the anxious call from Ricky James. At the captain's request, he was sending an emergency message to Miami, demanding a train be sent to evacuate the workmen on Lower Matecumbe Key.

"They'll be too late," Horrocks said. He spoke loudly, nearly a shout to be heard over the storm. "In clear weather the train takes two hours to get here, and if they intend to stop at the northern camps... Too fucking late."

Instead of contradicting him as would have been typical of Bainbridge, the man remained silent. The infirmary walls let out great tortured whines against a particularly vicious blast of wind. A piece of driftwood, the length of my arm, sailed through a window, shattering glass and rocketing to the far wall, where it hit with a thud before dropping to a cot. Rain followed, a steady stream running parallel to the plank flooring and the bellowing wind cried in triumph. "Are they ever going to sound the siren?" Bainbridge asked. "There are still dozens of men in their cabins."

His concern was understandable. The cabins had been built with an eye on efficiency and functionality; they hadn't been constructed for durability, certainly not against weather this serious. A couple of good men could tip one of them over and hardly break a sweat. I had no doubt the shacks would be coming down soon, the whole lot of them, and the planks that had proved ineffective as shelter against the weather's attack would snap and splinter, making more than adequate spears when carried on the vicious wind.

"Maybe we should get our asses up to the post office," Horrocks said. "I don't think this place is going to hold."

Behind his words, the long-awaited siren began to wail. At first it was slow as the operator cranked the handle to build the klaxon's momentum, and then the horn's voice grew steady and insistent.

"Well, there it is," Bainbridge called. "Lon, take up that lantern. Arthur, send a message to the hotel and let them know we're out."

Once the call was made, the three of us walked to the door. I led the way with the lantern, its yellow cast falling on the dead Lieutenant's wrapped form and then leaving it for the shadows. Bainbridge stepped forward and opened the infirmary door and the raging storm blew across the opening like a runaway locomotive. Debris filled the screaming wind. Bits of wood, scraps of paper, entire books, and articles of clothing soared by, momentarily captured in the lantern's cast. My fear notched up as I imagined the damage such garbage could cause when traveling at locomotive speed.

"Stay close," I called. "The guide ropes are on the far side of the motor pool."

Walking into the storm, an immediate disorientation fell over me. It seemed as if the world was indeed flat and God had seen fit to tip it on end. Gravity no longer pulled us earthward but rather pushed us from the east. The force at my back was unassailable. If we'd had to move against it, I imagine we would have failed, but our destination was to the west and the wind proved eager to get us there. Arthur Horrocks went tumbling and for a moment he lifted off the sand, and fell away as if dropping from the side of a building. He remained in the lantern light only a moment and then glided beyond its reach. We found him at the motor pool, dragging himself to his feet, using the side panel of a truck for leverage. He squinted into the lantern, clutching madly for the door handle to get a secure grip. Bainbridge and I joined him and received his bellowed assurance that he was uninjured.

Peering through the chaos, I saw lights on the slight rise above the camp, near the highway where the school and post office and depot waited. The lights were weak and seemed very far away, match flames in a maelstrom. All else was roiling darkness a turbulent sea of air, rain, sand and trash. I clutched the fender of a Buick and waved the lantern to get Bainbridge and Horrock's attention.

"Turn on the headlights," I yelled. "All of them. Start the engines and turn them on."

We wouldn't be the only men needing light. Those who emerged too late from their cabins would be fumbling around in the dark, trying to find the guide ropes, and every additional moment they spent in the storm had the potential to prove fatal.

Noting the confusion on Horrock's face, I handed him the lantern, struggled to open the truck door and climbed inside. The door slammed shut the moment after I'd pulled my leg clear. In seconds I had the engine running and headlights burning. They cut some ways into the storm, far enough to illuminate the first of the guide ropes.

Men in glistening black slickers pulled themselves across the sand, beetles ascending a spider's thread. The air about them was yellow and foul like gauze ripped from an infected wound.

I slid across the seat and climbed out of the truck, went to the next one, set its lights to blazing. Behind me, another pair of beams ignited and then another. More of the camp was revealed in the growing bath of light. My hands clutched the steering wheel and I looked out at the men struggling along the ropes, making their way up the incline toward the white box of a post office. I felt a moment of pride when a man emerged from the shadows by the back row of shacks and grabbed hold of the rope, knowing my ingenuity had played some small part in his salvation.

Then he was gone.

A dark form, which I first mistook for another worker in his rain gear, flew from the shadows, striking the man I had been watching. But instead of falling to the ground, the two men rose into the air, sailing over the heads of the others struggling along the guide ropes and vanishing into the gloom above. My heart skipped into my throat, and I questioned what I had seen.

And then I saw it again.

One of the grim sailors wearing strips of pale frayed fabric dashed into the light and leapt at another of the workmen. He knocked the man from the rope and carried him through the air, straight at the truck in which I sat. As they grew larger in the windshield, the sailor used one hand to furiously rip away the black slicker while holding tight to his victim with an embracing arm. The two bodies collided with the front of the truck, sending it rocking on its wheels. The workman tried to scramble away, climbing the hood of the truck toward me, and I recognized the man's round, neatly shaven face.

Dee Dee Macaby, eyes wide and mouth open, faced me. He might have been screaming but I couldn't say. The roar of the storm and the blood in my ears were too loud. He reached a hand toward me, his fingertips just grazing the glass. Then the grim sailor, who clutched at Dee Dee from behind, scrabbled forward like a starving insect and buried his face in the crook of Dee Dee's neck. The workman's mouth opened further, showing the holes where molars had been lost to battle and bar fights.

Then the men were gone. They rolled off the truck hood and across the motor pool as if no more substantial than sheets of newspaper.

In horrible awe, I saw another man plucked from the guide rope and another. It felt as if the hurricane had found a way into my head. It battered my thoughts and dislodged memories of trenches and explosive bon fires and men screaming through the blood filling their throats, and I sat there, paralyzed by what I was witnessing, past and present playing like two different motion pictures projected on the same screen—the sound so loud it blasted incomprehensible noise.

Another of the sailors emerged at the far reach of the headlights. Beneath his black wool cap, his face appeared as nothing more than a white smear. He observed the row of men, now scrabbling desperately up the hill toward the post office. The body of a workman rolled across the sand at his feet, pushed along the wet beach like a child's ball discarded in the sand. The sailor watched the body roll by, his head following the corpse's progression like a disinterested turtle. He lifted into the air, rising higher while the wind and rain pressed him as if trying to surface in a raging river, and he hung suspended over the row of men below.

A broad sheet of wood, either the roof or the side of a cabin spun into the flood of headlights and struck the sailor before whipping into the darkness. The sailor came apart from shoulder to hip, a ragged diagonal wound bisected him, sending blood and organs into the wind to be cleansed by the downpour and carried away. The segments of his body followed his fluid and tissue like two unmanageable kites lost to the gale.

And I was in a trench and men screamed and rifles cracked and a fire erupted over the ground, tearing two men into ribbons of flesh and viscera, and the man next to me doubled over to vomit, and the man ahead of me lost the back of his head to a German's bullet, and I shouted and aimed my gun into the night firing wildly, aimlessly, targeting any disturbance in the darkness, and that's when she appeared. A woman crossed the field, appearing in silhouette against the flame of a mortar detonation behind her one second and then being bathed in light front another explosion in the dirt to her side. She carried a baby in her arms, held the infant to her breast in feeding, and bullets peppered them both, but the woman didn't fall. She never fell. Pain startled me from my fugue. A sharp tingling rose on my cheek and I looked around in a panic, thinking one of the sailors had come for me, and I struggled irrationally, slapping at the air in the truck's cab, shouting incoherently. The pain came again and I found myself facing Horrocks, who was already cocking his palm back for a third blow.

"We have to go," he screamed. "Lon, the whole camp is coming apart. We have to get inside."

Bainbridge appeared at the front of the vehicle, holding tight to the fender, yelling at the top of his lungs. The wreckage of cabins, bits of wall and window and furniture flew behind him in a barrage of dangerous debris. He jabbed his finger at the post office and then secured his grip on the side of the truck.

"We have to go," Horrocks bellowed in my ear.

Holding the guide rope, moving hand over hand toward the post office, the wind shoving me along as the rough hemp tore at my palms. I saw souvenirs of the men who had gone before us, smears of blood and bits of skin left behind on the bristling line. The lights from the carpool provided sufficient illumination, but I refused to observe my surroundings. I focused on the rope—hand over hand. I didn't want to know what was coming, because I would be helpless against it, whether it came in the form of a substantial piece of structure, a lethal shard of glass, or the quickly moving and unnatural sailors who had arrived with the storm. Even if I had wanted to look, I couldn't. Fear had stooped me over and fused my spine in a coward's crouch. A shirt struck my back and wrapped around my torso. I imagined myself in the clutches of the sailor who had murdered Dee Dee Macaby, but the fabric ripped away and sailed on to strike Bainbridge and climb over his back before continuing to the west where it was pasted against the side of the post office. The slack came out of the rope and it jerked downward violently and then returned.

Finally we made it to the front of the post office and Bainbridge threw open the door. The tight grip on my spine released and I could look up and around. I felt as if a brace had dropped from my neck and back.

Forty men crowded into a space that would have been uncomfortable for half as many. Some squatted against the walls and others stood. They all looked shell shocked, an expression my mirror had tutored me in for years. A counter split the room on my right. Five men used it as a perch, dangling their legs over the edge. The windows on the east and north sides of the building had been boarded over, and the south side had no windows at all, but the western wall, the front of the post office, still wore a broad pane of glass. The odors of wet hair, sour sweat, motor oil, and damp clothing pushed into my nose like mud. There seemed to be no oxygen in the room, nothing left for me to breathe with so many other hungry lungs devouring the atmosphere, but it was dry and though the building creaked, the complaints were hardly noticeable, unlike those of the infirmary when every squealing nail seemed to announce the building's collapse. And even with the continued intensity of the storm, it was somehow quiet inside the room—almost peaceful in comparison with the pandemonium outside.

I turned to make sure Horrock's had made it inside and found him standing on the narrow porch, hands wrapped on the door-jamb for support. The fact that the door remained open surprised me as I'd considered the room so quiet, but I had little time to wonder on this phenomenon. Horrocks' posture and face made me uneasy. He wore a queer expression, part uncertainty and part amusement. A smile tugged at the corners of his mouth and then he was hauled upward off the porch. His head collided with the eaves, cracking like kindling under a boot. Then he fell away, landing on his feet—a bit wobbly but otherwise appearing in good health. He stomped forward, smiling again.

"Cock sucking storm about sent my ass flying," he said.

Just as he finished the statement, a hand crept over his face and fingers gripped his cheek so tightly they broke the skin. Horrocks' eyes doubled in size as confusion gave way to fear. A black form fastened onto his side, and another of the grim sailors crawled forward to clamp its mouth on his leg. A third emerged from the bleak evening at his back, and the sight of this third whitish face stunned me.

It was Graham Rowe. His skin retained the doughy pallor of death but his eyes were as black as a sharks.

Horrocks struggled against the three men. I stepped forward with the intent of helping the foul-mouthed communications officer, but I couldn't have moved fast enough. Before my boot even hit the floor, the doorway was empty. Horrocks and his attackers were gone, vanished like a magician's rabbit to be replaced with a black foaming gap as the storm's intensity climbed.

Two men closed the post office door, and they threw a wooden slat across a couple of L-shaped brackets to lock it. The men who had witnessed Horrocks's last moments all shouted, demanding answers, but I knew no more than they did. They'd seen the grim sailors and Graham Rowe as clearly as I had. I held no secrets or answers, and I wanted to be left alone. The door was closed and locked. The storm continued to thrash the camp and send refuse against the back wall of the post office in great crashes, and out in the storm were men, who weren't really men though one of them had been a good friend of mine only a day ago.

The hurricane returned to my head, battering and blasting away reason, showing me pictures of war buddies dismembered by explosions, and punched by bullets, and showing me a woman who carried a nursing child through the carnage, and my sister with her arms opened as a pack of crazy bald women stood above her and giggled at the pretty redness—the color of the fanciest of lipsticks—pooling about her wrists. And my legs went out from under me and I sat hard on the planks of the post office, ignorant and indifferent to the continued questions, some shouted and others hushed, that filled the room in a ridiculous mimicry of the merciless wind.

Bainbridge touched my shoulder but I didn't respond. I stared at the floor, wincing with each new image kicked up by the tempest in my head. I wanted the train to come. If the train came then it would take me away from the fear and anger, and I could leave the storm behind my eyes with its weather-born parent, and when we reached Miami I would find a safe room with no windows where nothing—not even a good friend—could find me.

"You shouldn't ought to hope," a dry, reedy voice whispered in my ear. I turned to find Leonard, the old man from the infirmary sitting at my side. "Hope is the fucking carrot that keeps us working, convincing us that there's something grand and tasty at the end of a rough road. But that's not right, is it? It's all rough road. Often enough, the path never evens out. It just stays nasty and ugly, and the carrot gets gnawed down by flies and gnats and rot until you can't hardly see it, and you're left trudging along, following the memory of it. You think one day you'll get that carrot. But you won't. Hope is a cold-hearted and lying bitch. We're better off without her."

"You gotta have a reason to open your eyes in the morning," I muttered.

"Why?" Leonard asked. "Either way you're just dreaming, but you don't have to work so hard for the lies that lead you when you're asleep."

"Sleep sounds good."

"Might as well get you some," he said. "That train ain't never gonna make it here in time. Best to just close your eyes and let the world take its course. That's what I'm gonna do. I just wanted to say my piece, because you seen what I seen. You know what I know."

"Thanks."

And I did know what he knew, and I believed him when he told me that train would never arrive in time, and the reason I believed him was because I could picture the train in the depot. I could see it pulling into camp and see all of us climbing on board and breathing our sighs of relief as the locomotive dragged us north, and I could hear Bainbridge in my ear, telling me he never doubted the evacuation for a second, and men would joke and blow raspberries at the hurricane and we'd reach the station in Miami and be greeted by brilliant, warm sunshine and bottles of whiskey and claps on the back, and congratulations for surviving the worst that nature could throw our way. All of this I had imagined with such clarity that I knew it to be a lie. Like Leonard had said, it was a carrot my mind hung out of reach, distracting me from the fact that I was trapped in the mud and sinking—my journey at its end.

Leonard stood to remove himself from my company and left me on the floor where I wandered my thoughts, like strolling along a city street, peering through a variety of windows, each showing me a place and time. The men shuffled around me and I noticed their legs, their dirty and wet trousers, and the muck on their boots, and I remembered my childhood with Marjorie.

Our family gathered for Easter Sunday and we moved through the forest of legs, sneaking bits of chicken and savory roast pork and snatching sweet crumbs from the plate of cookies in the kitchen aware that mama would scold if she caught us scavenging morsels before the meal was served. Marjorie guided me, and I followed. And at a point she turned to me in a panic, tears glazing her eyes, and she whispered, "What are they all doing here? What do they want?" For her, all of the familiar faces suddenly belonged to malevolent strangers. Marjorie only recognized me, trusted me alone. She grasped my hand and dragged me from the house, and we raced into the fields and Marjorie cried, because the wheat was too low for us to tie the stalks together. There would be no tunnels in the wheat. No rounded hut, like a womb, for us to retreat into.

Then a bomb went off, shredding Marjorie and the field and the sunlight, making it dark, and the legs I saw were clad in hoary frayed uniform trousers. The scents of wet wool, blood and rot filled my nose and throat, covering me like a fouled shroud. Once my rifle was reloaded, I returned to the lip of the trench and sighted, but the nursing mother, naked and peppered with wounds from scalp to toe strolled through the mayhem, walking directly for me, and when she reached the edge of the pit, she looked down on me and smiled. The bundle at her breast squirmed and kicked. I asked, "Who are you?" and she told me she was the Mother of Blood, and a bullet clipped the top of my helmet, yanking it from my head and sending me to the sucking black floor of the trench. The Madonna laughed cruelly and then hissed like a perforated canister of mustard gas.

Then lightning struck and I stood on the beach, facing the grim sailors, but they were gone the moment the air cooled to black, and I stood at home plate in Hilltop Park and Graham Rowe stood on the mound, and he was naked and striking—his skin the color of death. In his hand, something small and red dripped crimson to the pitcher's mound, and I waited for the pitch.

Then glass shattered and my mind tried to recall the image that accompanied the sound, but there was too much shouting in the cramped post office and the legs about me took on a frantic shuffle like cattle in a pen. The dreams broke apart in my head.

"It's got Carlson," a man shouted.

I sprang to my feet and was jostled to the left by the uneasy herd. A man lay across the window frame, his enormous legs grasped in the filthy hands of workmen while his torso and head extended through the jagged remains of the pane. The workmen heaved; dragging the large man someone had called Carlson back into the post office and with him came one of the grim sailors. His fingers raked into the fabric at Carlson's shoulders, its face pressing close to the man's scalp. The workmen heaved again until Carlson was fully inside the room and the monstrous sailor, clad only in strips of gray fabric hung over the sill. Through all of this, I had been moving, my legs carrying me without instruction toward the window.

The men not holding Carlson had cleared the space around the window, cramping themselves into tight huddles. I climbed onto the counter. The sailor twisted his emaciated face in my direction, revealing a gaping mouth and snake-like fangs curling into his mouth and dripping with spit or venom. I kicked at the mouth. Once. Twice. The workmen hauled the devil deeper into the room and I jumped from the counter, landing solidly on the sailor's back. A satisfying pop erupted at impact and the sailor yipped like a wolf in a trap. We dropped to the floor, and my boots sank into his ribs with further satisfying cracks as we hit the planks. Men moved in at my sides, delivering violent kicks to the man's face and torso and stomps to his arms and hands. Carlson wriggled out of his slicker and rose to his full height, appearing like a giant in the small room, and he produced a knife from his belt, and then other men produced knives, others held clubs devised from the legs of a shattered chair, and I again found myself pushed by the tide of men, shoved off of the sailor's back and pressed to the counter.

Carlson gripped the hilt of his knife in both hands and dropped to his knees before the sailor, driving the blade with tremendous force through the back of his neck. Blood sprayed from the wound bathing the surrounding men and more came as Carlson worked the blade free for a second blow. The sailor's extremities, having endured dozens of boot stomps, lay pulped and useless at his sides. Carlson drove the knife home a second time, piercing the dimple at the base of the sailor's skull, and he worked the blade back and forth, slicing and chipping away at the spine connected there.

I backed onto the counter, lifting my feet away from the spreading pool of blood, but the other men waded in; it seemed they all wanted to have a turn at the sailor. Shouted obscenities ricocheted from one wooden wall to another given ominous accompaniment from the howling storm and the clatter of debris striking the exterior of the post office.

The display of rage seemed perfectly natural to me. We had been attacked and we were simply defending ourselves, but the assault against the prone man continued long after the threat of him was gone. Carlson ripped the head away leaving a ragged stump at the neck, and he placed the head at the feet of two men who took it upon themselves to crush the face under their boots. An eye came free of the sailor's socket and teeth flowed from the mouth on a crimson stream. Bits of hair came away, stuck to the soles of boots.

A frenzy built as men tried to get close enough to the sailor to deliver punishments of their own, but I continued to back away. The ritual of retribution seemed endless and might have continued all night, but a wailing noise, sounding miles away and yet so close froze everyone in the room.

The evacuation train was pulling into the depot.

The angered voices and the tromping boot heels abruptly silenced, leaving the torturous sounds of the storm. Every man stood mutely. Heads cocked in attention, listening for confirmation. The horn sounded a second time and the wail of the camp klaxon cried out in response. Celebratory cries rose in the post office and the men threw their hands in the air victoriously. Smiles cut through expectant expressions and men embraced in joy, their recent brutality already forgotten as they gathered their canvas kits and sang the praises of the Captain and the government and the Florida East Coast Railway.

Bainbridge, whom I'd completely forgotten, placed his hand on my shoulder and gave it a squeeze. He appeared relieved though he didn't smile, and he gave my back a sharp clap before setting off toward the door.

In my mind, I calculated the distance to the depot. There was a short path, maybe fifty feet, to the highway and the tracks lay twenty yards beyond that. I could already picture the women grasping their children's hands tightly as they led them from the schoolhouse to the station. I could picture men climbing onto the train and taking their seats and laughing in relief, and I could picture myself nestled comfortably in one of those seats, drifting off to sleep with the rumble of the wheels on the track.

And it was this last fancy that served to convince me that any escape was impossible. Still, I waited with my heart in my throat as Bainbridge and another man knocked the locking plank from the brackets and pulled open the door. The storm howled but no battered sailors drifted into the room on its cries. If they had given up for the night, finally acquiescing to the power of the weather, I couldn't say. The evening beyond the doorway was still black as pitch.

The men filed out of the post office, some of them hesitating at the threshold, checking either side of the porch before bending forward against the elements and committing to the outdoors. I took up a position in the middle of the exodus, but I did not pause at the doorway. Instead I ducked my head and charged onto the porch and the walk beyond. The back of a broken chair flew by my head, hit the ground with a tumble and vanished in the gloom. Then I was clear of the post office and the wind slammed me low in the back, lifting my feet from the ground. Sand from the beach, carried like birdshot on the gusts, peppered my back and hissed as it blasted against my slicker. I caught my footing and managed three more steps before another gale threw me head first onto the highway. The world again tipped and I rolled with the unrestrained momentum of plummeting earthward from a dizzying height. I scrabbled for purchase, scraping my hands over the macadam I'd helped lay, and then I bounced into the air and came down on softer material. I yanked a clump of grass free and then another. Finally I managed to fight the wind and lay flat on the ground, staring upward at myriad shades of deepest gray churning like a vat of liquid charcoal. Rain sliced into my exposed face at sharp angles and began to fill the hood of my slicker. I took a moment to compose myself, breathing deeply and regularly until my wits had returned, and then I worked my way to my feet and continued the race to the train, which I knew must be ahead of me, though I could not yet see it.

Eventually a pinpoint of light emerged from the darkness. I fixed on it like a lighthouse beacon.

Soon enough the train appeared. Beside it, a man with a billowing oilcloth coat held a lantern in one hand and motioned with the other, waving me toward the engine, which appeared to be facing the wrong way. It's nose pointed north into the line of train cars and I wondered if the locomotive had traveled the entire distance from Miami in this backwards manner.

A gust of wind like a giant mallet struck me then. I flew through the air and collided with the side of the engine, pinned there by the merciless force and suspended three feet off the ground.

Another river of wet sand blasted the side of the locomotive. I felt it slash my slicker, tearing innumerable holes in its fabric and the shirt beneath, but leaving my skin ostensibly unharmed. The signalman took the blast in the face. The grit shredded his cheeks and his eyelids. His lips peeled back and then vanished revealing a sickening grin before his flayed hand released the lantern and the scene went dark.

The force slackened and I dropped to the ground before another gale pressed me again into the engine. From reflex I grasped a steel handle and held tightly.

Water hit me at the knees. This was not a shower of hard rain spit at me from above, but a solid wave pushed across the camp from the ocean. In seconds I stood in a flood, holding onto the metal handle with all of my might as the tide rushed over my shins. So great was the current the train appeared to be moving, running southward through a pond, but the train was motionless. Water gushed over the sand and the tracks like a furious river, and my legs tore out from under me and I held tight to the side of the engine.

Feeling an ebb in the pounding current, I managed to get my feet back on the ground. The only safety—if such a thing still existed—would be in the train, and I had to make my way to the west side where the cars blocked the worst of the wind if I was to have any chance of getting inside. I struggled along the side of the engine, fighting the wind and the water. Then I slid around the back of the engine and left the ground again. The flood pressed me hard to the tail of the engine but the wind tried to snatch me away, creating a painful jostling that rolled me over the coupling and the pronounced metal ridges. The storm had trained my body, and once the conflicting elements again allowed me to set foot on ground, I crouched and leaned back and managed to waddle around the west facing side of the engine, which blocked me from the worst of the blow.

Lantern lights burned in the depot, though the place was clearly empty, except for three corpses that floated face down in the water rising there. The ocean pushed in with one insistent wave after another. Another signalman stood in an open doorway halfway down the train, his lantern swinging frantically to guide the workmen. More men from the post office raced around me, using the flood to build momentum as they hurried for the safety of the cars and I saw them pile in by the depot lights, most ignoring the gesturing signalman and making their way into the first car they reached.

I stumbled forward, hoping to join them, but as I neared the front of the engine, which nosed against the first passenger car, a hand slammed down on my shoulder, and I felt the puncture of fingernails in my skin. I was spun in the air and slammed against the iron siding of the engine again, but this time it was not the storm that held me.

I looked down into the face of Graham Rowe. Water pooled and pushed at his knees. His open mouth revealed the same snake-like fangs as the grim sailor we'd destroyed in the post office.

"Graham," I said, my voice a whisper, weak with resolve.

His head dropped to the side like a dog that doesn't understand its command. His jaw slackened, and his eyes narrowed momentarily before flashing wide. Then I was falling and he was gone.

It was then that I understood the nature of his malady; the long days of illness had been a transformation into this thing, this man unnatural in the manner of the grim sailors who emerged from the ocean to feed. Had this same monstrous fate befallen the other workmen, those who had vanished from the northern camps? Though possible, I didn't think it the case, as no reports of debilitating illness had come with the news of their disappearances. If anything, I found it more likely that the other men had ended as the Lieutenant I'd found beneath the cage of a Mangrove's roots had. Though whether Graham shared his inhuman state with the others was of little concern. Before his flight, he'd looked upon me with eyes scoured of humanity. I wanted to believe that he'd remembered our friendship, our camaraderie, and that was what had convinced him to spare my life, but I had nothing to do with his decision to soar away from the train: He feared the storm and the towering wave it was sending over the beach to devour us all.

Aman bellowed down at me and I felt fingers on my slicker, and they forced me away from the train, fearing Graham or another like him had returned to finish me. I spun and saw the train's engineer in the open doorway. His mouth was open as wide as any human's I'd ever seen and he waved desperately in my direction, throwing quick glances over his shoulder as he did so. I waded another step away, still confused.

To my amazement two glowing orbs rose above the train. They seemed to be the faces of angels, gliding through the night, radiating the soft glow of salvation amid Hell's maelstrom.

They transfixed me. I stood in awe watching them rise higher and higher, and for a split second I imagined they belonged to the Mother of Blood and her infant, returning to bring me some fresh message.

But the lights were not faces. They were the headlights of a truck snatched from the motor pool. As the vehicle rose higher, the lights dulled and flickered before burning strong again. I saw the wall of water on which the truck rode. It climbed taller than four men, seeming to fuse with the sky above, woven by ropes of vicious rain.

I sloshed forward, pushing against the current and leapt at the waiting hands of the engineer. My shins scraped over a metal step, and I scrambled forward knocking the engineer off balance as I fought my way into the train's engine, and I didn't stop until I reached the far door, where I curled in a fetal ball and awaited death.

Across the way, the engineer righted himself and slammed the door closed as the wave crashed over the train. The coalman stared at the window behind me, his thumbnail clamped between his teeth. The great iron compartment shivered and shook and teetered and the world beyond its glass went black as the depot lights drowned in the wave. Metal shrieked in my ears as the wheels beneath us bent with the force, and then all was oddly silent.

I woke shivering in a cold puddle of water, still curled like a baby. My muscles throbbed a uniform misery through my body and bright flares of pain erupted on my brow and shins and neck when I uncoiled myself on the floor of the locomotive engine. I blinked rapidly because a glare of gray light hurt my eyes. I shielded them with a palm and another great anguish erupted at my shoulder. I groaned and tried to get to my feet, but only managed to slide my legs around, effectively propping myself against the wall until I was again ready to attempt standing.

In time the harsh grayness resolved into morning light playing through the screen of the window. A few dark clouds stained the white sky. I wondered on the whereabouts of the engineer and the coalman, but the consideration proved little more than a mental blink as I came to realize neither the storm nor the sailors who'd come with it had ended my life. The last thing I remembered before the womb of sleep had enveloped me was a rush of water leaking around the door. Then my mind had seized like an overheated engine, stalling all thought and sensation. My eyes had closed, expecting never to open again. But now it was morning and while my body felt as if it had gone under the wheels of a car, I was alive, though I refused to believe I was safe.

Eventually I made it to my feet and found myself looking east, where the choppy ocean waves bit only the share of beach they were typically allotted. The camp, however, was gone. Cabins had been washed away, leaving behind only fragments of wood where modest quarters had once stood. Debris from the ocean—strands of spinach green seaweed and foul looking timber—lay where my shack and those of my friends had once stood. Nature had taken the highway project to trial, and had found us reprobate. For our guilt the evidence of our existence had been erased by wind and wave.

Turning away, I winced at the knife-points of pain in my legs. Upon recovery I gazed through the far window of the engine and encountered a vision of atrocity.

Unable to trust my eyes, believing the train's window to be nothing more than a movie screen on which a lie had been projected, I crossed to the door and opened it. With great effort, I descended the stairs into a cool morning breeze and found that indeed the sliver of land had become the site of a massacre. To my left a stand of mangroves had survived the storm, and men, like pieces of drying laundry, draped the topmost branches, left there in the wake of the massive wave. Slabs of devastated housing littered the land before me. Splintered fragments and walls hardly blemished, lay sprawled amid the beach grasses and sand as if the entire camp had been lifted into the sky and thrown earthward to shatter. But for as terrible as these sights were, the worst awaited me when I completed the sweep of my gaze.

On my right I saw the rest of the train. Ten cars, many still connected to one another lay on their sides fifteen yards from the tracks in a jagged line. Smashed windows faced skyward. I walked toward this nightmarish vision and tears burned along my cheeks.

All of those people—the workmen, their families, Bainbridge and Leonard and the others who comprised the fraternity of the past year of my life—had found their salvation in the seats of those cars, only to have it cruelly washed away. The weight of the locomotive engine had kept it upright and protected from the wave, but the passenger cars had fallen like a toy cast aside by a bratty child. I wanted to believe some of the people had survived, but that would have been a concession to Hope and she had manipulated me for the last time.

So I walked toward the north, veering away from the worst of the wreckage. The post office still stood as did the school. A few of the heartier buildings further along also remained, but the camp was decimated. Gone. Erased from the face of the earth. And when the engineer called for me to stop, I ignored him and continued northward, following the highway I'd helped build through a landscape of grief as the sun burned through the light film of white clouds to gloat over the magnificence of life's cruelty.

Tuesday

The irony was lost on none of them as they drew straws. Six of them sat before the fire, hands trembling as they plucked the matches from one boy's fist. Outside their attackers groaned and pounded on the walls of the cabin.

They'd thought the mountains would give them isolation from the plague, and to some degree it had. There weren't many of the ravenous dead at their door, but there were enough, especially since those inside were fragile.

The food had run out last Tuesday—a week ago, now. Empty cabinets and cupboards.

Even the occasional insect eluded their desperate fingers and their saliva-soaked tongues. The six understood the hunger fueling the dead outside. The short straw would fix that hunger, if the remaining five were brave enough to eat.

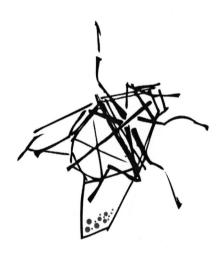

About the Author

L EE THOMAS is the Bram Stoker Award and two-time Lambda Literary Award-winning author of *The German, Ash Street, Torn, The Dust of Wonderland, In the Closet, Under the Bed*, and many other books. He lives in Austin, TX with his partner, John, his cat, Buster, and his dog, Mina. Find him on the web at leethomasauthor.com